A Nose For Trouble

A Scanner and Max Mystery

Jonathan H Kemp

CRIME WAVE
PRESS

A NoseFor Trouble
Copyright © 2014 Jonathan H Kemp
This paperback edition first published in 2015 by

Crime Wave Press
Flat D, 11th Fl. Liberty Mansion
26E Jordan Road
Yau Ma Tei, Hong Kong
http://www.crimewavepress.com

ISBN 978 988 13511 1 1

This book is a work of fiction. All names, characters,
and other elements of the story are either the
product of the author's imagination
or else are used only fictitiously.
Any resemblance to real characters,
alive or dead, or to real incidents
is entirely coincidental.

Cover Design by Hans Kemp

"And the woman said unto the serpent, of the fruit of the trees of the garden we may eat: but of the fruit of the tree which is in the midst of the garden, God hath said, Ye shall not eat of it, neither shall ye touch it, lest ye die.
And the serpent said unto the woman, Ye shall not surely die: for God doth know that in the day ye eat thereof, then your eyes shall be opened, and ye shall be as God, knowing good and evil."
Genesis 3

"Although the patient was prepared by both prolonged sensory isolation (35 days) and by repeated depatterning, and although she received 101 days of positive driving, no favourable results were obtained."
Dr. Ewen Cameron – President of the American Psychiatric Association in 1952–1953

"Free your mind… and your ass will follow"
George Clinton – Parliament Funkadelic

Milwaukee, April 30, 1978

Death is the ultimate killjoy.

Seated in the back of the Maverick, the teenage boy observed the driver's fragmented reflection. The rear-view mirror framed a familiar pair of eyes; eyes focused on the road ahead.

"It's gonna be a great game, right dad?"

"Yeah, it will be."

He could hardly believe it. They really were on the way. Tickets for the game were snapped up within hours of going on sale yesterday morning and his father had managed to secure two.

"Today is the day, Dad."

"It sure is."

The man's gaze drifted to the rear-view mirror and to the road already travelled.

"I hope we win, we gotta win, else we're out. We have a chance, don't we Dad? A real chance."

"A real chance," the man repeated wistfully, as if wondering about roads yet to be travelled. "I guess."

He slid a cassette in the deck, turned a corner. The tune that filled the Maverick brought a faint smile to the man's face.

"You know what day it is, son?"

A simple question. Why did his dad ask? They were on

the way weren't they?

"It's game day, dad, it's kick ass game day and the Bucks are gonna win and then we're gonna win game seven and then we're gonna go all the way, Dad."

The boy rhythmically swayed in his seat, unable to control his excitement.

"Yeah, but what DAY is it?"

"Sunday April 30."

Concern crept into the boy's voice. What was wrong? They had spent a big part of the afternoon yesterday discussing the game, analyzing odds and tactics, what they would do if they were the coach, how Winters would carry the game and how many three pointers would sink the Nuggets.

"April 30", the man whispered, "April 30."

The boy, alarmed now by his father's absentmindedness, leaned over the front passenger seat, quivering with trepidation.

"The tickets, dad? You have the tickets, right?"

Sugerloaf's chorus kicked in again. "Dressed in love, she lives for life to be…"

His father continued to rock along with the melody and the boy realized the question hadn't registered.

"THE TICKETS DAD!"

"Yes, yes, sure, yes, I put them in my…"

Silence. Dreaded silence. Even the song had faded out.

"Oh no dad, we're gonna miss the game." Tears welled up. "We're gonna miss the game, we're…"

"No we're not. Don't worry son." Snapped out of his revelry the man glanced over his shoulder, sending the ghosts of nostalgia packing. The boy sensed it, felt intimidated and simultaneously comforted by it and when his father commanded *Sit back Scanner, sit back*, he knew better than to continue grumbling.

The man expertly executed a screeching hi-speed U-turn. The engine roared and revved and the Maverick burnt rubber as it sped home, back to Bayside.

"We got plenty of time son, we're gonna make it, I promise."

It had taken them thirty minutes to get near the MECCA Arena. The game would start in fifty. As they raced back, the boy, pinned in the back seat, once more searched for his father's eyes. He loved his dad, loved him so much. He had been acting strangely earlier, but now he was back, his dad, HIS dad. He KNEW they would make it.

The car came to a halt in front of the restored colonial home. The man honked the horn to announce their unexpected return, jumped out of the Maverick with the engine left running and, before sprinting to the front door, turned to the boy: "Stay in the car son, I'll be back in no time."

No time turned into minutes that stretched an eternity.

"Where are you? Come on dad."

The boy climbed over the front seat and opened the curbside door, ready to get out of the car and check up on what was taking his dad so long.

An apocalyptic fireball spewed shards of glass and splintered wood into the air. The force of the explosion catapulted the boy back into the passenger seat. The door slammed shut. His house rained down on the hood and roof of the Maverick in a thousand torn and mangled pieces.

The car rocked violently, like an almost empty candy box in the hands of a sweet-toothed monster checking if there was anything left inside worth devouring. He wanted to scream, dad, mom, but there was no sound. There was only silence, and people running in slow motion, running up to the car, opening the door, turning off the ignition. The engine died.

PART ONE
CHICAGO, 1999

NOT ALL GOLD GLITTERS

There was a hard rain falling. A real rain. A Robert De Niro rain. A rain with the power to wash the scum off the street. Problem was, Scanner thought, the real scum stayed mostly inside these days.

Probably just as well, otherwise he'd be out of a job.

Not that there was a flood of work coming his way. The summer had been slow. Hot weather, short skirts, long legs and cold beers kinda had that effect on people. Mellowing them to the point of lethargy. Even criminals enjoyed their holidays.

Three cases. That was all he had worked on. A mere three cases. In what? As many months? Even to call all of them cases was stretching it a bit, though it made him feel better.

The insurance fraud had taken a while to figure out. Clever bastard that one.

Evil son of a bitch. Killed his institutionalized twin brother with a drug overdose, the coroner's verdict was accidental suicide. He dug up the body one month after the funeral, used it to fake his own death in a crash and burn. The wife got a huge insurance payout but instead of joining her deceased husband, as planned, in some tropical paradise, she finally realized her own dream and took off with her massage therapist. This caused a certain degree of suspicion so soon after her beloved husband's death, but what could they do? The DNA matched. Still, Scanner was brought in and he had done what had so often proved to be the best course of action: wait. Wait and smell.

He knew straight away that the whole episode stunk, literally. While alive, the man had suffered from a rare metabolic disorder known as fish odour syndrome. Medical records showed he had a very mild case, not noticeable under normal conditions but exacerbated by raised stress levels or by excitement and sweat. Poor wife, Scanner sympathized. Having sex in a fish market wouldn't appeal to him.

The burned corpse carried no fish scent at all; Scanner had thought that odd, given that immolation was generally considered to be stressful.

Before long the waiting paid off. Deprived of cash and Eve, paradise turned to hell, the dead husband returned to exact revenge. Afterwards, Scanner put the police on his fishy trail.

After that case, he'd done a new tenant background check. Second generation German immigrant. Psychiatrist. Renting a penthouse in one of the city's prime spaces.

Business must have been booming. The man looked like a Freud wannabe on uppers. But he was clean, no records, and rich. Independently wealthy, Scanner had written in his first report, the beneficiary of a well endowed trust fund. As soon as his client, the building's property agent, had found this out, the case was closed. No need to probe further. Money was often one giant cataract.

Mrs. Kowalski's missing cat was, well… It had shown him that his heart still had soft spots, at least one, a revelation he had found strangely comforting. He couldn't bear telling the fragile Polish immigrant concierge her beloved Misty had been the main supporting actress in a local youth gang's voodoo play, sacrificing heart, liver and eyes. So when he had found what was left of Misty, he'd placed the corpse in a Gucci shoulder bag a wealthy ex-client had left in his office, hoping he would call her to collect, weighed the bloody bag down with a couple of bricks, and dumped it in the lake. That sure solved the problem.

A friend at animal welfare gave him a replacement cat, a lovingly cared for pet named Milky. Not a twin, but close enough. Counting on Mrs. Kowalski's failing eyesight he brought Milky back, told her the missing cat had obviously gone through a harrowing ordeal, was severely traumatized and desperately needed her TLC, never mind Misty's occasional off-kilter behavior.

Three cases, three months. No gravy train. But he didn't worry. People would soon come off summer's high and return to their normal criminal selves.

The sound of trouble being pushed under Scanner's door ended his daydreaming. Mail, bills probably – they never cut you any slack, no matter the season. He gathered up the envelopes. What was this? His eyes picked out a yellow colored window envelope. Printed on the front was a semicircle, like an emblazed rising sun, with the words FRIESIAN GOLD underneath. He checked the window. Mr. Scanner Grant PI. The address matched.

Damn these bankers with their investment funds, they must have felt the squeeze as well, coming after a guy like him. He crumbled the envelope into a neat little ball, steadied himself, eyed the trashcan across the room.

"And theeeere is Winters" Scanner shouted, in his best announcer imitation, "Relentless intensity out there, the Bucks keep up the pressure, Brian Winters, Winteeeers!" Just as Scanner released the 16 feet shot he caught a faint hint of some familiar scent. Something feminine. He couldn't quite place it but he had learned to trust his olfactory faculty above any other sensory input. He rushed to the basket and shouted "Winters has done it again."

Upon closer inspection the rising sun wasn't a sun at all but a glowing, beaming half a wheel of Gouda cheese. Femininity and cheese. Scanner was intrigued.

CHEESY

*D*ear *Mr. Grant,* the short letter began, *you don't know me, but a kind, elderly taxi driver I met suggested I get in touch with you. You can help, he said. My father is missing. He is the only one I have in this world. He went to China, selling cheese. He never came back.*

The letter was signed "Max Zwoelstra". Scanner looked at the building and street address but he didn't recognize it.

***

Even after all these years, the '77 Maverick handled itself well. Scanner decided to drive to Milwaukee rather than take the short commuter flight. He felt safe in this car. Powerfully modified way beyond the original specs. He smiled. Kinda like him, still recognizable on the outside.

After reading the poignant cry for help a few times over, he had called the office of Friesian Gold. The appointment was for the afternoon, and with a little luck he'd be back by nightfall.

Music flowed from all four corners of the interior. The tape with his father's favorite songs had long gone, but Lobsang had given him an exact copy, on compact disc. *Lobsang, you crazy Lama, what are you up to?* A kind, elderly taxi driver, Max Zwoelstra had written in the letter. *Who else?*

Scanner had a state of the art sound system installed in the

Maverick. The least he could do for his dad. And besides, this music had to be played loud. He dialed up the volume; let the music blow his thoughts away.

"She's got it, yeah baby she's got it…" Scanner knew all the lyrics *by heart.*

Shocking Blue, they were Dutch, most likely not from Gouda though.

***

When Scanner stepped out of the elevator, 34 floors up, he entered into a little piece of Holland. Posters of windmills decorated the walls, the carpet radiated a grassy shade of green and three life-size fiberglass Friesian cows confronted him head on. It felt – what was the right word? – cheesy.

"Welcome to Friesian Gold", the smiling secretary said. Scanner was a little disappointed she wasn't dressed in a milkmaid's costume, wooden shoes, the whole kit. Would have looked good on her.

"Please go in, Max is expecting you."

The floor-to-ceiling windows at the opposite end of the office framed a spectacular view. Scanner stood for a moment, the doorknob firmly in his hand. Max was a woman. Why hadn't he considered that? His mind was getting rigid; he had assumed the whiff of fragrance originated with the secretary who handled the letter, not with the heir apparent of a multi-million dollar cheese empire.

"Come in Mr. Grant. I am sooo happy you could make it."

Never-ending legs wrapped in black tights supported an hourglass silhouette. Black lace-up ankle boots, heels higher than a pet Chihuahua, marked one end. The other… Scanner was breathless. Lush, golden angel hair cascaded down between bare shoulders to just above the waistline of a tight black knit mini dress, stretched to bursting point over the perfect reclining eight of Max's buttocks.

Get a hold of yourself Scanner.
Now!

"Quite a sight isn't it?" Max continued to look out of the window.

Scanner realized he still held on to the doorknob, knuckles turning white.

"Lake Michigan."

Now!

"Yes, yes, stunning."

He staggered to the far end of the office, barely able to command his buckling knees. When the angel finally turned, she revealed a flawless China doll face, a classic Rubens bosom and mind-blowing emerald eyes.

"Hi, I am Max."

Without a doubt, Scanner thought, without a doubt.

Rebirth

"Actually, it's Maxim, that's the name my father gave me when he adopted me."

Max extended her arm and walked Scanner to a couple of steel frame designer chairs, positioned on either side of a table Scanner recognized from a magazine picture as a Rietveld.

"Take a seat Mr. Grant, and I will tell you my story."

The contrast with the cheesiness of the reception area couldn't be more pronounced, Scanner thought, now that he was actually starting to pay attention to the interior. Art covered most of the walls. He recognized Andy Warhol's four renderings of Dutch Queen Beatrix flanked by a set of brightly colored, medium-sized lithographs; both depicting heavily stylized naked women and exotic animals. He particularly liked the one with the tiger.

"That's a Corneille" Max explained. "*La Femme avec le Tigre*, it reminds me of our dualistic nature, the animal in all of us."

Scanner had never heard of Corneille, the style seemed familiar though. Art was mostly a closed book to him. The stellar prices paid for some of the stuff were incomprehensible. Good job if you could get it, though you had to be dead to get paid the most.

Scanner didn't need a painting to remind him of the animal inside and the sort of art he appreciated most was talking to him right now.

"Call me Scanner, please."

"Sure. You know, Mister, eh, Scanner, before coming to the city looking for someone, anyone, to help me, I felt so alone, abandoned. I needed help, I mean, I was going to do it on my own, I am not afraid or anything like that but this voice in my head told me someone out there knows what you're going through, I mean really *knows*, so go and find this person."

Scanner settled back in the chair, a gesture meant to tell Max that all was fine, that he was here to hear her out.

"After landing, at the airport, I felt really stupid though. Having acted on a whim like that. The best I could hope for was to find a professional who would take my money and tell me to go to Interpol, leave it to other professionals."

"That's sound advice."

"Yes, perhaps. But then I took a taxi to my hotel and the moment I sat down inside I felt, I don't know, this may sound weird to you, I felt reassured."

It didn't sound weird to Scanner. He nodded.

"We just drove around, I mean, the driver asked me what I was doing in the city and I told him everything. It didn't feel odd. It never occurred to me to tell him it was none of his business, I just spilled the beans. And he just kept on driving. In the end, we were back at the airport, he handed me a piece of paper with your name on it, told me to write to you, make sure to dab the envelope with a few drops of Shalimar by Guerlain and have a nice flight home."

Max's entire body had shifted to the edge of the seat and now meandered back into its centre. She shook her head as if she herself could barely believe what she just had just told Scanner. "You must think I am insane."

Maybe, Scanner thought, but he wasn't gonna tell her, he enjoyed her spirited monologue, her body language. "So here I am. Tell me about your father."

"Right. You must wonder how an Asian girl ended up on a Wisconsin cheese farm. My dad, he's Dutch. He adopted me when I was five years old."

Max took a deep breath and exhaled purposefully.

"In the summer of seventy-nine, a ramshackle, barely seaworthy fishing boat set off from the port city of Vung Tau, Southern Vietnam, under cover of a moonless night. You see; they had no intention of going fishing. They already had a catch, a cargo, a human cargo. Tired of the countless brutal incursions into Vietnamese territory by the soldiers of the Khmer Rouge, the Vietnamese communist government had decided enough was enough and sent in the army to not only defeat the invaders but to liberate Cambodia from their oppressive regime. Much to the chagrin of communist China, at that time the Khmer Rouge's ally, the Vietnamese succeeded. A bunch of bad losers, the Chinese invaded the North of Vietnam, which was a pretty bad idea because the battle hardened Vietnamese kicked their butt. You still with me?"

Scanner nodded, he hadn't expected a history lesson. It hadn't been his favorite topic in school. Then again, they didn't have teachers like Max back then.

"After the fall of Saigon in 1975, living conditions for the Chinese Vietnamese citizens of the city, in fact for most of the people, deteriorated rapidly. First many ARVN officers, sorry, that is the name for the South Vietnamese Army, you know that don't you?"

"Yes I do" Scanner whispered, not so sure anymore that he really wanted to go there.

"At first, many officers, rather than accept their imminent capture, committed suicide. I don't know, maybe my real father did the same. I never met him. Tell you the truth; I can't remember anything from that time. I've read a lot of course, but remember nothing. Soon the shortages set in. There wasn't enough food to get by. Around that time I was born. Like I said, those years draw a blank with me. When the war with China started, ethnic Chinese really got it bad. So a lot of them decided to escape, by boat."

Max paused, picked up the phone from the table. "I need some water, sorry, I am such a bad host, I haven't offered you anything." She dialed zero for reception. "Could you bring us some cold water, Hilde dear?"

"You like your art." Scanner decided small talk would ease the built up emotions.

"Those are all my dad's." Max smiled. "He is a farmer but that doesn't mean you can't appreciate art. And everything except the Warhol is Dutch. A lot of talent for such a small country, don't you think?"

There was a knock on the door and the receptionist entered carrying a tray with two glasses of ice-cold water. She was a tall girl; at least five seven. Short-cropped blond hair accentuated a resolute jaw. Pale blue eyes, a sharp nose and thin lips added to the projected determination. In fact everything about Hilde was full of purpose, Scanner noticed. Pretty, in a martial Northern European kind of way. Not exactly his type, but someone else's for sure.

"Thanks Hilde dear."

Scanner's eyes trailed Max's secretary as she marched out of the room.

"It's her first day as a temp, she should have offered you something to drink the moment you arrived. Sorry, my long-time assistant is absent, twisted her ankle yesterday when some guy late for an appointment bumped into her. Where were we, oh yes, talent. The Dutch seem to have a disproportionate amount of it. Dad has it, his cheeses are consistently ranked amongst the world's best."

Max sighed and sipped from the icy water.

"My mother must have felt desperate at that time, with a little daughter, not enough to eat, the future a black hole. So she decided to escape. It was a lucrative trade, refugees. The Vietnamese government distrusted the ethnic Chinese and would rather see them leave. Not before extracting a price though. Three to four thousand dollars in gold seemed to have been the going rate. I don't know where she got it, but we made it onto that boat, that night, out of Vung Tau, into the unknown."

Silence. For a fleeting moment, Scanner stared into the unknown through Max's eyes; dark blue shifting to jungle green and back to blue, depending on how she turned her head, how the light fell, like the fathomless depths of the deepest oceans, sucking you in, wondering if you'd ever be able to descend far enough to see the bottom.

"At that time dad was working on an exploration vessel in the South China Sea. Hard work, he told me. But he was young, adventurous, single. It was a Dutch ship, drilling for a German-Vietnamese joint venture. The name of the Vietnamese company was Petro Vietnam, communist owned of course. Not many people back in Holland were aware this was going on. There was an embargo. Not only the Chinese were sore losers, you know."

Scanner shifted in his chair. By now he was fully engrossed in this young woman's life story. She knew how to bring it on. Measured passion, at times on the brink of boiling over, but always in control.

"One morning, it was during monsoon season, strong winds and ash-laden skies, the crew discovers a small fifty-foot wooden fishing boat, packed to the hilt with refugees, attached to their anchor line, on starboard side, somewhat protected from the elements. The contract signed by the mother company with Petro Vietnam explicitly forbade them to take any refugees on board without the approval of the communist authorities. There were these people on board of my dad's ship you know, these eh, what do you call them, these communist agents."

"Commissars," Scanner interrupted.

"Yes, yes, thank you. Commissars, that's what they were called. There to check on the Vietnamese laborers, looking for signs of dissent. One of these guys, this commissar, he starts to argue with the captain, telling him not to take anyone on board, ordering him really. The fishing boat was absolutely packed. More and more people started to rise from its bowels and climb onto the roof shouting *Com, nuoc soi, xinh moi.* They wanted rice, water. It must have taken them at least four days to get that far. They were filthy, covered in shit and vomit. So the crew starts lowering food and water, as much as they can. By now the captain and the commissar are really at it. *This is my boat*, the captain shouts, *and I do as I bloody well please.* Suddenly the fishing boat starts taking water and precariously tilts to one side. Panic and fear grabs hold of the refugees. They shout, they cry. People jump in the ocean, young, old, mothers with children; it is complete and utter mayhem.

Take them on board. Now! The crew only needs half a word from the captain and immediately lowers the lifeboats. The commissar protests, in vain. *Do ma, get out of my way motherfucker!* The captain has picked up enough Vietnamese curse words from the local crew and is fuming. My dad is down with the first lifeboat. As it hits the water the fishing boat starts sinking rapidly. There are waves, high waves, shouting, screaming people, drowning people. Dad doesn't know how to lift them out of the water, he has to hold on with one hand else he will be tossed overboard. Then he has an idea. He hooks two fingers into the nose of a drowning man. He is skinny, they all are skinny. Dad hooks his fingers in the man's nose and manages to lift him out of the water long enough for one of his shipmates to grab him and drag him on board. All around people are drowning, screaming, disappearing. The scent of fear is palpable. *Cong co em, cong co em!* A woman, a young Vietnamese woman, eyes like eggs, round, filled with fear, hope, determination. *My baby, my baby*, she shouts. *Help me, my baby, help me.* Dad looks at her, she barely manages to stay afloat, she holds a little girl, pushes her upwards, pushes her towards my dad. He hangs over the railing of the lifeboat and hooks his arm around me. *Cam on nhieu*, the woman whispers. *Thank you*. Then a wave rolls in and swallows her."

PRINCESS

Scanner averted his eyes, got up and walked over to the Corneille. She shouldn't see his eyes. He felt tears well up, had to keep it down, invisible. He didn't know this woman. Couldn't let her see his emotions, couldn't let her in. Was that really true? He had just witnessed her birth; he knew all there was to know.

"That day, two hundred and twenty people boarded my father's ship", Max had moved beside Scanner. "More than eighty found peace beneath the waves, my mother was among them."

For a few moments they both stood there, staring at the naked woman, the tiger hovering over her ochre-colored body. Duality was a bitch sometimes.

"My dad wouldn't let go of me. Back on board. He kept holding me, rocking me, saying *I'm so sorry, I'm so sorry.* Finally the doctor took dad and me into the ship's infirmary for a checkup. I had no papers, no identification, no name. I was wrapped in a large sheet, turned out to be a tablecloth. In one corner there was a name, a logo really. A crown, and written underneath in capital letters MAXIM'S. My dad later found out that this was the logo of a nightclub and restaurant in downtown Saigon. For him it was a sign, there was no alternative. My name would be Maxim. I was his little princess. And now he has disappeared!"

THE PRODIGAL SON

Max slumped back in her chair. Trembling hands cupped her face, only letting the occasional muffled sob pass through. Scanner was at a loss, not something he experienced often, and not something he allowed to happen frequently. Not anymore. It's gonna be all right, he wanted to say. Put his hand on her shoulder, show her someone cared. He waved the thought away. Unprofessional conduct, taking advantage of a distressed client and more such bullshit. Who was he fooling?

"How did you manage to get to Holland after that, that's where you went right?" Back on the job.

"Yes, yes. That's where we went, finally. It was a long ordeal. We were on the ship, safe, but the ship couldn't just leave, they had work to do. Though with all those refugees on board that had become next to impossible. There was a lot of diplomatic fencing I guess, I don't really know. Dad never told me, and I guess he didn't really know either. In the end, all the refugees were picked up by a supply vessel, brought to Singapore, flown to Holland. Dad too. He'd had enough. He was more traumatized than I, never wanted to work on a boat again. He had grown up on a dairy farm, his parents wanted him to continue the family business. Young and rebellious, one day he had packed his bags and announced he was going to the Far East, to seek his fortune in exploration. Opa and Oma must have been heartbroken, but they knew better than to cage a free spirit. When he returned with me, there were no questions, no we told you so, there was an acceptance, there was family. Life has its seasons, in one you sow, in another you reap, they knew better than most."

"So how did you end up in Wisconsin?"

Let's not talk about family.

ABODE OF LOVE

"What did you tell her about me?"

Scanner entered the taxi in front of his building. He had made the call earlier. Not via the telephone though. He had told Mrs. Kowalski he needed a ride. She knew. All she had to do was to put the red geranium in the window of her little cubicle instead of the purple violets.

"I did not tell her anything. That's not what Lobsang does. You know me Scanner. By the way, nice to see you, how are you Lobsang? It's been a while."

"Yes, sorry, I am sorry. You look good." Scanner smiled, slightly embarrassed. How long had he known this man? Lobsang was like a father to him, ever since... But the question burned in his mind, hadn't left since he returned the previous night. "Yes, I know but, man, did she push the right buttons."

"I didn't tell her anything about you. That is up to you. What and when and where. I only facilitate meeting. The river runs but the yaks only drink when thirsty, we say in Tibet" Lobsang shifted into first gear and the taxi joined the widening stream of morning commuters.

"Talking about meeting. How did you meet her in the first place?"

"You know, she came to the airport."

"And you just happened to pick her up. Shalimar by Guerlain, that sure was a nice touch."

"How long I know you, eh? You were fourteen. I see you grow up, I know what ticks you."

"What makes me tick, Lobsang, what makes me tick."

"Yes, yes, that too. I know. Lobsang knows."

"It was my mother's perfume, wasn't it?"

"She loved it. Didn't care for anything else. Jack, your father, always returned from Paris with a bottle. Straight from the source, for his very own queen, he would say, nothing less would do."

Scanner relaxed in the back seat. A scent was like a time machine. It had the power to transport you instantly to a bygone era. Nothing more than a trace was needed, if you were sensitive. He was sensitive. By the force of his extraordinary willpower and under the guidance of Lobsang, his olfactory faculties had developed beyond a mortal man's capability. It would never happen again. That day. Never.

"So what about Max? You gonna help?"

Scanner smiled; the old lama would continue to point at the river until he got down to drink.

"We will fly to Hong Kong in a few days. That's where her dad was the last time they spoke. Attending a cheese conference or something like that, a Grand Prix du Fromage. China's the next big market for Friesian Gold. An uphill battle Max told me, but those are the ones her father enjoys fighting. Tell me about China, Lobsang. You were there right? Isn't that where you met dad?"

"Tibet, Scanner, Tibet." Lobsang spoke forcefully. "Not China. I met your father trying to keep my country free."

GAME OF CHICKEN

"What was he like, my father?"

Scanner had asked Lobsang this question many times over the years, and the old Tibetan had never grown tired of weaving a different story each time he'd answered. Scanner was grateful for Lobsang's patience, the tales that kept his father alive. The comfort he found in Lobsang's stories had pulled Scanner back from the abyss more than once.

"I met Jack Grant for the first time in *Dhumra*, the Garden, back in 1959. That's what we called it, Camp Hale. It reminded us of our home in Tibet. The home we no longer had. I was young, full of fighting spirit, a Khampa, a Tibetan cowboy. I wanted to fight the Chinese invaders, kick them out. But we had nothing, no weapons, no rifles. Just our horses and our knives."

Lobsang chuckled. It was obvious he enjoyed these trips down memory lane. Stuck in morning traffic, the taxi wasn't going anywhere soon. The driver and the passenger though had embarked upon a journey across time and space.

"Knives. Ha. Your father wanted to impress us. Define borders, right from the start. Who was in charge and all that. He was strong, athletic, confident. Perhaps a little too much. So he challenged all of us, Baba, Jamba and me. We had signed up together; you know as childhood friends we were inseparable. So Jack says *let's see what you're made of, one on one.*

Back in Litang, during the summer, we had big competitions on the grasslands. Archery, equestrian skills, knife fighting. For three seasons in a row I was the champion, very popular with the girls. So I step forward and he sizes me up, from head to toe, laughs, says *let's go cowboy* and hands me a switchblade. Now I was still wearing my sheep-skin-lined *chuba*, the traditional Tibetan winter coat, long sleeves tied around my waist, cause the sun was out and it was quite hot. I shake my head, refuse the offered weapon, my hand disappears inside my coat and when it comes back out it holds my father's sixteen inch knife, a family heirloom given to me before we left for the border. Then I repeat, *let's go cowboy*." Lobsang was beaming, laughing loudly. "You should have seen the worried look on your father's face. We all nearly rolled over laughing!"

"Did you fight, after that?"

"No, no, never meant to. It was a game of chicken, see who would retreat first. But the ice was broken, we became friends, Jack and me, real friends."

The traffic started to move and Lobsang put the taxi in gear. The trusted Chevy coughed forward, reluctantly joining the morning zombie caravan. Scanner felt very much alive though, basking in his father's presence

"Of course Jack was by far the strongest, especially in upper body strength. You see; he was a smoke jumper, a daredevil parachuting in front of out of control wild fires, digging trenches, combating the flames, saving lives. It was off-season and he was hired to teach us the finer points of paradropping over rough terrain."

Scanner knew the story, had read the accounts. They had called it Operation St. Circus. Inserting US-trained Tibetan fighters back into Chinese occupied areas of Eastern and North Eastern Tibet. Causing a nuisance to the People's Liberation Army, was how the US government described the mission internally. Liberating our homeland, as the Tibetans eagerly anticipated. The diverging goals only became apparent later, after the massacres. *Realpolitik* triumphed; idealism was no longer useful or needed, the Tibetan fighters were sacrificed, pawns in a game they had failed to comprehend from the start.

"Life didn't turn out to be as black and white as we thought back then." Lobsang seemed to pick up on his thoughts. "I was naïve, privileged. My father, he was a trader, we had a good life. But others were not as fortunate, were kept as serfs, mistreated or worse. Still, the Chinese should have kept out." Lobsang shook his head. "Enough reminiscing for now, there is something else I want to discuss with you, something that worries me and, if I am right, something very evil."

For an almost negligible instant Scanner noticed a hint of fear in the old Tibetan's eyes. Too short to be certain, he waved it away. "Sure, but first, pull over, there, around the corner, it's time for a toast. I brought you some, better than last time, I think."

The taxi came to a halt in the deserted side alley and Scanner handed Lobsang a five-liter plastic jerry can.

"You think? You want Lobsang to try? Not vinegar like last time?"

"No, it's good. I know. I took my time, lowered the temperature, slow and low, just like you told me. This time my *chang* is the real deal. Try it."

Lobsang opened the glove compartment, took out a gleaming polished wooden bowl and filled it with the thick, milky white liquid from the container. Both men got out of the taxi and silently faced each other on the sidewalk.

"For heaven, for earth, for those who have left us," Lobsang pronounced solemnly, flicking a drop of the traditional barley brew into the air with his ring finger each time, before downing the contents in one large gulp. "Good," he finally uttered, "you make an old man happy." He filled the bowl a second time and handed it over to Scanner.

"For heaven, for earth, for those who have left us."

Scanner drank. The two men hugged.

Before getting back in the taxi Scanner noticed for the first time the brand new yellow license plate, RINPOCHE stamped across in blue capital letters.

Nice touch, you old lama, nice touch.

"Now what is it you want to discuss with me?"

Amnesia

"A teenage girl from our community has disappeared."

"I've heard." Scanner replied. He maintained an amicable relationship with local law enforcement. "That was last week, right?"

"Yes, ten days ago exactly. But she was not the first Tibetan girl to go missing lately, there were five more girls before that."

This surprised Scanner, Sue hadn't told him about other girls. Was the rookie detective holding out on him?

"They weren't reported," Lobsang continued, "because they all returned home within two days. We are a pretty tight knit community you know and don't like to wash our dirty laundry."

"To air, Lobsang, to air one's dirty laundry in public, that's the idiom, but yes, I know what you mean." Scanner had grown up in the Tibetan community, considered them his extended family. His only family.

"All five girls returned to their homes and acted as if nothing had happened. Just a normal day, doing normal things. When asked where they had been for two days they thought their families were taking them for a ride. As it turned out not one of the girls could remember anything. For them, those days were not missing, they never existed, all recollection wiped out."

JONATHAN H KEMP

Lobsang accelerated and overtook several slow moving vehicles. Traffic had eased, cars moved into allocated slots in parking garages, the passengers into the tinier cubicles above. Another day at the office. And make it a productive one. Scanner was glad his office was in his head, unbound by physical restraints, not compartmentalized. The thought that files could go missing, whatever the reason, was somewhat upsetting though. Maybe he should start writing down more.

"None of the girls showed any sign of physical harm being done. No bruises, no cuts, no forced penetration. A psychiatrist examined them, didn't discover any clues. It was odd, disturbing, but life went on. We all opted for collective amnesia, until Dolma didn't return."

"I need all the information on the girls you can get. Family records, school, friends, activities, you name it. Can you do that for me? I mean I'm gonna go to Hong Kong with Max the day after tomorrow, but we'll keep in touch. If anything shows up you've gotta let me know. I don't know how long I will be away for, but anyway you can scan files and email them to me. Or use Fedex if you're worried someone might be snooping. In the meantime I know Sue is aware. She might be a rookie but she's no fool, she has a good heart and I'll tell her to put as much time into Dolma as she can get away with."

"Thanks Scanner." Lobsang sighed. "I am worried, really worried. I sense an evil spirit at work, it is strong. I can't mention it to the police, they'll think I am mad. But you know Lobsang, I can tell you, you understand."

Scanner understood. The world was a materialistic place, people's motivations primarily selfish; greed, fear, power, even love wanted a return most of the time. Life as a whole made little sense to him, though under the old Lama's guidance Scanner had started to see connections where before only chaos had ruled. He had no problem with spirits.

"I'll do what I can, I promise. We'll get to the bottom of this."

The taxi stopped and Scanner looked up. They had returned to his residence. Lobsang's timing was impeccable, as always, a legacy of the training with Jack.

"Pass my regards to Mrs. Kowalski," Lobsang rolled down the window before driving off. "Tell her I'll come and play bingo at the club soon."

***

"Mr. Scanner, this was just delivered for you. Are you going on a trip?"

The fragile Polish concierge handed him a Friesian Gold envelope. The window unmistakably revealed an airline ticket. *Next time you'd better obscure that window, Max.* That Mrs. Kowalski knew his movements was not a problem. *But who else?*

"Yes, I am going to Hong Kong. Got myself a job. By the way, that's a very nice perfume you're wearing today."

Keeper

The wooden stairs creaked under Scanner's feet. It wasn't so much that he was overweight – his exercise regimen was starting to pay off – but the stairs were old, ancient. In fact, this whole place was way past its expiry date and would have been torn down years ago if it hadn't been for a dispute over an inheritance. Funny, Scanner thought, how the dead can keep things alive. *Concentrate on the ascent, move from your hips.* By no means as graceful as a skilled Balinese temple dancer carrying a tower of fruit offerings on her head, he nevertheless did somehow manage to eliminate the heavier grunts. The ones that persisted carried on even after he reached the third floor.

He found the door to room 304 at the end of the gloomy hallway slightly ajar, spilling patches of red light onto the stained carpet. He gingerly pushed the door inwards and stepped into a nearly empty room.

"Smell this you creep."

A woman's voice emanated from behind the door. Before he could turn around she had jumped on his back and covered his nose and mouth with a cotton cloth. It was a familiar scent. Scanner smiled and passed out.

When he came to a few minutes later he had no problem recognizing where he was. He'd been there before. He was stripped of his clothes, lying on his back, legs and arms shackled to the four-poster bed, the only piece of furniture, endlessly reproduced in the opposing mirrors.

"One of these days you're gonna overdo it officer and I will be under for so long you're gonna have to go downstairs and pay for another hour." He joked with his uniformed assailant who sat astride his legs.

"Fat chance, I'd go insane having to wait that long for you to get up."

He was getting up alright. Sue noticed and smiled.

"I hate waiting, you know me Scanner, I am a punctual girl." She slowly unbuttoned her jacket, slid out of it in two highly choreographed movements and dropped it gently to the floor.

"So I have noticed," Scanner replied as the topless rookie cop inched forward.

"I like my man to come on time."

Scanner was more than happy to oblige.

Afterwards, unshackled, the raging fire reduced to a soothing afterglow, he pressed her tightly to his chest. He totally dug this girl. Smart, sharp, a good sense of humor, no nonsense. Petite, adorable, dangerous. Able to floor, cuff and book in one fluent motion. And she knew how to handle a gun. That's how they had met, at the range. A keeper by any standard, sometimes Scanner wondered what was holding him back.

"So you are leaving me, Mr. Private Investigator?" Emphasizing the 'private', Sue angled her head upwards, kissing Scanner's nipples on the way.

"Just for a while, gotta go to Hong Kong. Missing person case. I could really use the money."

"I have heard your new employer is quite a looker."

No use hiding anything from a police officer.

"Max? Yes, she's something else altogether, a bit, eh, overwhelming."

"Don't get overwhelmed too much." Sue laughed. "Don't worry, I am not jealous. Just a bit worried. Remember what we talked about after we met, the first time we made love?"

Scanner remembered, they were free, consenting adults, enjoying each other's company, a joy that would not be diminished by notions of possession.

What I am asking, Sue had said, is that when we are together, physically together, there is only us, that's all I want, our moments together, unburdened by anything or anyone else.

Truly a keeper.

She gently bit his lower lip and let her tongue wander inside.

"It's going to be a while then, I guess," she finally whispered. "Let's opt for paying the overstay."

***

Sue was ready to leave, looking radiantly girlish in her flower dress. The uniform folded and returned to the wheeled pink carry-on she had come with. "I am going to miss you, do return soon." She reached for the doorknob.

Taking his cue from Sue's words, Scanner walked over and leaned against the door. "I almost forgot; Lobsang told me there have been more missing girls, but unlike Dolma, they returned home after about two days, before anyone filed a report. I promised to ask you to look into it. He seemed truly worried, almost scared, I've never seen him like that before."

"I'll do what I can, I know how to get a hold of him. By the way, I have heard leather is cheap in Hong Kong, bring me back something sexy."

HONG KONG HERE WE COME

The airport buzzed with activity. More and more people traveled these days. The concept of holidays was a strange one. Escape the daily grind, recharge your batteries, visit exotic destinations and immerse yourself in other cultures. Cold feet often preceded the immersion and most people happily sheltered in the comfort of a hotel room with running hot water, a bathrobe in the closet, CNN on the TV and a percolator next to a basket filled with 3-in-1 coffee sachets. There wasn't anything wrong with comfort as such, but you've got home for that. Holidays were also a fertile breeding ground for marital problems and many divorces found their origins on a sun-filled beach where dear hubby couldn't keep his eyes from wandering. At least the part of escaping the daily grind was true. Escape permanently.

Scanner checked his watch. Where was Max? They had agreed to check in together so they would be seated next to each other. Use the long flight to discuss strategy. He scouted the departure area, rotating on his heels like a human lighthouse, all the while focusing his beaming eyes on the ebb and flow of people. Lots of tour groups. Asian mostly, Chinese probably. They were getting richer, so they spread their wings, and all wearing identical travel agent bags and sporting red baseball caps, they traipsed in the wake of their guide who feverishly waved a yellow triangular flag. Nothing glorious about that, Scanner thought. And no Max. Damn. He had cast her as the reliable type. He didn't like late, never had, ever since he was a kid.

"Hey stranger, are you looking for me?"

Scanner turned around. The woman who had, since he'd arrived, been sitting on the bench not far behind him stood up and walked over.

"You guys are all the same." Max laughed. "Wave something long and blond, wear something short and tight and the mind gets all mushy. You weren't seriously considering the possibility my hair was real, were you?"

Scanner looked at Max. He recognized her now. Vaguely. The golden locks, the black tights, the black boots and the emerald eyes were replaced by short cropped spiky hair, blue track suit pants, flower patterned Converse All Stars and dark brown eyes behind rimless glasses. She looked like an Asian exchange student, a sports major, maybe a volleyball player. Her sleeveless white top fitted like a second skin and Scanner noticed that at least two of Max's attributes weren't fake.

"I, eh, you were hard to spot. And you left Shalimar at home."

"Ah, I see, well that is not my favorite anyways. I seldom put on any fragrance, I am a natural girl, but if I do I like something younger, more energetic, bordering on the subversive, something like this."

Max delved into her *Free Tibet* shoulder bag, extricated a palm-sized pink porcelain bottle, shaped like a hand grenade, *Agent Provocateur* written across its face.

"What do you think? It's a pre-production sample, I know the designer. It will be out soon, I'm testing it."

Two short puffs and a tiny droplet of fragrant juice collected in her delicate jugular notch. Scanner's brain flashed a warning. *Complex, flowery, hints of wood, animalistic, sensual, direct, tough love, rough sex, sweet talk.* "It suits you," he replied neutrally.

***

"Any check-in luggage?" the girl behind the counter asked.

Scanner traveled light. Always had. There was no knowing how long they would be in Hong Kong or where they would travel afterwards. Bring the necessities and pick up what you need along the way.

"How about you madam?"

AIRBORNE

"The blond wig was the idea of the PR department. They came up with this great TV Commercial for Friesian Gold." Max loosened the airplane seatbelt buckle and folded her legs underneath. "Meant for the Chinese market of course. Trying to get a foothold there is our greatest challenge. It's all about image, projection. Do you know they drink Petrus over ice?"

Scanner was well into a bottle of '93 Bourgogne, courtesy of Cathy Lee, chief purser. Flying up front had its perks and Scanner wasn't going to let them go to waste. Petrus was out of his league though. Always had been, ever since the priest at bible class had introduced that treacherous SOB to him.

"It's a sign of status, of power. Price trumps taste in this game. The more you can afford to pay, the higher your prestige. Friesian Gold is one of the best mature Goudas out there, gold medal you know, but by itself that doesn't mean a thing in the Chinese market. So we are trying to project an image of success, of glamour. Perhaps even a bit of cheese-induced sexual prowess. That's where my blonde alter ego fits in. Girls dig it when you eat Friesian Gold, that's the message."

Scanner held up his glass for a refill. Cathy was digging him, Scanner Grant. Wasn't his good looks. Last time he confronted himself in the mirror they hadn't returned. Gone the day his mother stopped breastfeeding. Average height, average build, average clothes, not so average female companion. Must be doing something right, chief purser Cathy Lee probably figured, and so continued to lavish her attention on him.

"You're up against shark fin, rhino horn, deer antler, tiger penis and other such delicacies." Scanner wanted Max to know he had done his homework.

"Disgusting isn't it? I mean, you got to be kidding. Shark fin is tasteless, rhino horn has the same composition as your fingernails and tiger penis? Castrated to extinction. It makes me furious, ashamed to be Chinese. If I can help reverse the tide, if Friesian Gold can become the next hot thing, the next limp penis implant and stop the sharks from getting killed, hey, I'll wear a wig and shake my booty."

Scanner had to hand it to her; the girl had morals. In her position, she didn't need them. Most people would consider them a hindrance. Most people would never get to her position weighed down by morals. With her physique she could just about shake anything at anyone and entire fortunes would be surrendered voluntarily. Scanner didn't worry. Max was probing at the fringes but he had locked up pretty tight. Time for another refill.

"She fancies you."

"Wouldn't count on it. I think she's hedging her bets. I think she can't, for the life of her, figure out what you're doing with me unless I am somebody or am someone who knows someone who is somebody."

"Give yourself some credit, Scanner, you decided to come with me on this crazy mission, to help me find my father. Your heart is in the right place, women can feel that intuitively, that makes you attractive."

"You're paying me well."

"Don't be such a hard-ass, Mr. Grant." Max playfully ruffled his hair and gently pushed his head away.

"Where was your father the last time you guys talked?"

Scanner decided it was time to get on with the job.

"At the convention center. He had been in Hong Kong three days already, meeting with distributors, finalizing the ad campaign – the one I am going to be in and he was doing some hands-on market research, he told me. That was depressing him a bit, I could tell. There is this entire area on Hong Kong Island, to the West, where shop after shop sells bags full of shark fin and other alleged medicinal and aphrodisiacal stuff. Just walking around the area made him sad, and upset too."

"What was he doing at the convention center?"

"Looking after his booth. They were holding a gourmet fair, luxury food items, delicatessen, fine wines. Golf too. It was all part of a larger event, unashamedly aimed at the mainland China market. People with money and people with access to money, which isn't necessarily the same thing under communist party rule. Here, take a look."

Max handed Scanner an A4 sized glossy booklet. The cover showed a scene that could have been photographed at one of Marie Antoinette's more decadent garden parties, had the camera and the game of golf been invented. What bright, young and promising talent had come up with this, Scanner wondered. Embossed in some oversized golden curly font across the front it read: TASTE OF OPULENCE. And in a smaller font underneath: *The Ultimate Affluent Lifestyle Fair*.

"I need to stretch my legs."

LIQUEFIED AIR

"How are sir and madam doing? Is everything according to your wishes?"

"Actually, I need some air, can you open a window or something?"

Cathy Lee was smiling. "It does get stuffy in here sometimes doesn't it? I am afraid I have to disappoint you there sir, windows are to remain closed, orders from the captain. Last time we opened one a rather corpulent passenger got sucked out. I wouldn't want that to happen to you sir, not when we are having such an interesting conversation. And not that I consider you corpulent, don't get me wrong, that would be an impertinent falsehood." The impeccably dressed stewardess winked at Scanner. *Was she blushing?* "Perhaps sir would like some liquefied air? It's the next best thing we have on board."

"The next best thing eh? Are you sure, chief purser Cathy Lee?" Scanner enjoyed the verbal sparring, wouldn't give it up for any amount of affluent opulence or opulent affluence or whatever the fuck these mind jobs would come up with next.

"Absolutely sir, I would be tempted to try it myself were it not to result in my immediate dishonorable discharge. You see, I quite like my job sir, I get to meet nice people like you."

"You'd better keep it dry then, I'd hate to see you get sacked, the airline industry would absolutely be the poorer for it."

"Thank you sir, I appreciate your encouragement and understanding and will heed your advice. Once I am off the job though, I can consume what I want. Now what will it be, sir?"

"I'll have a single malt then, and I like it straight up."

"Good choice sir, I'll be with you in a minute."

When Scanner lifted the glass from the silver tray, filled with a double measure, he noticed a hastily scribbled number on the paper coaster underneath."

"Enjoy, sir."

HELL'S CLUTCHES

"Are you ok? I am sorry, it's horrible isn't it?"

Scanner had returned to his seat. "Much better now, went and got some air. Was close to throwing up our very own gourmet meal but managed to sedate the impulse just in time."

It had taken him a refill, courtesy of nurse Cathy Lee, to completely suppress the feeling of nausea. Or was it the sparkle in those dark brown eyes, solicited by his request to hit his oxygen-starved soul once more, that was the real medicine?

"Air, eh?" Max frowned. "I'd like to go where the air smells like that. Talking about smelling, what is it with you and your olfactory faculty? You have some kind of super nose?"

Scanner hesitated. His first reaction was to wave it off. It's nothing. I'd rather not tell. It's none of your business. But the alcohol had somewhat smoothed the sharp edges of his usual defensive parameter. *What the hell Scanner, you can share, she's ok. You haven't told her anything about yourself. It's not exactly a secret.*

"When I was fourteen my dad took me to a basketball game." Scanner crossed his legs and turned to face Max. "It was a playoff game, Western Conference. Our team, the Milwaukee Bucks against the Denver Nuggets. Game 6 in the series. An all important game. Losing would mean the end of our championship dreams. While we're driving to the arena my dad starts to behave rather strangely, absentminded, starts asking me weird questions about the date. So I get worried

47

that maybe he has forgotten the tickets. As it turns out he has, and we have to scramble back to our house to get them. He tells me to stay in the car while he runs up to the house. A few minutes or so pass and I am totally impatient. I mean, what is taking so long? I am about to get out of the car to go and check, when the entire house is engulfed in this enormous fireball, followed by the loudest explosion I wish I had never heard." Scanner slowly shook his head. "That Maverick saved my life you know. That's why I still keep it."

"I... I am sorry, I... didn't know." Max stammered.

"It's okay, that was twenty-two years ago, a long time..." Scanner shook his head once more. "It was a gas explosion, there had been a leak. Our house was completely destroyed, only parts of my father and mother were found."

Max took a hold of his hand, pressed it firmly in between hers. Scanner let her, for a few seconds.

"They found me huddled on the driver's seat. I couldn't hear a thing, everyone moved in slow motion. I refused to leave the car, kept rocking back and forth. Finally Lobsang came, your kind taxi driver. My dad and him were best friends, close as brothers. They had met in the fifties, in Colorado, training the Tibetan resistance. Lobsang was the only one who could get through to me, he just grabbed me, lifted me out of the Maverick and carried me home. He and his wife took me in as the son they never had. Lobsang had connections, it was all instantly approved."

It felt kinda good telling his story to Max. Most women he met never knew. Most women he met didn't stay long enough for him to bother. Except for Sue. Scanner smiled. Sue never stayed, but she also never left.

"I was angry, blamed myself for my parents' death. If only I could have smelled the leaking gas. Why didn't I? Why couldn't I? Lobsang helped me to channel my anger. He told me guilt would not bring my parents back but with the right diet and the right mental training I'd be able to honor their lives in my own special way. Lobsang is amazing, he knows so much, he's just an eccentric Tibetan cowboy, a long way from home, but it makes me wonder. Where does all that knowledge come from? Sometimes the idea of reincarnation doesn't seem so far-fetched to me." Scanner paused, took a deep breath. "So there you have it, Scanner Grant PN, Private Nose."

"Can I ask you something? Did you ever find out why your dad was so, eh, how shall I say, so lost in his own world that day? What was the date?"

"It was April 30," Scanner replied. "April 30, 1978. Exactly 3 years after the fall of Saigon."

For the remainder of the flight Scanner entered in and out of a restless slumber.

***

The little boy Scanner parachuted out of the back of a C130, strapped to his father. An intense fire raged below and they were heading straight for the inferno. *Steer away dad, steer away*, he shouted, but his dad couldn't hear him, he was wearing headphones and completely absorbed in his favorite music. Scanner felt the scorching air engulfing them. *Too late he cried, it's gonna be too late.*

Out of the blue Lobsang appeared. Take the boy, his father shouted, take the boy. Lobsang drew an enormous knife and cut Scanner loose from his father. No, no, dad! Scanner was crying. His dad looked at him, touched his forehead with his hand. It was cold, so cold. It's okay, his dad said, it's okay. It's okay.

"It's okay, sir, it's okay."

Scanner woke up. For an instance all reference to time and space was lost. Until he saw a familiar pair of deep brown eyes, clouded over by a worried look. Chief purser Cathy Lee kneeled by his side, dabbing his head with a cold towel.

"You're having a bad dream sir. Probably one whiskey too many. I thought it prudent to wake you. Here, I brought you some water."

Scanner adjusted his chair to a more upright position. "Are you an angel?" he asked, only half jokingly.

"No sir," Cathy Lee laughed, "but I am here to take care of you, steal you away from Hell's clutches so to speak, sir."

"And just in time it was," Scanner whispered softly.

PART TWO
HONG KONG

Role reversal

" "Welcome to the Mandarin Sir. Welcome back, Madam. If you just leave your passports we'll do the check-in formalities for you. We'll get your signatures later. The bellboy will show you your rooms. Oh, by the way sir, someone called half an hour ago. Left a message. Here it is sir." The receptionist handed Scanner an envelope.

"So you've been here before?"

"Yes, The Oriental is my usual residence when I am in Hong Kong."

"Did your dad stay here too?"

"No, no. He prefers something a bit closer to the exhibition center when he is in Hong Kong for a fair. The Shangri-La, I didn't book us there, thought it better not to announce our visit."

"Your floor, madam, sir." The bellboy gestured towards the open elevator doors.

Amazing, Scanner thought. He hadn't even felt the acceleration of the lift car. Smooth wasn't covering it. More like a time machine. Couldn't say he was feeling comfortable though. This wasn't exactly his kinda joint. He much preferred to stay somewhere more low key. Bumpy elevator rides inside a stale smelling stained steel interior or even just a cold concrete stairwell. It was hard to blend in when everything was so designer sanitized. Comfort dulled your senses and that could be fatal for a PI, fatal for anybody, though most people probably were beyond noticing. Scanner was already considering moving.

"Your room, sir. Can I have your key?"

The bellboy seemed ready to introduce all of the room's features to him but Scanner waved him off.

"I got it, it's okay. If I am lost I'll call you. If I can find the phone. Now go and take care of the young lady."

"There is a phone next to your bed sir, and one on the desk. Another one is in the bathroom, on the wall near the toilet." The bellboy didn't miss a beat.

Gotta move.

"I am two doors down," Max laughed. "I'm going to freshen up and have a nap. See you at five, in the Captain's bar."

The room was everything Scanner expected it to be and nothing he had hoped for. From somewhere a phone rang. *What the…* The source was multi directional. *Fuck.* He hurried to the location he foremost remembered, lowered the lid, sat down and picked up the receiver. It was Lobsang.

"You got my message?"

"Yeah, I did. Haven't read it yet. Just got in. Man, this place is cold, you know, no soul. Don't think I can stay here. They got bathrobes and slippers and a walk-in safe and…"

"They found Dolma, Scanner."

"That's great! And, did she remember anything?"

"No, she didn't remember anything at all." Lobsang turned quiet and Scanner immediately regretted his overly enthusiastic response.

"She is dead, Scanner. They found her this afternoon, Sue just told me."

More silence.

"She… she is…she is messed up, Scanner. Very… messed up. Somebody done her real bad."

It didn't sound like Lobsang. The voice on the other end of the line was broken, in shock, fear palpable in the short, rapid breaths. Scanner tried to imagine his old mentor in his current state. He couldn't. Lobsang was the very essence of mindfulness and serenity. Unperturbed by even the most adverse circumstances, he remained calm whenever danger reared its rapacious head, long after the rats had abandoned ship. To picture his friend and teacher this distressed, gripped by some unfathomable dread, sent an icy chill racing up and down Scanner's spine. He shuddered.

"Calm down, my friend. Breathe slowly, be aware, like you used to teach me. The grasslands, you're back in Kham. It's spring. Every day the sun reaches a little higher. The dark mountains can no longer hold the rays back and a golden light spills over the ridge, into the valley. Ice is melting, the air is fragrant with new life, with budding hope. You take a deep breath, inhale the hope, smell it, embody it, breathe slowly." Scanner had spent countless hours together with Lobsang, working on visualization techniques just like this. Playing reversed roles felt weird.

"Is Sue still there, Lobsang? Pass me on to Sue will you."

"Hey."

Silence.

"Hey." Scanner paused; silence would always beat words hands down when it came to expressing emotion. "Is Lobsang gonna be ok?" he finally asked, "Are you ok?"

"He will be, you know him, he won't collapse, though the foundation is shaken, I am shaken. I haven't been with homicide for very long, haven't seen what some of the other guys have, but I tell you, even Don had to take a breather."

Don Cockburn was Sue's partner. A rookie teamed up with an old hand, making sure experience didn't just walk off at retirement age.

"Some kids called it in. They went fishing over by the old warehouses. Making out is more likely, though we didn't press them too hard on it. Shocked out of their wits, might very well be the last time they engaged in unencumbered lovemaking, probably traumatized into impotence by the stiff."

You could say a lot of things about Sue, but tactful wasn't one of them. Scanner liked her that way.

"They went out in a rowboat. A nice, sunny afternoon, an icebox filled with cold brews. Skinny-dipping weather. Casanova himself couldn't have picked a better day."

More silence. The kind that comes before the inevitable storm. Scanner knew the moment well.

"She was still tied to the chair, Scanner. The bastard. He had strapped her in, legs at the ankles, arms at the wrists. And her head too, locked in some kind of metal vise. Maybe he was in a hurry, maybe he was just being lazy. The entire contraption was dumped in the lake, chained to a concrete block. The accumulated gasses made the body buoyant after being submerged for a few days. The chain was a little too long. Keeping the chair and body just below the surface, where the rowboat bumped into it."

Scanner pictured the scene in his mind. How many times had his dad taken him fishing on the lake?

"Dolma was naked. The autopsy is taking place as we speak. So I don't know yet if she was raped or not. And her head... it's.. There are all these holes you know. No hair. And holes. Someone drilled holes in her head. It's... Why would someone do that?"

Why would someone? Why would someone kill, murder, maim, rape another human being? Greed was usually in the top three of motifs, vying for pole position with envy and revenge; the dual-faced expression of love gone wrong. But the signs weren't there.

"It seems cold and calculated, Sue, not an act of rage. Methodical comes to mind. Or maybe this is how he gets his rocks off, a sadistic psychopath."

"I know. I know. I wanna get the evil son of a bitch who did this, Scanner."

"And you will," Scanner cut in. Always best to leave the

emotions out. Or at least under control. They clouded your judgment and when dealing with a calculating, murdering psycho, one slip could be fatal. "You'll have to wait for the coroner's report. Keep me informed will you? And keep an eye on Lobsang."

"Sure, don't worry. How's things on your end? How was your flight?"

"All good, settling in. It's a comfortable place." His aversion to the hotel's packaged luxury suddenly seemed trivial, pathetic even.

"You're not the comfortable kind." Sue knew him well.

"I'm fine, nothing to worry. Might move tomorrow, I'll let you know. Be careful."

"And you."

Scanner remained seated long after the echoes of Sue's goodbye had stopped reverberating in his head. He closed his eyes. *Keep the world out. If only for an instant.* There was way too much shit out there.

Scanner got up, flushed the toilet. He needed a drink.

BE MY BABY

"What can I get you sir?"

"Macallan, please, the sherry oak 18 years one. Make it a double, straight."

"Certainly, sir."

Seated at the far end of the curved bar, out of sight of anyone casually strolling in, Scanner watched the bartender pour his choice of poison. He was early, it would be a while before Max showed up. That suited him fine. Gave him time to sort out his thoughts. Scanner slowly swirled the dark, amber liquid inside his glass. Fine teardrops descended along the inside, indicating a rich, viscous, oily single malt. The fragrance was mysterious and complex, like an exotic and experienced lover, only giving up her secrets to the man who, patient and skilful, knew how to treat her right. What a joy she promised, hidden beneath that sensuous bouquet, alternating between darkness and light, maturity and youthfulness. Finally, at the apex of anticipation, Scanner made his move. He leaned back, closed his eyes. She had yet to disappoint.

Indulging in his favorite Macallan was a pleasure he permitted himself only occasionally. Abstinence sharpened his senses and heightened appreciation. The smooth nectar exorcised the icy chill left by Dolma's murdered body and gradually lubricated his stagnant mind. One thing was certain; the lazy summer had come to an abrupt end. *Be careful what you wish for, Scanner.* Now he had two cases to solve. Not that anyone had hired him to look into the Tibetan disappearances and Dolma's murder. Wasn't necessary. They didn't come more tailor-made for Scanner Grant P.I. than this one. He smiled faintly and emptied his glass.

"One more, sir?"

Scanner looked up at the bartender. "Sure, hit me again, eh... Trueman."

People in Hong Kong chose their own English first name. Chose their own spelling too. Official Chinese names were not used very much in everyday interaction. It was a rare outlet for individuality in a society that put conformity high on the virtue list. It was a good idea, Scanner thought. Names, consciously chosen, reflected a person's character in ways most Western monikers did not. Notwithstanding some notable exceptions, Caucasian names were usually dull and unimaginative. No, the system here was much better, certainly more enlightening and entertaining, as people tended to gravitate towards choosing what fitted best. Kinda the same way that dogs could reveal a lot about their owners. Gucci Yu, one of the other stewardesses on the plane, didn't need to tell you her favorite pastime. Mojo Man, the taxi driver from the airport, probably knew all the city's happening and hot live-music hangouts and far too many female guests entering the hotel stared just a bit too long at the handsome and gallant Mandarin doorman Ivan Ho.

Trueman Wong placed the double Macallan on the bar in front of Scanner. "Your first time in Hong Kong, sir?"

Scanner nodded. He wasn't game for small talk, not now. Fortunately the bartender had logged enough years and had developed a keen sense of his customer's needs.

"Let me know if there's anything, sir," he said, before turning to polish the bar's array of crystal wine glasses.

Scanner picked up his drink and gestured to Trueman that he was moving to one of the tables set against the grey back wall. More comfortable. More protected from lonely strangers wanting to talk. He needed to draw up a battle plan, search for clues that would lead to Max's father's whereabouts, hopefully current, probably past. But Dolma prevented him from concentrating. Her chair-strapped naked body kept floating up to the surface of his mind. What was the connection? Why was this girl killed while all the others had returned home unscathed? A connection wasn't even established yet, though highly likely, of course. Before leaving, he had asked Lobsang to courier him photographs and information on all the missing girls. With a bit of luck he would get the files tomorrow. Part of Scanner wanted to be back home. Murder had a way of changing priorities. He was worried. The dread in Lobsang's voice was unmistakable. And no one who had failed to heed one of Lobsang's premonitions would repeat the mistake a second time around.

"There you are."

Scanner looked up to find his field of vision obstructed by Max standing within a foot of his table. *So much for sitting in the back where he could observe whoever approached.* Admittedly, Max moved with great stealth and even at thirty feet she would have blocked his view. *No excuse.*

"Hey. Wow, you look…"

Absolutely, mouthwateringly stunning.

"…different."

Let's keep it neutral, Scanner.

Gone were the tracksuit pants and sleeveless top, the All-Stars. The Max in front of him didn't play volleyball. There was just not enough room in that contour-accentuating little black dress for any muscle to flex, even with the revealing side slit. Designer no doubt, though brand names and logos were absent from anything she was wearing. Max's hairpiece was sculpted beehive style. Scanner remembered the look from the Ronettes' albums his dad had listened to. *What was the name of that song again?*

"I'll take that as a compliment, coming from you," Max

laughed, "Care for another one of whatever it is you are drinking?"

"Absolutely."

Max swiveled around and floated to the bar. The Japanese businessmen seated at the far end turned their heads and stopped talking mid-sentence. *Turning their heads...* Scanner's mind flashed on cue. *So won't you, please...* There. Now the song was in his head, impossible to erase. Great tune. Gorgeous women, all three of them. Gorgeous woman. It was hard to concentrate when Max was around. Concentrate on something ELSE. Max had style, no doubt, and she was sexy as hell. Leaning into the bar like that, two elbows on the counter, knees slightly bent, one foot on the brass rail, knowing all eyes in the entire establishment were on her, from all directions. But what about substance? Scanner had met a lot of lookers on the job – not quite like Max, but somewhere up there. He could have taken advantage of most any one of them had he wanted to. But he never wanted. The anticipation of carnal pleasure was often rather more stimulating than the act itself. Good sex originated in your head. Sue certainly had substance and he had sensed it in Cathy Lee too. Scanner felt the urge to check his pocket for the chief purser's lifeline. He wasn't drowning or anything, at least not yet, but it was reassuring to know someone wanted to come to the rescue if you were. Feeling the edge of the paper coaster drew a smile on his face. And Max? Perhaps. But she was too young, too self-conscious, too vulnerable. She was looking for her father for fuck's sake and on top of all that, she was his client.

"You didn't have a rest? No shower?" Max put his Macallan on the table and settled in the opposite seat. "I got you something. It's the latest model, just out this year. It has a local SIM card." Max slid a Nokia 3210 across the table. "I have got an orange one. My number is the first in your speed dial menu."

Scanner wasn't very keen on carrying a phone. He wasn't

averse to technology per se; it could make life a lot easier. But it could also make people lazy, rely on machines for human interaction. Besides, you'd never know who would be listening in. It was prudent to be careful.

"So how long have you been sitting here drinking?"

OH CAPTAIN! MY CAPTAIN!

"That is… I don't know what to say. That is so horrible, so, so…evil. Who would do that? Why? What kind of sicko? The poor girl. What are you going to do?"

Scanner had tried to convey the story of Dolma's murder in as detached a manner as possible. Leave out the details, just sum up the basic facts. But Max had been inquisitive, skilled in drawing him out. Now, as she had sunk back in her chair, deflated, on the verge of crying, he felt somewhat sorry for spilling the beans. It was hard to stomach, even for him. And over the years he had learned what Max was most likely yet to discover: human kindness was heavily overrated. *Well done Scanner, swell way to start the evening.*

"Nothing. At this moment. There is nothing I can do. Hopefully tomorrow Fedex will deliver the files on all the missing girls. Maybe I can find a clue. Something they all had in common. Not so likely though. Lobsang, Sue, homicide, they have all been going through these files with a fine-tooth comb. The autopsy might reveal something, who knows. As for me, I am not even on the case."

"I know, but Lobsang seems to have taken it rather personally and you're concerned about him, aren't you?"

Max was right of course. Lobsang was family. If he was affected, so was Scanner. His eyes wandered around the bar. Strategically placed glass partitions enhanced the place's intimacy without making the patrons feel completely boxed in. Etched on each screen was a chessboard. If there was a game being played here, the moves, hell, even the rules eluded him.

"I am thinking of moving," Scanner announced. "It's hard to stay sharp with all that carpet around here."

"But… No, you can't. How are we going to work together if you're not staying here? I am not going to move, all my stuff is here."

"Listen Max." Scanner said sternly. "First of all WE are not working together. I work alone and YOU go shopping or get your nails done or do whatever it is that you do as long as it doesn't involve me." This was a missing person case after all and it could turn ugly. Scanner had had a graphic reminder of that only a little over an hour ago.

Max pouted and for the first time Scanner saw her spoiled little girl side. Used to getting her way. Not taking no for an answer, never getting a no for an answer. Daddy's girl. Of course he sympathized with her. Probably more than she realized. All the more reason to go it alone. A world without Max's bubbly presence would most certainly be a lot less enjoyable and Scanner didn't want to be responsible for the resulting loss in cosmic karma if something happened to her.

"No, don't move. Stay here. You can't leave me here all by myself. It's a big place, it's… I like talking to you. You wouldn't want me to be lonely, would you?"

Scanner looked straight at Max and kept quiet. Saying something, anything, would only make things worse. He had been there before. Hell, he was more than qualified to write the definitive handbook.

Max changed course; "You work for me, I have hired you. I have paid for your room. I am not going to spend more money. What a waste. You make me waste all this money."

Scanner continued to stare blankly at Max. He knew what would come next.

"Arrrgh. You're… you're freakin' impossible. And selfish.

You're only thinking about Mr. Grant. I am going back to my room. I am not hungry anyway, thanks for asking."

Max got up and storm-trooped out of the bar. For the second time that evening the Japanese businessmen interrupted their animated conversation and turned their heads. Mouths dropped open as they followed Max all the way to the elevators before slowly rotating in Scanner's direction. The incredulous looks on their faces said it all. *You stupid fuck. Are you insane to let that piece of ass get away?*

Scanner quite enjoyed the moment. He remembered one of Lobsang's arcane proverbs: *Only a thirsty wolf howls when the river freezes over.* With his eyes fixed on the stunned Japanese, he slowly shook his head, the corners of his mouth slightly curled upwards in a semblance of a smile. He shrugged, palms of both hands facing upwards, and pointed two index fingers at himself. *Not me*, he mouthed silently. Then he directed his gaze to Trueman Wong under whose command, no doubt, heavier storms had been weathered. The captain didn't hesitate.

"A double Macallan sir, on the way," he announced purposefully from behind the bar.

A RAMBLING TRAM

The evening had barely started and Scanner felt pleasantly buzzed. The episode with Max didn't worry him. She would come around. It might take some time, but in the end she would realize that he really didn't care, one way or the other. That was the message he had worked hard to convey. It was always best to set clear boundaries right from the start. Don't leave any room for a head fuck. He hated people messing with his mind, manipulating his sensitivities. Most women did it, naturally. Not necessarily because they were more controlling then men. No, Scanner believed that the desire to influence other people's behavior was ingrained in both genders. But women were better at it. And men were so much weaker. The reason why women had developed manipulation into a high art form was that, throughout history, men had consented. That's what having two heads would do to you. The reaction of the dumbfounded Japanese customers to Max's theatrical walkout was proof positive for Scanner.

Women had other buttons one could push. Most of them were variations on the security theme. As far as Scanner knew, threatening to withhold sex had never swayed any woman into following a man's wishes.

"Let me sign for the drinks, the lady's too."

"Certainly, sir. It's none of my business sir, but I don't think the lady was truly aggravated. I wouldn't worry too much. It doesn't seem to be anything a good night's sleep won't take care of."

"Spoken like a genuine connoisseur, Trueman. Your concern is very much appreciated. Now, since I am free for the night, where should I go?"

***

The hot and humid Hong Kong evening clung to Scanner like a wet blanket. A shower and a change of clothes had refreshed him after the four inebriating double shots in the Captain's bar. But now, outside the air-conditioned enclosure of the Mandarin, that shower was nothing but a fading memory. Hong Kong didn't cool down much at night. For some punters, it got noticeably hotter. *It's a Wednesday night*, Trueman had said, *you should go to see the races.*

It was only a short walk from the hotel to the picturesque tramway, a remnant of the colonial era and the island's cheapest public transport. Scanner boarded the Happy Valley-bound carriage and settled on an upper level wooden seat. The windows were down, the neon night rattled and shrieked past and a gentle breeze cooled his overheated brain. This didn't look like Hong Kong at all, Scanner thought, as they passed towering skyscrapers and glitzy designer name window displays. What exactly Hong Kong was supposed to look like was cinematically induced, courtesy of Suzie Wong, and Bruce, and his dad, who had introduced him to martial arts movies at a young age.

That had been a long time ago and cities like Hong Kong changed faster than an elected politician after Election Day. One of the biggest changes had occurred two years earlier, when the old colonial masters had returned the territory to its giant Northern neighbor. The so-called Handover had caused considerable anxiety amongst the city's residents. The moneyed elites had, of course, managed to secure second passports and Swiss bank accounts. If the shit hit the proverbial Chinese fan, those without assets would be left to front the bill. Scanner had read about it in the papers: the promises and guarantees of autonomy, the hysterical fear of communism. But for the rich and famous in Hong Kong, there was nothing new under the sun; two systems had always been their way of life, one for them and one for the rest.

Scanner caught a glimpse of a street sign. Queensway. Now there is something that hasn't changed, he thought – Queen's Road, Queensway. You would think a staunch communist would do away with all references to the British monarchy, especially on road signs, except perhaps for one-way or dead-end streets. Chairmansway didn't have a particularly nice ring to it though. Secretary's Road sounded a lot better and was sufficiently egalitarian.

Ding ding ding, the tram's bell woke Scanner from his nomenclatural revelry. Evening rush hour traffic was obstructing the rails. Pedestrians, often in an excessive shopping induced comatose state, crossed the road at will. The tram conductor reserved his deafening air horn for the worst offenders, those in danger of dying a second time that night.

The city started to change. You could smell it. Scanner inhaled greedily. Less money, more real life. Floating on top of the ocean of petrol fumes, he detected spices, fresh vegetables, human sweat. People rushed about on foot. They stopped at streetside butcher shops on the way home and selected enticing pieces of meat displayed from large hooks and glowing in the descending dusk with a reality defying redness. Chinese had a love affair with red. The communists got that right. A lucky color. An auspicious color. Wealth, fortune, happiness, love, revolution.

The tram trotted onwards, swaying its passengers gently back and forth. Occasional glimpses down narrow side alleys revealed bustling street markets before shop fronts closed in once more, unashamedly intimate in their closeness. If the tram would have stopped long enough, the street could have been one long public transport drive-thru.

Scanner looked upwards. Along this particular stretch of road it was hard to see much of the evening sky. Laundry, hung out to dry on bamboo poles, obscured the thin strip of darkening blue that was left exposed along the top edge of the tenement building. The vast majority of people lived small, as space came at a premium. So like true proletarian flags, each household proudly waved their shirts, trousers and bras, lending identity to otherwise indistinguishable windows.

They made a sharp right turn. The insides of the tram's steel wheels scraped the edge of the rails with an eerie screech. No one paid any attention. An impatient taxi driver honked his horn at a transport van blocking the road while the bare-chested and heavily tattooed co-driver got out and shouted instructions for parallel parking, leaving but a hair width of space between their beat-up Toyota and a brand new, black Mercedes S-class. The hole in the wall wonton shop attracted all strata of society, old and young, rich and poor. Down the road, a jackhammer bombarded Scanner's eardrums as crews of dark skinned Pakistani laborers worked on yet another systems overhaul. In Hong Kong there was always something to upgrade.

Finally the cacophony of high-density living subsided. They passed a high wall, an enclosure of sorts. Scanner picked up the scent of freshly mowed grass even before he spotted the racetrack. From the top floor of the tram the turf looked immaculate. Taking his cue from the other passengers, he got off at the final stop and crossed the road. The powerful floodlights illuminating the grounds attracted the punters in droves, like insects to the light of a flame. And just like insects approaching the light too recklessly, some, no doubt, would get burned tonight.

WANNA BET?

"She's a beauty isn't she? I mean, look at those quarters, just the right amount of curvature. And that chestnut mane. She's well in but I dunno mate, see them cheekpieces? Means she's nervous. Still, you'd be hard pressed to ride anything more exciting, I reckon. Great stamina, likes coming from behind, a real stayer and a swooper on top of that. Care for a wager? Stuart is the name."

For an instant Scanner wondered whether he was actually looking at the same thing as his bold and squat neighbor whose beefy hand was momentarily squeezing him in a vise-like grip.

"Scanner."

"Pleasure. First time eh? I can tell, your eyes are all over. Understandably. So much beauty in one place. It's about as much as a man can take, I know. Beats the telly and Fashion TV hands down, hell, it tops anything in them clubs in Wan Chai. Don't get me wrong mate, I like pussy as much as the next guy, but this here, this transcends pussy by a few levels. Ever ridden a juvenile?"

"Can't say I have, no."

"Wouldn't think so, you don't have the gait. I can tell, saw you coming in."

"Did you?"

This was one of those one-way conversations that only

needed a few drops of verbal oil to keep the motor running. Scanner didn't mind. It was shaping up to be a fine evening and if anything, he would pick up some interesting jargon to lay on Sue once he got back home. *Cheekpieces? What the hell were cheekpieces?*

"Sublime mate, absolutely sublime. Right out of the barriers. The usual guy got jocked off. I was just a claimer, a bug boy, but there wasn't anyone else around. It was my first real race. Halfway through, I came in my pants. Her name was Third Base; I remember it like it was yesterday. Any doubt I might have had about becoming a full-fledged jockey instantly evaporated and I crossed the finish line in a post orgasmic haze. The horse's owner and trainer came up to me after the race and even though I had finished last they were laughing. It was all arranged and I had behaved as hoped, if not entirely as expected. I had passed my initiation with flying colors and now I wanted more."

For the first time Stuart seemed to trail off, the distant memories still vivid enough to leave him choked. Scanner noticed the hard swallowing.

"You're not riding anymore?"

"You're kidding? At my age, with my weight? I had a few good years but in the end I struggled to keep my racing weight. That, and the constant threat of injuries is what did me in. You know what they say about falling, don't you?"

"Can't say I do."

"It's not the fall that hurts but the sudden stop at the end."

Stuart's laugh was infectious and drew Scanner in. He was starting to like this outgoing Aussie.

"So what are you doing now?"

"I became a trainer for a while, couldn't leave them horses alone. Then the bad people showed up. No love for the animals, just in it for the money. Big money, big egos. Fucking criminals, that's what they were. I don't fucking care if they off each other, the world would be a better place for it, but

71

they better damn well leave my horses be."

Stuart was visibly agitated and had started swearing. Scanner liked him even more for it.

"It's irony supreme isn't it? Years of top tier racing and I never once break my leg. Fell off plenty, but as far as breaking a leg, never. Then I become a trainer, look after my stable, love them beauties, all of 'em. Some fucking wannabe Lanskys walk in wanting me to screw up this filly called Lonely On Top, drug her up or something, make her go slow, so him and his mates can rake it in. Those fucks. I refuse, they break my leg. Half a year later I spot them at some races. It's obvious they're still at it, driving a big flashy Merc convertible with wire wheel covers and surrounded by big fleshy boobs on stiletto heels. Money has no taste. Did you ever notice that? Anyways, as these lowlifes are so full of it I fill up that pimpmobile with some fresh horse manure while they're trackside. God, wish I could have seen their faces but there was nowhere safe to hide. The shit wasn't the only thing fuming, I'll tell you that."

The PA system announced the start of the first race of the evening.

"Let's move track side," Stuart suggested. "Get a couple of brews and watch the action, I am getting thirsty. I ain't talking too much am I?"

They moved away from the Parade Ring and settled for one of the few remaining high tables that weren't occupied yet, offering an unobstructed view of the turf. A few minutes later Stuart was back carrying a pitcher of beer and two plastic cups.

"Now let the games begin."

In Deep

A roar of excitement emanated from the throng of punt-ers as the first field of the evening burst out of the start-ing gates. Trackside was jam-packed now and Scanner and Stuart squeezed through the crowd to get to the edge of the turf, as close to the action as possible.

"Exhilarating isn't it? See the red and blue silk, number nine? That's my girl."

Scanner scrutinized the racing program he had received at the entrance. *Bodhisattva* he read out aloud. *Interesting name for a racehorse.*

"Yeah mate, that's her. Put a wager on her too. Nothing too complicated, just a tierce, Bodhisattva first of course. Long odds, I know, but those are the only ones worth it. Go for the impossible. Shoot for the stars, that sort of stuff. Vic-tory is only sweet when you don't have to share it."

Scanner wasn't about to contradict the Aussie punter with the finer points of Buddhism's compassion and enlighten-ment. Stuart wouldn't get it. His love for the animals seemed genuine, but something in his demeanor indicated a razor sharp competitive edge when it came to fellow humans. Scan-ner shrugged it off. He didn't know the guy and was probably never gonna see him again. So why over analyze a perfectly enjoyable evening? Still, there was the scent. He hadn't no-ticed it earlier but now, sardined into this large oval can, Scanner picked up a trace of, *of what exactly?* Struggling to identify the smell he bent down, closer to Stuart, feigning the Aussie's words had drowned in the heightened euphoria.

"Sorry, I couldn't get you, what did you say?" It wasn't Stuart's scent.

"I like winning," Stuart smiled "and without losers there ain't no victory. That's why I go for the long shot. Losers are the sugar in the victory cup. GO BODHI GO, GO."

The horses were now at the opposite end of the track and the race only visible on the monstrous monitors placed in the center of the oval.

Scanner looked around him as he tried to locate the source of the exotic fragrance, but there were too many people packed in close proximity for an accurate reading. I don't have a sweet tooth, he thought, before turning his attention to the final stages of the race.

"I told you she was a swooper, look how she's moving forward. GO, GO, COME ON BODHI, YOU CAN DO IT. GIVE IT TO ME, YES, YES, GIVE IT TO ME."

Stuart's exhilaration seemed to grow exponentially with every nose length Bodhisattva gained on the competition. Scanner wondered whether the man would ultimately come in his pants, just like all those years ago. Money would never buy you love, but an orgasm was to be had on merely a promise.

With the race in its final stage, any attempt to communicate with Stuart was futile. The beefy ex-jockey was jumping up and down as if skipping a rope, his verbal output alternating between grunts and encouragements, a barely audible distinction that became muddier by the second. He was not alone in this. The entire crowd was up and rooting for their favorite. Like a drug induced mass hysteria. That or they were all hired as voiceover actors for the final thrust in some cosmic porn scene, a galactic orgy of stellar proportions, the soundtrack for the Big Bang.

Scanner suddenly felt the urge to close his eyes. An image

of Sue appeared and he felt an erection working its way up. It didn't bother him the least. *Everyone is riding their own race.* She had asked for something made of leather, a saddle and whip perhaps. *Do they sell tandem saddles?* He was definitely hard now. *And cheekplates too, if only he could find out what the hell cheekplates were.* Something Sue would sit on, naked no doubt, something for the dinner table. He was getting hungry. *Gotta eat something. What about those hot dogs they were selling near the entrance?* Visions of hot dogs in the night sky replaced Sue, who had taken off, straddling her own Pegasus. *Wait a minute, those are not buns.* The hot dogs, sandwiched between what closely resembled Sue's buttocks, were being served on white ceramic plates. *They look like UFOs. Familiar point of view too.* Acutely aware now of the Apollo in his trousers Scanner tried to shift it upwards from its sideways position. Soon the race would be over and he'd have to walk away, rather hard to choreograph elegantly with three legs. The anxiety over this imminent predicament took a hold. He started to sweat profusely. And there was that scent again.

"Why don't you go back home? This is no place for you to be. You're in way over your head. Go back home and bonk that sweet little lady of yours."

"Stuart?" Scanner opened his eyes. *What is happening?* The race had finished. Scanner had no idea who had won and he didn't care. Where was Stuart?. Some lucky punters used the break in between races to replenish empty glasses, others sauntered back to the Parade Ring, going over the what ifs and should haves in their mind, hoping to pick a winner the next race. Everyone was moving. *Where is Stuart?* More and more people bumped into Scanner who had remained motionless from the moment he had opened his eyes. *Where was Stuart? Did he warn me, did he threaten me? WHO was Stuart?*

Gripped by paranoia, Scanner searched all corners of the public area. In vain. The Aussie punter was gone. Scanner wasn't even sure anymore he had actually met the guy. Nor, for that matter, was he sure that he was where he seemed to be. He scanned the crowd for familiar faces but found none. In need of a piss, the beer had quickly worked its way through his empty stomach, Scanner set off for the toilets. *You're in way over your head* the voice had said. *Whose voice? Stuart's? His own?*

Walking to the bathrooms proved challenging. Scanner couldn't decide where to put down his feet, there were too many choices of brightly colored stepping stones. Just as he had decided to go for the red ones they changed to green. Damn he hated green. Scanner barely managed to suppress the urge to piss right there on the spot. *Forget the colors man, forget the colors.*

The bathroom door swung open violently just as Scanner was getting ready to reach for the knob. He had stood in front of the door for some time, positively convinced that a touch would jolt him with a heart-stopping electric current. Scanner found that ironic, as his bladder would no doubt relieve itself upon death and all his squeezing efforts would have been in vain not to mention the substantial energy it had taken him to get rid of the colors.

"He's dead! There's a dead man in there. Somebody call the ambulance!"

Great, Scanner thought, staring at the open door, problem solved. Aware that the door was on a spring Scanner quickly slid through the slowly closing gap and took the stairs down to the lower level.

Stuart lay on the floor next to the urinals, arms and legs spread out.

"There you are," Scanner said. "Dude, this is no place to take a nap. Come let's get out of here." He bent down next to Stuart's motionless body. "Let's go man." *Dead man. Hadn't someone shouted dead man?* "Oh fuck, Stuart!" Scanner grabbed the Aussie's head, tried to shake him awake. *Pulse, pulse, got to feel his pulse, oh god, Stuart.* "STUART!"

Return of an Angel

"Get a hold of yourself Scanner, NOW." Scanner turned around to see who had so severely admonished him until it hit home that the stern voice had been his own. A couple of slow, deep breaths dissipated enough of the psychedelic mist in his head to realize he really was in a world of shit. "This is not good, NOT GOOD."

"Son."

Stuart's eyes beckoned. Words struggled to escape from the man's lips and Scanner stretched forward to catch the verbal absconders before they got away.

"You... look like him... I... I couldn't... drugged... I am so sorry... Not safe mate... they got me... Go... You gotta go."

"Look like who? Who are they? Who are you? Hang in there buddy, help is on the way."

Stuart had closed his eyes again and slowly removed a crumpled piece of paper from his shirt pocket. "Too late... no antidote... take... this."

Scanner spotted a round black plastic token folded inside the betting slip. He postponed further scrutiny and slid the package into his back pocket.

Outside an approaching siren indicated the imminent arrival of more trouble than would be good for Scanner. Leaving now was not an option, however. Stuart's migrating spirit needed all the help it could get in this moment of greatest danger. Lobsang had taught Scanner that at death, the presence of a noble spirit would greatly assist the wandering soul of the just departed in the crossover. Scanner was far from certain he was qualified but there was no alternative. Not knowing what else to do, he quietly mumbled the Universal Mantra *"Om Mani Padme Hum, Om Mani Padme Hum."*

Stuart's eyes popped wide open in the final moment of mortal lucidity. "She did it mate. I told you. We won!"

In the end Bodhisattva had beaten the odds.

With Stuart dead, the authorities on the way and the second wave of drug induced hallucinations edging closer, Scanner realized he had precious little time to make it out of the racecourse. He had to make it back to a safe environment, let the drugs run their own course with as little chance of going on a bad trip as possible. He had to be with someone he could trust, someone familiar. He had to get back to Max. But first he had to make it out of the toilet.

"The man had a heart attack, I'm afraid it's too late. Let's all step back and respect the dead." Scanner had opened the door to a large curious crowd and immediately flashed his PI license. "I am a medical doctor. As you can hear, my colleagues are very close. I'll walk to the gates and get them."

Scanner stepped out onto the street just as the blazing ambulance pulled up. *Nice lights.* Stuart was dead, murdered most likely. Was he gonna be next? Transfixed, Scanner stared at the flashing blue beam. It resembled a lighthouse on steroids. *Safe haven.* The thought of dying horrified Scanner, he wasn't ready. Not here. He had promised Sue to take care. They had gotten to Stuart, he had better make sure they didn't get to him as well. Who were they? And who was Stuart? Parked along the curb a taxi beckoned, Scanner jumped in. "To the Mandarin," he mumbled.

***

"Stop, stop! Now!"

The taxi had barely pulled away from the curb before Scanner panicked. The guy was in on it, he was certain. Just one look at the driver's face reflected in the rear mirror, checking Scanner out as he lay slumped across the backseat, filled him with dread. The man was gonna drive and drive until the drugs had sufficiently comatosed and immobilized Scanner and then he was gonna make him disappear. *Don't close your eyes. Do NOT close your eyes.*

"I want you to stop. STOP!" Scanner yelled.

"*Chi sin*", mumbled the driver, crazy gweilo. "*Puk gai!* Drop dead"

Instead Scanner dropped a twenty Hong Kong Dollar note on the front seat and got out. They had made it barely fifty meters down the road. He was alone. He felt safer being alone. Easier to notice strangers. This section of the road was obscured in darkness. A large concrete overpass blocked most spillover from the streetlights and towering high rises with their neon emanating windows that were the city's equivalent of a starry night. Scanner started to walk. He had no idea which way he should be heading but at least he was moving, going somewhere. *Concentrate on walking, stop the mind from wandering.* On his left, a large stone wall obscured what or whomever did not want to be noticed, or perhaps it was there to keep him out. Why would someone want to keep him out?

In the distance a group of men approached. Positive that they were coming for him Scanner turned around only to see another murder squad heading his way from the opposite direction. *Now what?* His heart raced faster than Bodhisattva. He should have stayed at the track. At least his death would have been well documented. Now he would just be disappeared. Stuart had gotten it right, dead right. *There,* Scanner spotted an opening in the wall a few meters ahead. The locked cast iron gate blocked his only chance of survival. Closed doors, shut windows and locked gates had never deterred Scanner, and spurred on by thoughts of a less than glorious demise it took him ten seconds to pick the lock. *Ten seconds!* He had timed every break-in he had ever done, it was good to realize when essential skills got rusty. *Ten seconds!* Appalled at his sluggish performance, Scanner contemplated for a moment shutting the gate and giving it another go. *Get the fuck in!*

Breathless, backed up behind the large wall, Scanner watched as first one group of would be assassins passed and then the second. Well, in dealing with death, one could never be prudent enough.

***

They would be back! Scanner shot up straight. He had no idea how long he had dozed off, slugged against the inside of the enclosure. Time was a meaningless concept, especially the linear version he was brought up with and even more so on drugs. He decided to stay put, it wasn't safe out there. Better to wait for daylight to scare real and imaginary suckers back into hiding. *Don't hang out too close to the gate*. He jumped to his feet and moved deeper inside.

Away from the overpass, Hong Kong's signature celestial glow cast an eerie light over the assorted dwellings that sloped uphill before Scanner's eyes. The population density of this particular piece of real estate was amongst the city's highest. It was also one of the quieter areas. Real quiet. Dead quiet.

"Good evening miss, lovely evening isn't it?"

Scanner tried to befriend some of the residents as they sauntered on the porch of their home. They were a well-behaved lot, civilized really. And the girls were pretty too. Their fashion sense got stuck in the sixties but that actually made them more attractive Scanner felt. Lorna was a prime example and so was Marjorie.

"Hey, how you're doing Marjorie?"

What an inviting smile this girl had. Full lips, sparkling with a dab of moisture, parted to reveal a perfectly chiseled row of pearly whites. Her bob cut raven hair asymmetrically separated in cascading sides that curled inwards at chin's height, accentuating a delicate and slightly elongated neck held steady by the stand-up collar of a black cheongsam dress, cut unusually low in front to offer but a glimpse of the indentation of her spectacular jugular notch. Oh that most underrated part of female anatomy. Scanner was a sucker for the jugular notch. *Ask Sue*. He couldn't think of a better vessel for his sherry oak Macallan. How many liters had he sipped, hunkered at her bosom? Like a wild animal, quenching his insatiable thirst at that little pond only to be devoured by an even wilder beast the moment he let his guard down. From jugular notch to jugular vein. I miss her, Scanner thought.

"I apologize ladies, it's kinda rude of me to keep staring at you but you see, I miss my girlfriend. And my whiskey."

Scanner wandered onwards along the winding path amidst the residences. Occasionally he paused to strike up a conversation but for the most part he tried to decipher names. They were not all Chinese. W. Toole, T. Whitley, J. Grant, S. Boswell. Scanner imagined priests and pimps, bankers and gamblers, farmers and pilots, whores and spinsters. Hong Kong sure was an exciting place to live.

J. Grant?

"What are you doing here dad? You're not supposed to be here, you're…"

Scanner sunk to the ground and broke down in an uncontrollable sob.

"Dead, you're all dead. It's all my fault, I should have warned you. I am so sorry dad, mum. I… Everyone's dead."

It hit Scanner like a horse's kick to the head. His father, his mother, Stuart, even lovely Lorna and Marjorie, they were all dead. Scanner curled up against Marjorie's tombstone, his head just below the youthful portrait of the deceased Chinese girl etched in the cold black marble. The graveyard, now revealed before him, terraced uphill as far as Scanner could see.

No longer in control of his emotions, Scanner rocked back and forth. A world of grief bore down on him in a ferocious assault and crushed whatever defenses he had managed to construct since that day all those years back.

"It's all my fault, it's all my fault."

***

What? Someone had touched Scanners forehead with an ice-cold finger. *There, again. Now he's coming for me.* Petrified with fear for having to answer Death's call, Scanner remained motionless on the young woman's grave. *Who are you fooling?* The icy cold sensation repeated itself with ever shortening intervals. Death was an impatient motherfucker. Rapacious really, devouring all in the end, without regard for wealth, status, beauty and religion. It dawned on Scanner that he had none of life's customary trappings. Immediately he felt liberated. He had nothing to lose. Energized by the rekindled fire of defiance, he let out a primeval roar and opened his eyes.

"Arrrgggghhh! You talking to me punk," he shouted, combining two of his favorite movie scenes, determined to take possession of his life once more and fight to the death if needed.

The dark eyed angel stared back at him. It had been her tears that had redeemed Scanner, pried him loose from Death's mauling jaws. She had taken pity on him and now the heavens joined in. Scanner gratefully accepted the torrential downpour unleashed to cleanse him of the sin of his near surrender. "I got it, I got it," he shouted. "Thank you." He wanted to hug the angel, all the angels. There were so many.

***

The caretaker of St. Michael's Catholic Cemetery found Scanner at daybreak; sound asleep at the feet of one of the larger marble cherubs. Firm in his faith, the old man praised God for the miracle of redemption, for the return of a lost soul. There was no need to call the police. After God, what could they do? He found a phone in Scanner's pocket and speed dialed the second name in the address book. He didn't speak much English and Cathy Lee sounded local.

Famous

The blades of the nouveau-colonial-style ceiling fan cut through the heavy air with audible exertion. The grunts and squeaks had woken Scanner from a dark and dreamless sleep. For the first few semi-conscious seconds he had been back at his usual lovemaking joint, deeply disturbed that he couldn't remember any of the untold pleasures he had no doubt experienced. A mind disconnected from the past would never generate the joy associated with anticipation. Scanner knew that the best orgasms originated in your head. He hated morning after amnesia.

His feisty police friend had probably left answering the call of duty. But on closer inspection Scanner noticed that the other side of the bed was cold and unruffled. Besides, he failed to detect even the slightest trace of the usual post intercourse aroma.

Scanner's restless eyes settled on the revolving fan. *Are there three blades or four?* Frustrated at not being able to answer this existential question he got up and switched off the problem. Three.

He was naked, a state congruent with his earlier assumption. Maybe the bathroom had been the steamed up battle-field, the lovemaking erect under the stimulating assault of thousands of pin sized water bomblets, sky semen vigorously attempting to penetrate the entangled bodies of Sue and him.

It was an arousing thought. Scanner did vaguely remember water, lots of it. *A true clusterfuck Mister Grant. What happened? How messed up did I get? Where am I?*

The shower revealed no clues other than the near physical impossibility of two adult bodies standing side by side in the enclosure, let alone doing an Indian Headstand. Scanner opened the tap and tried to cold start his brain.

***

"Welcome back to the land of the living, Sir."

Scanner had slipped into the white cotton bathrobe that he had found hanging from the bathroom door; having had no luck locating his clothes.

"Chief Purser Cathy Lee. I am… What am I doing here? Where am I?"

"This is my apartment Sir, and no, we didn't have sex, if you will excuse me so directly and indiscreetly imposing on your private thoughts. It would not have been any fun at all, being immobilized as you were and for all practical purposes it would have been impossible to stir things up. If you don't mind me saying so, Sir, you were pretty deflated."

The quick-witted stewardess had immediately disarmed Scanner with her frontal approach. He wasn't quite ready to spar with her; his mind was still too fragmented.

"No Sir, it would never occur to me to take advantage of an attractive gentleman such as yourself, utterly defenseless and drugged out of his mind. Quite frankly I don't think I need to."

She had a point there, Scanner thought. Out of uniform, unspoiled by excessive make-up and seated on the twin sofa, Cathy Lee exuded a quiet, girl-next-door beauty. Cocooned in a huge oversized home knit pink sweater, knees pulled up high and pressed against her bare bosom she oozed the kind of confidence that would get just about anyone into trouble.

Scanner recalled the black belt hanging from the bedroom wardrobe door. If there were any trouble, it would be highly unlikely for this woman to be on the receiving end.

"How did I get here? Where are my clothes. Did you remove them?"

"You went to the races, put down a substantial wager, won an even more substantial bundle, found God and ended up naked in my bed. And you don't remember a thing. Oh, and I forgot to mention that you're on T.V. Not bad for a first night in Hong Kong Sir."

"Are you pulling my leg, Cathy Lee?"

Time for a little dance.

"No Sir, I wouldn't dare, that would be extremely impertinent. Not to mention that it would be more akin to pulling a string."

Another knockout blow.

"Look Sir, they are mentioning you again on the news!"

Cathy Lee turned up the TV's volume and translated the anchorwoman's words.

"They say that last night an Australian punter was found dead on the floor of a bathroom at the Happy Valley Racecourse. No foul play is suspected, the most likely cause of death a gambling related heart attack. Witnesses did describe seeing a foreign doctor leave the scene shortly before the arrival of the ambulance and the police are asking anyone with further information related to this doctor's identity to come forward. The name of the deceased will not be released until next of kin has been notified."

"Stuart," Scanner mumbled. A flare had been fired into the blackest recesses of his mind exposing distinct forms and shapes where moments before only darkness had ruled.

It took another hour for Scanner and Cathy Lee to reconstruct most of the tumultuous events of the past night. Scanner had been trailed from the moment he had exited the Mandarin. At Happy Valley Stuart had spiked his beer with a

86

potent hallucinogen. Whether this was meant to scare Scanner off or worse was debatable. Whatever task Stuart had been given, the punter's death had resulted from his failure to deliver. His dying, remorse filled words had indicated a past acquaintance with Jack, Scanner's father, but the intricacies of that relation remained a mystery. Stuart had the answers, unfortunately he was no longer able to respond to questions.

"Who is Stuart, who was he working for and who killed him?" Scanner reflected. "And, chief purser Cathy Lee, who are you? Why are you not the least bit distressed or surprised by my adventures?"

"I am delighted you're finally inquiring, Dr. Grant. And awfully relieved."

FAMILY

"I detest lying sir, but I was told not to be forthcoming unless expressly asked."

"Told by whom?"

"My great uncle Sir, your stepfather, Lobsang."

Scanner dropped down in the chair opposite Cathy Lee. This was wholly unexpected. Lobsang. What was his game?

"And I thought it was my charm that persuaded you to give me your telephone number. I don't like being messed with. Suppose you're not really a stewardess either, are you?"

"I can understand your aggravation Sir, I really can, but not all is what it seems, Sir, and I most ardently hope that you will let me elaborate."

"Well, I guess you'd better do that before I am going to elaborate in my own way." Scanner started to get pissed off, "and stop 'Sir-ring' me, it annoys the hell out of me right now, makes me feel I have to behave towards you in some gentlemanly fashion and at this moment nothing could be further from my mind."

"Most certainly Sir, eh, Mr. Grant. Kindly proceed to that table over there and peruse the photographs while I slip into something a bit more, what shall I say, deterring, since you're getting all piqued."

With a passing wink and a disarming smile Cathy Lee removed herself from the sofa and disappeared into the bedroom. Scanner shook his head. It was hard to remain agitated with this woman for any length of time. After all, she had collected him from the cemetery this morning and nursed him back to life." *Nursed? You wish Scanner, you wish.*

***

The vast majority of framed photographs on the antique Chinese altar table were old black and white portraits, printed with a thin white deckle edge. Scanner used to collect baseball cards like this, when he was a kid. He recognized his savior, Cathy Lee, in some of the images. A little child held up by proud parents. In another one, slightly older now, she was wearing a white martial arts uniform trying, in vain, to strike a menacing pose. Yet another photograph, in color this time, and Cathy Lee, black belt and all, had taken centre position on the winner's podium. Cute, Scanner thought. And in debilitating shape.

The picture with Lobsang seemed fairly recent, the two of them positioned next to his taxi. *Where else?* Scanner picked it up for closer inspection.

"A little over a year ago. Chicago airport. I really am a stewardess."

Cathy Lee approached. Hair gathered in a tidy bun that Scanner remembered from the plane, part of the airhostess uniform. The rest of her outfit belonged to a different airline. One Scanner had yet to fly with. Black gym shorts topped her trained and toned legs, formidable weapons no matter what the battle. *Free Your Mind…* was written across the front of her T-shirt. Scanner tried but his eyes kept wandering south.

"We only met last year. My mother had passed away and I received a letter from the US. It was Lobsang. I have absolutely no idea how he knew. He introduced himself, said he was my mom's uncle; his sister was my grandmother. I had never heard of him, and naturally wondered whether this was some kind of sick hoax. But he knew things, stories about my family no one was supposed to know, unless…"

Cathy Lee paused and picked up one of the framed photographs. A handsome young couple stared at Scanner. The Chinese man, dressed in the uniform of an army officer, tried to look stern while the girl, Tibetan, with long, braided strands of hair flowing down her *chuba*, beamed with a radiance that transcended time and space. Scanner couldn't help but smile.

"Theirs was a doomed love from the start. What do you say we sit down and I'll tell you my parents' story? That is if you are interested of course, Sir, eh, I beg your pardon, Mr. Scanner. Before we do though I'd like to inform you that it was Lobsang who made me scribble my telephone number on that coaster. It was your charm however that made me actually hand it to you."

Cathy Lee turned and walked to the sofa. *And Your Ass Will Follow*, the back of her T-Shirt said.

SELFLESS LOVE

"My father was a P.L.A. soldier. He belonged to the so-called 'Entertainment Corps' of the People's Liberation Army, the military arm of China's Communist Party. He was a famous acrobat and a skilled Kung Fu Master who, together with other artists, performed to boost the morale of the troops. In 1959, while he was stationed in Kham, Eastern Tibet, near the town of Markham, he met my mother. It was love at first sight, his daring somersaults and muscular physique utterly dazzled my mother while her blue eyes instantly bewitched my father."

"Blue eyes?"

Scanner had never heard of natural blue-eyed Asians. Nowadays, colored contacts were all the rage, as Max had showcased so devastatingly the day they had met. But surely not in 1959, in China?

"Yes. They got married that same week. Mom told me later that when they met for the first time she was absolutely certain that she had known him her entire life. All around them Tibet was burning. The Dalai Lama had escaped to India earlier that year and the PLA was in the midst of a no-holds-barred assault on Lhasa."

Scanner remembered the horror stories his adopted family had impressed on him.

"My parents wanted no part in this tragedy and dad put

in for a transfer east. He was approaching forty and well liked so his superiors not only granted his wish for relocation, they sent him into early retirement from the Corps and gave him a martial arts school in Shanghai to manage on top. It truly seemed the gods were watching over the newlyweds."

Scanner didn't believe in fairy tales. The gods were a cruel and unpredictable lot, negligent at best, more likely sadistically inclined. He felt he was more qualified than most to judge. Lobsang had tried to instill in him a sense of life's interconnectedness with a higher consciousness, death merely a transit to the next level. Sometimes Scanner could almost see it. But the pain never really ceased. *Lobsang, where does he fit in?*

"Am I boring you already? Mr. Grant? I am truly sorry, you must still be exhausted, I shall immediately refrain from bothering you."

Scanner detected the disappointment in Cathy Lee's voice. It was obvious she had been brooding on her story for a long time.

"No, no, please do continue chief purser Cathy Lee, I want to hear it all. It's just that, well, I ain't much of a believer in divine virtue."

"Understood Sir, and I must say that I tend to concur; it's far too dangerous to assign goodness exclusively to the realm of divinity. We have to accept our own responsibility. I guess I could have used a different metaphor to describe the vicissitudes of life."

Cruel. Unjust. Bigoted. Savage. I could help you.

"Life was good. Simple, but without much hardship. My father and mother managed to save up a small sum and contemplated having a child. Then the shit hit the fan. Chairman Mao unleashed the monster of the Cultural Revolution that raped and ransacked and pillaged the country. My parents were accused of being bourgeois elements. You know, just wearing glasses made you a suspect, and both of them were teaching at that time, dad his Kung Fu and mom Tibetan language. Anyway, they were forced into struggle sessions, humiliated, beaten by their former students."

Heinous. Horrifying. Barbaric. The usual stuff.

"It's a miracle they survived physically but perhaps more so mentally. You know, families were torn apart, broken and discarded like filthy useless garbage. Children denounced their parents, husbands their wives. But their love never faltered, it kept them alive. Perhaps it made them stronger. I don't know. The torture…"

Cathy Lee stared at the historic photograph, pressed it against her heart and closed her eyes.

Did she try to forget or fail to remember?

"My father and mother had worked out a plan, a strategy to survive the indiscriminate madness and carnage that raged and roared and devoured souls with the ferocity of an out of control wildfire gorging on tinder-dry forest. When the inevitable knock on the door would come, they had decided to fool their persecutors, knowing that nothing would please the monsters more than turning husband against wife. You see, fear would do that. Fear and self-preservation. Blinded by an insatiable appetite for destruction and the hubris of unchallenged power the arrogant beast failed to recognize the absence of self and therefore the ineffectiveness of its methods. Mom and dad were one in spirit. The Red Guards could never break them.

Mom used to show me the scars on her back. Marks of selfless love she called them. Sometimes, talking to acquaintances, she would mention that her husband had left a deep impression on her and then she would look at me and wink. It was our private joke. Dad had struck her hard, drew blood, had to make it look real. But he knew from his Kung Fu to avoid the vital organs and so he saved her, saved them both. Deemed to be successfully reformed, they were eventually sent to the countryside, with the other vegetables. From there they escaped to Hong Kong. They were called freedom swimmers. One year later, in 1968, I was born."

"It seems your mother was an amazing and courageous woman. Why did she never tell you about Lobsang?"

"She didn't know about him. Right up till a few weeks before she passed away she had always maintained that her own mother had died from complications during her birth. A wealthy Khampa trader took pity on the orphaned child and raised her as his own."

"But this was not the whole truth?"

"No, you see sir, after my dad passed away, it became apparent that my mother would follow him soon. The love that had sustained them both through all the horrors now beckoned from beyond his grave. Her will to live was inextinguishable, but the flame could not be divided. One day, she called me over and without trepidation informed me of her desire to continue life with dad. That's what she said. Continue life. Death never intimidated her. It was as uneventful and straightforward as changing trains; the next leg of the journey was the exciting part. There was, however, one piece of luggage she didn't want to carry any further. I had a right to know, she informed me, what she had told no one, not even my father."

"And that was the same story Lobsang conveyed in his letter?"

"Yes, the same dark and ominous tale."

LOBSANG'S LETTER

"I am going to make us a nice pot of coffee Sir, in the meantime, here is Lobsang's letter. You should absorb the entire story in his words I think. My version will only be a watered down summary and will not have quite the same effect. Do you take sugar and milk?"

Cathy Lee handed Scanner a plain white envelope cleanly cut open at the top. Scanner alternated between excitement and dread as he fished out an A4 sized sheet of paper, densely covered on both sides with Lobsang's familiar slanted longhand. Never one to waste anything. He switched from his chair to the sofa, nestled in the stewardess's lingering warmth and started to read.

Dear Miss Lee, you must wonder who is this letter from. I hope in the end all will be clear as the turquoise waters of Lake Yamdrok. There is a time for everything. We don't shear our sheep in winter. Now that your mother has left and you have become an orphan, it is time for Lobsang to tell his story. Please do forgive me for waiting so long.

I was a five-year-old child in Tibet before the Second World War, in 1939. At that time, our knowledge of the world was extremely limited; we lived very isolated, cut off lives. I never saw a white man, only heard about them in stories. One day, many white men came to my village. A large group, like an expedition. With a lot of bags, transported by mules. I was afraid, but I was curious too, so I followed them around as they collected plants and animals, filmed and took photographs. One of them carried an instrument, I do not know the exact name, but it looked like a ruler. He put this instrument against people's heads and wrote down the measurements in his book. He also covered their faces with mud and removed the mask after it had dried. Me and my friends thought this was very funny, especially when one of our neighbors got mud into his nose and could not breathe.

We had no idea who these people were and why they had come to visit us but they seemed friendly. I heard my parents talking about a place called Deutschland and a man named Der Fuehrer. As a kid I assumed he must be their religious leader, you know, like our Dalai Lama. His sign was the swastika, similar to the symbol in our religion. Not until much later, after I left Tibet and traveled to the US, did I find out about Hitler and the atrocities committed under his watch. But I am getting ahead of myself now.

My eldest sister - we come from a large family, and we are eleven years apart - she and her friends were constantly talking and gossiping about our foreign visitors and one of them in particular. Maha Siddha they nicknamed him, Grand Master. I had seen this man. He was older than the rest and unlike the others he didn't seem to have a particular task to perform. It was clear though that he was in charge. He moved with an air of authority and spent a great deal of time with the abbot of the nearby monastery. I also noticed that he never once allowed himself to be photographed.

I should mention that, after my sister turned sixteen earlier in the year, my father often brought her to the monastery for studies. So when I overheard my sister mentioning a meeting with the Grand Master in the monastery later in the week I didn't think much of it. It was only when she failed to show up for some days afterwards that I recalled the conversation and inquired as to her whereabouts with my dad. Initially my father was evasive but finally he told me my sister had taken the vows and became a nun. This was not entirely unexpected and I didn't care much, I was just a little disappointed because I hadn't witnessed her head being shaved.

Two weeks later they brought her back. Or perhaps I should say they brought her shell back. My sister was gone. I mean, her body was there and it sure looked like her but there was no one home. The light in her eyes was extinguished and she didn't recognize any of us. We had to feed her, clothe her, bathe her. Her hair was gone. As you would expect from a novice nun. But her head was completely bandaged, like a mummy.

That night I sneaked into my sister's bedroom and unwrapped her head. I had to know. Now I wish I hadn't been so curious. You see I was only a five-year-old boy without a worry in this world. But the sight of my sister's perforated skull changed that forever.

Scanner stopped reading, leaned back on the sofa and closed his eyes. Lobsang's voice reverberated in his head. It was only yesterday he had talked to him on the phone. What had he said about Dolma? *Somebody done her real bad.*

Lobsang had been terrified, a state of mind his friend never displayed. And now this. Dread stepped into the ring and kicked surprise in the balls. This was turning into a fight without rules. It was time to smarten up.

Not once did I mention my horrendous discovery to my parents. Of course they knew. They did their best to carry on, maintain a happy demeanor for the sake of the other children. They refused to return to the monastery, neither to question the authorities nor to worship. As far as I can remember no one from our household ever went back there. The Germans? They had left and I never saw them again in our village.

They say time heals all wounds. Broken ice freezes over again and eventually will carry you to the other side. I ask you what good is that when the desire to reach the opposite shore is gone? My sister never came back. Her hair eventually covered the scars on her head, restored her familiar appearance. But without spirit there was only the illusion.

Approximately nine months after she was returned to us my sister gave birth to a little baby girl. It filled our house with joy. It was as if my sister had found her way back to us. Her baby cried: "enough with the sorrow, do away with the pain, life renews itself!"

That little baby girl, Miss Lee, that exorcist of our demons, was your mother. My parents named her Gyalwa Opame, a name roughly translated as The Victory of Infinite Light. Two weeks after Opame's birth my sister passed away.

It was clear from the beginning that there was something special about Opame. Her eyes were like the reflection of the midday sky in lake Puma Yumco. Both bottomless black and penetrating blue, depending on the angle she looked at you. Some people experienced an all-absorbing tranquility in her presence, others felt their darkest secrets were being exposed. Long before she could speak Opame had already made powerful enemies, especially in our monastic community.

My father knew her life would be in danger if she stayed with us. The abbot was an influential man, some even claimed he was a sorcerer. One day, Opame and my father were gone. Ostensibly he wanted to introduce her to some distant relatives in Amdo but, as I found out much later, he traveled further east and left my little niece in the care of an old and trusted friend.

Scanner picked up the scent of freshly brewed coffee. His brain could use the fuel. The other drugs had left his system but it was still hard to concentrate. He knew he had been lucky. The madness from the chemical slash and burn in his head had only been temporary. It could have been worse, much worse.

"Here you are, Sir, a cup of Blue Mountain. Careful, it's hot. Are you done reading?"

"Thank you. No, not quite, but it's good to have a break. It's an incredible story. Lobsang never told me."

"I think you've been around him long enough, Sir, to know he is not the garrulous kind. He will never tell a lie but he likes to keep his cards close to his chest. Only when questioned is he forthcoming and even then it'll take some probing."

"Seems to run in the family."

"You got me there Sir. Again. You know, all those years Lobsang knew, but not once did he contact my mother. At first I was upset but then I understood he was doing it for her.

He was protecting her. It must have been difficult for him, I think. He knew she was family, my mother never knew she had any."

"What was your mother's secret?"

"Ah, yes, you haven't finished the letter."

A PLAN

"So both your mother and Lobsang knew she was fathered by the Grand Master but exactly what happened to your grandmother remains a mystery."

"Indeed it does Sir. Until Lobsang's letter arrived I had no information at all about my mother's history. Her foster parents never told her. Right up till she got married she was unaware she was an adopted child, oblivious as to who her real father was. It was only the likelihood of a continuation of the bloodline that compelled her parents to part with this secret. As Lobsang writes, his father had instructed his friends accordingly when he trusted Opame into their care. Likewise, my mother kept this knowledge from me for as long as she could."

Scanner took another sip of the Blue Mountain brew. His head reeled with competing thoughts; perhaps the coffee could flush out the rubbish. Lobsang, Opame, the Grand Master and now, sixty years later, the web continued to expand with Cathy Lee and Dolma. And then his own case. He'd better stay alert. Stuart had tried to warn him, ended up dead as a consequence. The punter had known Jack, his dad. Wasn't that what he had said? *You look like him.* Whoever was behind it, they knew where he stayed. They knew where Max stayed. *Shit, Max.*

"I'd better call Max. Gotta let her know what is going on.

She might be in danger. Someone clearly doesn't want us to look for her father."

"Taken care off already Sir, I called her while you were asleep. The number was in your cell phone. She was out, something to do with shooting a TV commercial, hadn't checked in on you yet. Said you were being unreasonable and had upset her and she was waiting for an apology. But when I told her what happened her shell cracked. I don't think you'll have to worry anymore about her being all wound up, Sir."

Great. Get one woman to solve your other woman's problem. Nice going sport!

"Thanks, I guess."

"You're welcome Sir. She's a nice girl, very pretty, stunning in fact, but perhaps somewhat spoiled. I think she quite likes you."

"She is my client, for crying out loud chief purser Cathy Lee, as I am sure Lobsang told you. And I think you shouldn't project your own emotions onto her. It's not what I would expect from a woman like you."

It was nice being noticed, and a little rivalry never hurt. Scanner felt he was getting back in form.

"Touché Sir. One day I'd very much like to hear what it is exactly you expect from a woman like me. I'm not quite sure I'd be able to live up to your exalted standards, but trying could be educational. Right now, though, there are more pressing needs. Shall we get on with it?"

Didn't see that coming now, did you? Sport.

Scanner had to laugh. It was not often he encountered a feisty spirit like Cathy Lee's. Come to think of it she reminded him of Sue in many respects. A real find, worthy of respect precisely because she had such a low bullshit tolerance threshold.

"Sure, what's the plan?"

"Stuart is your best bet for finding Max's father, I think. You should check with the hotel Mr. Zwoelstra stayed in before he vanished but it is my educated guess that Macau holds the key. I found this in your back pocket Sir, prior to putting your trousers in the washing machine."

Cathy Lee handed Scanner the betting slip Stuart had relinquished in his final moments. It was a tierce bet. 9 – 1 –6. The Aussie punter had wagered one thousand Hong Kong Dollars. And won.

"The odds were quite long, I checked it. The ticket is worth close to four thousand US Dollars. But this is more significant. This is a chip from the Lisboa Casino in Macau. Stuart had folded it inside the winning ticket. Fancy an affair with Lady Luck, Sir?"

LAUGHTER

Macau housed a veritable pantheon of gods. True to form, the Portuguese enclave on China's Southern doorstep had hedged its spiritual bets. Fishermen in search of protection from the elements and a bountiful catch frequented the A-Ma Temple. Merchants and traders coveted the powers of Kwan Yu, the god of war and justice, who held court at the Sam Kai Vui Kun Temple. Children's health benefitted from a visit to the miniscule Na Tcha Temple. Luck, good fortune, prosperity, love; the gods and goddesses held the power to bestow such blessings on the mortal souls that came to worship. It was a simple trade-off, too good to pass up, really.

In that respect, the Portuguese colonizers with their plethora of saints had fit right in. Though they somewhat spoiled the party by introducing the concepts of original sin and guilt.

Bemused, Scanner watched the throng of worshippers shuffle their way to the main altar in the A-Ma Temple. Scanner and Max had decided to follow the only lead they had, a dead man's not so lucky chip. An inquiry at the Shangri La hadn't turned up anything useful besides the acknowledgement that indeed a Mr. Zwoelstra had stayed on the premises. He had checked out by phone after four days and his staff had come to pick up the luggage.

Macau was only a two-hour ride by high-speed ferry from Hong Kong. After having checked into the hotel, Max had expressed her desire to pray at the oldest temple in the colony. Pray that they would find her father.

Giant, slow burning incense coils spiraled down from the beamed ceiling, occasionally dropping a puff of ash on an unsuspecting devotee below. This was grass roots religion, stripped of lofty discourse and paralyzing dogma. Without pretentions and in that respect honest, direct and, for the most part, selfish. You ask, the gods give. Or not.

If all the piety still failed to deliver or protect, there was always Guanyin, the Goddess of Mercy. And of course there was the Lisboa, the largest and most opulent of the city's temples. Devout visitors to the Casino Lisboa fell in either one of two categories, the lucky bastards or the desperate souls. Life being impermanent, many punters migrated back and forth between the two, multiple times, during the course of a night in the Lisboa. Naturally the cards were stacked and most gamblers ended up in the latter category. Their misfortune spawned an entire secondary economy of pawnshops, loan sharks, human trafficking and hit men. Macau was a microcosm of the human condition. The end of the line for the greed express.

Avarice was the most reliable of human religions. Its temples and churches and megamalls packed with the faithful, you could count on it. In fact, you could bet on it.

"I think you should burn some incense, you know. You have been very lucky."

Scanner looked at Max. He couldn't detect any hint of irony. During the ferry ride on the way over Max had expressed her worry and relief that he was, in the end, unharmed. She had masked this, of course, in a preachy sermon berating his foolishness. After all, she had her own box at Happy Valley. Why hadn't Scanner informed her about his intended excursion? She would have arranged a limousine with chauffeur and perhaps even some champagne; it would have been a fun night.

Scanner had let it slide. To tell her they were not in Hong Kong for fun would be stating the obvious. Max's father had gone missing. She was only trying to be cheerful. He wasn't gonna rub salt into that open wound.

Sometimes though, you needed to provide an opportunity for providence to get in touch with you. Mysterious ways and all that. In Scanner's opinion there was no need to ask the gods. It didn't work that way. Give them some room.

"Let's get one of those huge coils then. They'll burn for two weeks, saves me from having to return and express my gratitude every time I am fortunate enough to survive."

"Yeah, go ahead and make fun of it. Never mind. I'll do it for you."

Max was a good girl. What had Cathy Lee said? I think she quite likes you sir. Scanner wasn't really into good girls. They were so, what was the right word? So, inexperienced. Not really her fault of course. Max was still young and, besides that, for most of her upbringing her father had kept the big bad world at bay. Scanner had the feeling that was all about to change.

"Thanks, Max, I appreciate it. Really. There's a kind of innocence in this approach don't you think so? Kinda like the tooth fairy of my childhood. Somewhere along the way most of my teeth got kicked out though."

"You know what your problem is Scanner? You're too analytical. It doesn't hurt to make a wish sometimes. And that is what I am going to do right now."

Max walked over to a nearby table supporting a large copper bowl, about two thirds filled with water. She briefly dipped her hands inside and started to vigorously rub the two protruding handles. Soon enough the vibrating vessel hummed along in a low, monotonous tone.

"Come over here Scanner and listen. Nearer. Put your ear

closer to the water."

Scanner approached and bent forward. Max's visible excitement was rather cute. She was almost like a daughter, or the younger sister he never had. Family, let's not go there Scanner.

The humming intensified, like an approaching car. Too late, Scanner realized the connection, too late to jump away. From four distinct areas inside the bowl water spouted over a feet in the air, blasted his face and soaked his shirt.

"Shit!" Scanner shouted. "You little…"

Max doubled over in a fit of laughter.

"Got you, ha ha, you never saw that one coming, I got you."

She sure did. Scanner wiped his face with the sleeve of his shirt. Max was holding her belly.

"Ha ha, oooh, it hurts, it's sooo funny. Look at you."

Max's exuberant laughing proved highly contagious. Scanner was not immune.

"You little rascal, ha ha, how did you know?"

"This, my dear Scanner, is called a Chinese Spouting Bowl. It grants the wish of those who manage, with the right vibrations, to cause the water to spout. And it works! Beyond the shadow of a doubt, it works. My wish was to see your face beam with laughter."

Scanner had to give it to her. Max was like a breath of fresh air. Actually more like a tornado. When had he stopped laughing? Simple, childlike joy was the best medicine for a jaded soul such as his. And Dr. Max knew the prescription.

"What do you say we grab something to eat before heading back to the hotel? Plenty of time left till the casino action kicks in and I feel kinda hungry."

"Sure, I know a great place. You like seafood?"

Martyrs

"So what is this part of Macau called? And what's that smell?"

The fifteen minutes taxi ride had taken them across a long bridge, a broad causeway and approximately seven decades of history. Urbanity, with all the associated stress and stench of mechanized progress, had traded places with rolling green hills and the stench of nature. *Fish odor syndrome?*

"We're on Coloane Island, the southern most part of Macau. It's a world apart isn't it? This used to be a haven for pirates and slave traders. Now it's mostly fishermen who live here. The dried salted fish is a local delicacy. We get out here."

Scanner followed Max onto the cobblestone village square. Arched colonnades bordered both long sides of the *largo*, creating a tunnel perspective that visually beckoned Scanner towards the cream colored chapel at the far end. Aware that physical sustenance was currently more pressing, Scanner and Max headed instead for the red-checkered tablecloths of Café Nga Tim, the restaurant housed under the left archway.

"It doesn't look like a fancy place." Max studied the menu. "But the food is heavenly. Let me order for us both. OK?"

Scanner had never been much of a gourmand. He tried to eat healthy and usually chose the TV Dinner with the most vegetables in it. This though was a whole different level of eating. Like the difference between a quick shag and a transcendental erotic experience.

Scanner kinda missed Cathy Lee. He had spent last night at her apartment. Fully conscious this time. Grateful he didn't have to return to the canned warmth of the Mandarin. And the slippers. Early this morning he had gone straight to the ferry pier and boarded with Max. Cathy Lee would be babysitting passengers on her flight to Chicago just about right now.

"What did I tell you? The clams with black beans and chili sauce were out of this world, don't you think so? And the *mexilhoes*, just thinking of those mussels makes me salivate."

Scanner leaned back as far as the blue plastic chair would allow and washed down the remnants of the steamed mussels with a nice cold Super Bock.

"Great choice Max. I could die now, I'm this close to paradise. We'd better be on our way soon, though. And, as you so aptly demonstrated earlier, I doesn't hurt to muster all the help we can. Let's have a look inside the church first."

Scanner settled into one of the front pews. The intimate chapel, dimly lit now that dusk had surrendered to darkness, exuded tranquility, in stark contrast to the earlier mayhem of the A Ma Temple.

Max had left, still craving sweetness. She wanted to buy some of Macau's famous Lord Stow egg tarts. Scanner didn't mind. He wished some of her enthusiasm would rub off on him. It would make life easier. He had to work hard to keep up with what came natural to Max. To regain what once had come natural to him too.

A cold draft raised the hairs on the back of his neck. Max had probably left the door open.

"The lord giveth and the lord taketh away."

Scanner turned around. He hadn't heard anyone move into the wooden bench behind him.

"That's a beautiful verse, don't you think? And to realize we are his tools. Wonderful. *Komban wa*, my name is Hideyoshi. I am from Japan, and you?"

"Scanner, Scanner Grant. From Chicago."

Scanner intently studied the elderly Japanese gentleman. He was well past pension age. Thick white stubble and a matching moustache and beard covered most of the bulbous head. Eyes unusually round for an Asian, set into a tanned face, gave Hideyoshi the cuddly appearance of a panda. A tiny white square at the base of his throat contrasted with the perfect upright collar of his black dress shirt. *A priest?*

"Ah so, USA. You know Grant San, we have a history here. Would you die for your faith? For your beliefs? They did. Happily. Eagerly almost. Now their bones are here. Powerful isn't it? That's why I like to come here. Soak it all in. Bathe in the glory of the lord."

Scanner vaguely remembered reading about Japanese martyrs. Crucified hundreds of years ago, their remains interred in this very chapel.

"I should be on my way now. Nice talking to you Grant San. Feel the power. The lord works in mysterious ways. *Sayonara.*"

Before the baffled Scanner was able to reply the priest had stealthily taken off and disappeared into the surrounding darkness.

Did that just happen?

Max rushed through the door. "Hey I got them. Tried one already. They're delicious. Let's go then.

Oops, I am sorry. I didn't mean to disturb your meditating. That's what you were doing right? God, you look so serious."

"Did you see…"

"See what? I didn't see anything. Let's go to the casino. I feel lucky tonight."

Never mind.

ZOMBIE SEDUCTION

"Remind me again what we're doing here."

Scanner had just burst onto the set of the Asian *Dawn of the Dead*. Or was it the psychiatric ward of a substance abuse clinic taken over by patients with access to an unlimited stash, totally wasted by their mad addiction-fuelled bender of financial debauchery? The dark and cadaverous room packed table after table with hollow-eyed junkies, lines of chips in front of them. Judging by the look on the punters' faces, money impeded happiness. Losers wanted to recoup their loss, winners wished to increase their gains. Both never had enough. Both filled their evening with an endless sequence of 'last ones'.

"It's pretty awful isn't it? Some nights are better than others but tonight it's particularly lifeless. We're here to find my dad, or at least pick up some clues, if we're lucky. Of course considering your adventure at the races, the clues are more likely to find us."

Max was right. The whole enterprise was a wild goose chase with a faulty rifle. The possibility of it all backfiring worried Scanner. But what choice did they have? At least Stuart had directed their aim. It was time to take a few shots, see what came crashing down, or who would return fire.

Scanner felt distinctly overdressed. Max had bought him a suit in Hong Kong. An impeccable fit. How did she do that? Matching white shirt and black wing-tip lace-up shoes complimented the elegant two-piece. The label advertised an exotic foreign name impossible to pronounce without stuttering. No doubt the price would have the same effect. The cash spent on the tie alone could probably replace his entire T-shirt collection.

Scanner never wore suits. He didn't own any. He had bought a sports coat once at a JC Penny sale. That was years ago. Only recently, Sue had made him cut open the side pockets. He checked his suit. Open.

"You look bad. Like you mean business. Like you know you're hot and desirable."

Was Max taking the piss?

"No seriously. I think you're sexy. Confident. Will you be my sugar daddy tonight?"

No shit. Scanner turned and stared intently at Max. *Agent Provocateur.* She had the Lolita look down to a tee. A short red plaid skirt revealed the almost endless length of her thigh-high-white-stockings-clad lower assets. The top buttons of her pearly short-sleeved cotton blouse displayed the visible strain of a spring flower, moments before bursting into full bloom. Thick black hair protruded sideways, just above Max's ears, like the handlebars on a thoroughbred Italian bike. *Sinful, seductive, dangerous.*

"You'll get me in trouble. Did you bring your I.D?"

"Don't worry, we're in Asia. What do you think?"

Thinking was the least of Scanners worries. It had been a good decision to forego his usual jeans.

"You're missing your lollipop." *Can't believe I just said that.*

"Couldn't find my favorite flavor unfortunately. Besides it would probably be just a little bit too provocative. Not to mention I'm a compulsive pencil chewer when I'm tracking my Baccarat scorecard. Let's walk over there."

Max hooked her arm in Scanner's and flicked her head in the intended direction. The unsteady wobble in her gait indicated that affection was not the only reason for this physical contact. More than once, Scanner's arm muscles tensed under Max's faltering weight.

"First day at school?"

"No, I had a few lessons but it is the first time on these."

Like a seasoned can-can dancer Max kicked up her right leg until a chunky black platform shoe appeared in Scanner's line of vision. He blushed as he imagined what, at this very moment, a gambler's line of vision would reveal. But no one looked.

"Put it down will you. We're not in the Moulin Rouge."

"Don't worry," Max laughed, "they all have their eyes on the money. There's no other game in town for them."

***

With a sweeping hand motion the dealer suspended all bets. Time to draw cards. Scanner had never played Baccarat but it sure wasn't rocket science. Banker, player, draw. He couldn't understand the attraction though. Max, on the other hand, had surrendered to the game with complete abandon. Like everything else she did.

"The trick is to understand that there is a pattern within the pattern of all shoes ever dealt and then to spot the deviation from this pattern in the current shoe. The opportunity to place a winning bet will present itself if you're patient enough. I am not a gambler, I am a player. Pay attention and you'll see."

To Scanner it sounded very much like wishful thinking, the prescription of some gaming quack whose job it was to convince gullible patients there was a method to the madness. But what did he know? Max was the one going to school.

Sure enough, while the other gamblers at the table placed bets on every hand Max remained practically motionless. There was nothing, however, that escaped her observation.

After each hand she religiously noted the outcome on her scorecard, chewed a few more dents in the beat up pencil and held back.

"Now."

With the ferocity of a wild cat having lied in ambush at the waterhole for hours, she pounced on the next hand. One third of all her chips migrated to the Banker field. All other bets on the table rode the chop sequence and favored the players. The sneers didn't seem to affect Max.

Are you mad?

Max drew a seven of Diamonds and a five of Clubs against the banker's seven of Clubs and eight of Hearts. Two against five. Not particularly promising, Scanner deduced with his basic knowledge of the game. Max's last card was a six of Spades. A nearly unbeatable eight. *But she has bet on the banker! Oh no.*

Then the dealer delivered the final *coup de grace* in the form of a four of Diamonds, and for the first time that evening all eyes at the table were on the little ponytailed schoolgirl in the red plaid skirt nearly biting her pencil in half.

RELIGIOUS FEVER

"That was amazing. How did you know?"

"Follow the pattern, like I told you, I'm a player not a gambler."

Max spotted a few more opportunities in the rest of the shoe. On the first bet she lost, only to double up and win on the following hand. Her winning streak continued unabatedly with the next shoe. Gradually, a miniature Chinese Wall rose in front of Max, two rows deep. Would it keep the barbarians out?

"What do you think, we got some attention?"

Scanner glanced over his shoulder. They were completely fenced in by curious punters.

"Word is out, it seems. You've got quite the crowd lined up. You might consider charging for private tuition."

"They all failed the entrance exams. Sorry. Besides, I don't think I need the money."

Max opened her purse, fumbled around inside, visibly annoyed.

"Where is it?"

Last time Scanner had seen a similarly branded bag there was a cat in it, a dead cat. He made a mental note to bring back a small something for Mrs. Kowalski. She had the key to his apartment and kept his plants alive.

"Argggh, this is impossible."

With theatrical zeal Max turned over her purse and emptied the contents on the table.

"What are you do…"

Scanner eyed the heap of assorted pads, brushes, sticks, tubes, and vials, unceremoniously dumped for all to see. Then he spotted it. Between the orange Nokia and a pair of matching Ray Bans, partly covered by the grenade shaped bottle of her favorite fragrance, Max's father looked up.

"There you are."

Now that she had the crowd mesmerized Max reached for the explosive French perfume, aimed in the direction of her cleavage and filled the air with a barrage of scented puffs. Tiny fragrant pearls formed and coalesced into a meandering rivulet.

Certain that her audience had taken it all in, Max leaned back, disposed the chemical weapon into her designer bag and with one nonchalant underarm swoop shoved the rest of the treasure inside, half of her winnings included.

"Time for a change. Here you take these. Try not to lose it all. I am going for a walk, see what else I can stir up in this twilight zone."

Scanner stared at the tower of fortune in front of him. It was enough money to cover his pay for a month. Most of the world could survive on it for many years, if not a decade. And he would probably lose it in a mere sixty minutes. What was wrong with society? Anxiety that the virus would contaminate him as soon as he touched the chips immobilized his body and almost paralyzed his mind. How did Max do it? Did she consider the ramifications or was it all really just a game?

"Are you a religious man?"

Again?

"Is the seat taken? Would you mind?"

Scanner looked up at a middle aged, well-built Caucasian man. A broad shouldered oversized cheap polyester suit failed to conceal he was packing. *Security? Hood? Cop? P.I?* The suit partly gave it away. A self-conscious and aspirational gangster would have gone for silk or cashmere, tailored in a Tony Montana three-piece. A salaried cop or guard, not to mention a freelance investigator, on the other hand, could only afford to dance in an off-the-peg Tony Manero. Not the real thing though. Scanner remembered reading about the astronomical amount paid for John Travolta's Saturday Night Fever suit at an auction a handful of years back.

Not waiting for an invitation, the man sat down next to Scanner. It was a tight fit for the shoulder holster.

"It is written that when God punished Sodom and Gomorrah, he instructed Lot and his family to flee without looking back. The wife failed to obey and was turned into a pillar of salt. Have you ever wondered why?"

Scanner was sure the answer would follow.

"Do not rejoice in the destruction of your enemies. That's what it says. When the inevitable occurs, for it always will, walk away, without glee, without second thoughts."

Religion was a funny thing. It could and had been used to justify just about every conceivable folly of human behavior. Notwithstanding its dogmas, however, it didn't provide an answer to the existential conundrum, the who, what, why and where of our presence. Believers just stopped asking questions. Their mouths stuffed with the giant pacifier called church, or temple, or mosque, or money for that matter.

"Do you have what it takes? To walk away?"

A veiled warning?

"I myself find the wife a lot more sympathetic. What's the purpose of enlisting God to wipe out your enemies and then you can't watch? Makes no sense. I would want front row. Bet you most people would."

Scanner did not detect any aggression in the man's voice, merely a nostalgic overtone. Still, it paid to be cautious. *Keep listening.* He needed more time with his enigmatic neighbor and the table provided good cover as long as he continued betting. *Alright then. Realize there is a pattern.*

***

Scanner managed to hold the fort fairly well. He wasn't exactly winning but he kept his losses at a minimum. Max would be proud. His burly neighbor on the other hand was losing money faster than the Fed could print. Small amounts, but constantly. He didn't seem to care or notice until the final chip. Scanner spotted the opportunity and slyly migrated a quarter of his chips to the left.

"Oh, thanks. I guess I should pay more attention. Your pretty girlfriend earlier had the game under control, hadn't she? Asians, it's their religion, man. She's sexy, young and headstrong. Just what he is looking for. She should be careful."

"Who is looking for what?"

CONFESSION

"They call him The Priest. He is a procurer of human flesh. Young women mostly, teenagers preferably, he supplies them to his customers in Japan. For sex, yes, of course, nothing unusual about that. But the prostitution is actually just a cover. I mean, the cover below the cover of domestic helper or marriage or whatever else they can get away with. In reality The Priest is pimping minds. Most of his merchandise is used for experiments. Dark stuff, unspeakable, unimaginable horror. Not everyone survives. They say he collects the thigh bones of the discarded victims. Uses them to meditate, to increase his power."

Scanner stopped breathing. An icy chill gripped his spine and crawled its way up, frozen vertebrae by frozen vertebrae. The cold draft he'd felt in the church when he met Hideyoshi hadn't been the result of a door left ajar.

"You should continue placing bets. Don't look alarmed, as far as everyone here is concerned we're just having a chat. Macau is a most convenient base for the slave trade, especially now. At the end of this year, the colony will return to Chinese rule, just like Hong Kong did two years ago. All the power-brokers are jostling for position. Lots of money at stake. And money works like a blinder on a horse. There is a grab-while-you-still-can attitude that has permeated all levels of society.

The Priest, he is elusive. He appears at will and vanishes

118

without a trace. Rumors endow him with supernatural power. I don't believe in that shit but there are plenty who do."

Scanner didn't believe in it either. He knew. The powers of the mind were virtually untapped in the Western world, where so-called mechanistic science ruled.

"I'm an investigator, I work for an NGO called Oriental Peace Collective. We have been following The Priest for quite a while now. All evidence we managed to collect thus far is circumstantial, nothing we can pin on him, he is a smart motherfucker, for a priest you know. But we are getting closer.

Macau is his favorite hunting ground; there is much unhappiness to exploit. People come here with dreams, hopes of making it. Most never climb past the first rung, just manage to hang on. And what do they do when the nightmare becomes reality? When the kids' college money is gone, the watch is pawned, the house mortgaged, the marriage destroyed? What people all over the world have always done when the shit piles up so high it covers the fan; seek solace in fairy tales, in promises of a better place over the rainbow, in other words, religion. Left with a choice between religion and suicide it's worth a shot so to speak, pun intended."

"You said he was looking for women mostly. Look around though, it's usually men who are gambling."

"True, but the same principle applies to women. You know how many Filipina girls are working in Macau? They have an added advantage. They are catholic. The Priest loves taking confession. And don't underestimate the power of youth, a baby girl can wipe out a large amount of debt."

Scanner felt nauseated. His stack of chips had dwindled. He had stopped paying attention to the pattern a while ago. It seemed trivial at best to worry about winning or losing. He didn't want to have anything to do with this Mephisthelean industry, peddling life but selling death. Why had this guy pounced on him? It couldn't be a coincidence, it never was.

"Why are you telling me all this?"

Best to take the devil by the horns.

"I believe you met my partner, Stuart, may his soul rest in peace."

WHAT A RIDE

"Stuart and I were working the case together. Been on it for over a year. Shuttling between Tokyo and Macau, occasionally to Bangkok. They know a thing or two about trafficking in Thailand. You been to Bangkok? Nice place. It's like the Walmart of sex on Black Friday. Deep discounts. If you like shopping."

The guttural substitute for a laugh that escaped from the investigator's lips urged Scanner to get up and leave. The failed 'buddy wink' that followed ignited ideas for a much more savage response. He didn't have enough chips left. *Stuart? You're getting paid for this Scanner.*

"A lot of bang for your buck right?"

Scanner loathed himself. *It's a game. You play it well. That's why you're here.*

"You know it, sure you never been? Anyways a month or so back I started noticing Stuart being increasingly preoccupied. Like he was leading a double life. Late to appointments, bags under his eyes, that sorta thing. He gambled. At least he used to. Had undergone treatment, apparently was on the wagon. No way they would have kept him employed otherwise."

Well, he isn't employed anymore. Sent into permanent retirement.

"We all have our vices."

"Of course we do, but in our line of business vices leave

one exposed and exposure leads to vulnerability."

What exactly is your line of business?

"And vulnerability gets a man killed?"

"Exactly, or even worse, gets a man's partner killed. I ain't paying another man's debt. I might settle it, but paying, no fucking way. So I figured Stuart got himself involved with the wrong people. Easy to do in this part of the world. It's candy store galore, whatever treat or trick you fancy and lack of cash ain't gonna stop the pursuit of temporary happiness. Paradise on credit, but when the devil comes collecting, you need a whole lot more than a prayer to save your ass."

"Amen." The man was on a roll and Scanner offered just enough encouragement to keep him going.

"Two nights ago I followed Stuart to the races. He'd been a jockey in his previous life. The ambiance at Happy Valley sucked him in. Sooner or later resistance would be useless. It is also a great place to have a clandestine meeting. So many punters, you share a few tips, exchange bits of information, who knows? I had taken up a position way high up in the public viewing gallery, took my field glasses. Stuart was easy to spot. Obviously he would be in the vicinity of the parade ring, watch them numbered ladies. Make his choice. It is exciting you know. It's a power rush. Just like them fishbowls in Bangkok. Only difference Stuart didn't get to ride his pick."

It was moments like these Scanner wanted to dump the compassion and mindfulness Lobsang had tried to instill in him and incarnate into Mahakala or any of the wrathful deities in the Tibetan pantheon, fangs and all. The principle to adhere to was not non-violence; that was such a crappy Western projection of Tibetan Buddhism. Scanner's transgression was that he would actually enjoy dishing out the pain and thereby eliminate the difference between himself and his victim. There was still plenty to work on.

"So what I want to know is what you and Stuart talked about. What did you want from him? I saw both of you trackside, obviously something went down. Stuart left to place a wager or take a piss or something and then you followed. When neither one of you returned, I came down to find my partner being carried away on a stretcher and no trace of you. Cardiac arrest. Possible, with the excitement and all that, but I didn't find no betting slip or anything on him."

Scanner's brain cells fired off scenarios faster than a computer could analyze. Was this guy telling the truth? Was he as much in the dark about Stuart's motives as Scanner himself?

"I wanted to enlist Stuart's help in tracking someone down."

Scanner decided to play.

"You saw my girlfriend at the table right? Her father went missing while on business in Hong Kong. She coerced me into helping her find him. She's headstrong, you said it yourself. Doesn't take no for an answer. Not that you wanna say no to her, cause that'll be the end of the ride and the theme park doesn't offer anything better if you get what I mean."

"Yeah man, I get it. She's up there. I saw the old man's photograph. So that's it. Stuart was freelancing on the sly. Makes sense, with our salary and his gambling habits. Still, you know, he shoulda told me; we could have worked together. I could use the extra cash. So now what? Someone wants the old man to stay disappeared. And he'll kill for it. Looks to me you could use some help buddy. You wanna keep the missus happy. Clearly you're in over your head, while all you want is to be in with your head. I can appreciate that."

I am sure you can.

"Here is my card, call Tony for your peace of mind. I'll settle your little problem, for a fee, of course. But hey, a great ride is worth every penny."

Scanner looked at the business card, *Oriental Peace Cooperative* embossed in gold across the top. TONY M. and *Don't settle for less* written on the next two lines. He could have guessed.

"And if you run into The Priest, gimme a shout too, but

remember he's a sadistic son of a bitch, a real mind fuck."

Scanner had known a few of them in the course of his job. He stood up from the table, pocketed his single remaining chip and put a hand on Tony's shoulder.

"Thanks Tony, I appreciate your concern and will consider your offer. Now I gotta find my girl, she's calling the shots, you know."

ALIVE AND KICKING

Where was Max? Scanner walked the entire floor in a grid, elbowed his way to the edge of tables obscured by curious crowds, even checked the slot machines. The provocative schoolgirl was playing truant.

The Lisboa casino and hotel connected to form a labyrinth of art-filled corridors, chandelier lit lobbies and soap opera stairways. Intricately carved jade statues and humongous Chinese porcelain vases projected the image of a seriously rich owner with an ego to match. Big money had a need to justify itself. Fortunately, in the myopic world of the mega-rich, justification and sophistication could be bought by participating in philanthropy and art acquisition.

Charity art auctions for the benefit of underprivileged single parent children in pauperized ghetto neighborhoods of high unemployment urban centers were particularly well attended. The patrons were, at best, blissfully oblivious to the fact that greed, expressed in the real estate speculation, stock market manipulation and workforce off-shoring that had contributed significantly to their Forbes rankings, was the root cause of little Jimmy's inebriated mother locking him up inside the filthy backyard shed while she, semi-comatose, out on her back, serviced the third John of the afternoon so that her son wouldn't be ostracized by the other abused kids at school for not having the latest trainers or joggers produced by another little Jimmy in some godforsaken off-shored Third World sweatshop. At worst, they were willing actors in a carefully orchestrated Public Relations whore's cynical wet dream.

Scanner called it the Misery Business. A fast growing segment of the world's economy. And just as the pharmaceutical industry had no genuine intention to heal people with its products, an equitable distribution of wealth and earth's resources was not on the agenda of the do-gooders of the corporate world. Scanner imagined this part of the planet to be no different. Less sophisticated perhaps, as greed looked to be more of a virtue in Asia and did not require the layers of packaging Western sensibilities demanded.

Another round past herded commoners gawking at the assorted treasures failed to turn up Max. Tired of the fruitless search, Scanner dug the small Nokia out of his suit pocket and speed dialed his employer. Rowdy noise overpowered the fading echoes of the fourth ring. Max was barely audible.

"Where are you? You're in some kinda party?"

"Something like that. I'm on the lower level, can't really talk, I think you'd better come down."

***

Scanner considered himself fairly jaded. Years of front row seating witnessing human folly unfold in an endless reprise had set the bar for surprise, pleasant or otherwise, pretty high. A single raised eyebrow or a barely visible headshake had become his signature response to all but a few extreme acts of depravity.

The scene Scanner was about to encounter in the lower level corridor would later be categorized as a double brow raiser/faint smile combo, a rare occasion indeed.

Scanner almost intervened and he almost felt sorry. Not for Max. She was, well, she was Max and he would have been surprised if she was unable to stand her ground. Just in case though, he kept a close watch. It was the two middle aged Indian guys he was worried about. They traipsed the circular corridor in the wake of Max's fluttering plaid skirt like a pair of horny goats raised on a diet of Viagra and fetish porn.

Scanner couldn't hear what they were calling her but there was no mistaking their intention when Max turned around and faced off.

"I warn you," Max was fuming. "You guys have your dicks in your ears? What planet are you from? I said NO and when I say NO I mean NO. Maybe your sister or your mother or your neighbor's donkey loves the attention but I don't. So fuck off or go and dump your load in the toilet over there, but leave me alone."

Max wasn't the only overtly sexy dressed female lingering in the corridor between the restaurant and the convenience store. Scanner knew that most of these stunning girls meant business and he could see how Max's attitude confused the heck out of the Indians. Still, there was no excuse for disrespect and No! was pretty universally understood.

Max continued her tour of the Lisboa's very own Parade Ring.

DON'T! Scanner suppressed the initial urge to shout as both of the Indian men reached out simultaneously and lifted the hem of Max's skirt, revealing the innocent white of her panties. As a male he could appreciate the extent of the punishment about to be dished out. Ouch. Scanner shook his head.

It was all over in a few seconds. Max swiveled around on her front leg and planted the chunky platform at the end of the other firmly in the one offender's groin before withdrawing in a fighting stance, three quarters of her weight supported by her rear right leg. The worst was yet to come. Without allowing the second offender to recoup from the shock of seeing his partner writhing in agony on the floor, Max jumped up, using her left leg in a stepping-stone movement to gain momentum. Hovering mid air, the right kick was executed with ball-busting force and precision. Scanner cringed as the impact registered a speechless "Oh" on the victim's lips, flabbergasted that such a pretty party girl could be so mean, before the pain registered, knees buckled and his slumped over body collapsed to the floor.

Max hovered over the unlucky punters, legs slightly apart and firmly grounded, hands on her hips, ready for anything that was stupid enough to come her way. Ironically the killer view the Indians had been lusting for was now right in their faces.

Max looked around, silently daring anyone to come forward, ready to unleash her wrath once more. No one approached.

"If you ever touch me again or if I ever see or hear you disrespecting any of my sisters here I will make you regret the day you were born, do I make myself clear?"

Scanner noticed tiny nods of approval amongst the sisters gathered, some, though, glanced around nervously. By now, trouble would be on the way. He didn't want to wait for casino security or worse. Mad pimps. Assertive merchandise and semi-castrated Johns were bad for the bottom line. It was time to split.

"Let's go. Now!"

Scanner grabbed Max by the arm and ushered her through the crowd in the direction of the stairs. Off her adrenaline high, Max trembled like a leaf in an autumn storm, clinging to the branch for dear life. She was close to tears.

On the way out they passed Tony M.

"Call me, really, she's got a mean kick, man. You wanna make sure she stays happy."

Tony M had a point.

SENSORY DEPRIVATION

"All in all it's been quite the night. Max was totally fired up. Can't blame her, we haven't really gotten anywhere yet besides the likelihood that Macau holds the key. It wasn't exactly covert, but it sure rocked the house. Now let's see what comes crawling out of the woodwork. Those two Indians though, man, I nearly felt sorry for them. Hold on a sec."

Scanner kicked off his shoes and threw his jacket on one of the chairs. He was on the phone with Sue. Earlier, he had taken Max to her room. The girl had been all shook up. Only after he had fed her a couple of shots of the Macallan brought from Hong Kong did Max relax sufficiently to allow sleep to take over the reins. Scanner had removed her neutering tools, tucked her in. Then he had waited for the slowing down of Max's breathing. On his way out he had dismissed a faint desire to kiss her on the forehead with the usual client-relation bullshit. The phone had rung just as he had stepped into the adjacent room. Sue.

"I mean, they'd probably won at baccarat or gotten lucky on the slot machines and were on their way to celebrate."

Scanner stretched out on the bed; it was soothing to hear Sue's voice.

"Looks like Max depleted their jackpot, but not in the way they had hoped. Will take a while to fill up the juice again, I reckon. And they will probably pussy out of anything but the one-armed bandit."

That's my girl. Scanner grinned. Sue's associating skills were second to none.

"That seems an accurate assessment, my dear. I marvel at your oral abilities."

"Ha, I am sure you do. Please come marvel soon, I miss you."

"Same here, the casino is a dark place. This much money; it attracts all sorts of shady characters. Some would cast a shadow even on a moonless night."

Scanner recalled his meeting with The Priest and what he had learned about this mysterious Japanese through Tony M. *Selling minds.* He then realized Sue didn't yet know about his own mind trip and Cathy Lee's amazing story. *The Grandmaster.*

***

"Wow."

Scanner remained silent. Let Sue digest all the implications.

"Wow, I mean, it seems all connected, somehow. Creepy. Now you've got me worried. Go with your instincts on this ok? Don't rationalize them away."

Sue knew him well.

"I won't, it's what I've got. Right now we need to wait, we've thrown out enough baited hooks to catch something. Hopefully it will be Max's father and we can get the hell out of here."

Hopefully. Hope was a dangerous intoxicant, a sensuous Delilah ensnaring and eventually disempowering knowledge, true knowledge, not the stuff you learned at school, but the lessons life taught those who questioned. In matters of life and death, hope wouldn't quite cut it.

"How about your investigation? Made any progress? I haven't got the files yet cause we left Hong Kong this morning. The hotel will forward any mail so I guess it could be here tomorrow."

"We managed to identify the chair Dolma was bound to when she was found. It is an original tranquilizer chair. A late 18th century design by some head doctor called Benjamin Rush. Used to stabilize patients by way of sensory deprivation. It really is something out of Edgar Allan Poe, gives me the chills just looking at it. Poor girl.

Other than that, no more missing persons and the selective amnesia of the other girls seems permanent."

Sue paused. Scanner didn't fill the void with any more words. He had told his story. Sue had to make the connections; this was her case.

"It's the Grandmaster isn't it? I mean Lobsang was mortified when he saw what had been done to Dolma. I can understand why now. He had seen it all before, with his sister. It's obviously something he'd rather forget but it might just give us an insight into a motive if not a perpetrator. You've got to talk to him. Better that you do it. I am actually waiting for him to pick me up right now. We're gonna drive to the lake, you know, where those kids found her. I'll call you back so you can ask him. You're like his son, why would he hide anything from you?"

The same thought puzzled Scanner.

GIFT HORSES AND THIRSTY YAKS

The smooth Macallan worked its soothing magic. Scanner poured himself another one. He had taken a quick shower, rinsed the cigarette stink from his hair and body. His clothes would have to go to the cleaners tomorrow. He filled out the ubiquitous hotel laundry form; made sure the suit was a dry-clean job. Then he scribbled his room number, 916 and signed. The stuffed laundry bag he attached to his suit hanger, which in turn he hung from the closet door. Draped in the hotel bathrobe, he sat on the bed, single malt in one hand, multiple thoughts in the other.

His mind won, for now. Lobsang would soon call and it was best to remain relatively sober till then. The glass stayed empty after the second shot.

***

"Good to hear your voice Lobsang. I don't know if Sue filled you in or what?"

"She told me you went to the races, were drugged and ended up in the apartment of my niece."

Silence. *Come on old friend, tell your tale.* Scanner knew making Lobsang volunteer his story was like trying to get blood from a stone; you needed a miracle.

"That's uh, an accurate though somewhat limited summary of all that went down."

"I guess in this case you should have looked a gift horse in the mouth."

Scanner smiled. Lobsang was getting better at his idioms; he even managed to throw in some humor. Time to break the ice.

"Look, I am not angry OK? You could have told me about Cathy Lee being your niece and all, but I know you well enough to understand you operate in a different way. You like to put things in place while at the same time leaving room for whatever it is you tried to arrange not to happen. I appreciate you were looking out for me, if and only if I needed help. You can lead a yak to water but you can't make it drink right? Well, now I wanna drink, I want to know, Lobsang, all there is to know about the Grandmaster."

FORGET ME NOT

"His name is Bruno Weber. I didn't know his name when I first met him. I was just a little boy. Cathy told you everything, didn't she? About my sister, and about Opame, her mother."

"I read your letter, saw the photographs and talked to Cathy Lee. That's what I am familiar with. But that's not everything there is to know, isn't it?"

"No. No, there is more, I…"

Scanner let the silence do its work. Patiently. Silence was essential nourishment for words to blossom into meaningful stories.

"I wish I could leave it in the past, forget what happened. But that is not up to us, is it? To forget, when we want, what we want."

It wasn't. How many times had Scanner tried to leave the pain behind? That his teacher was still grappling with the same conundrum was simultaneously reassuring and discouraging.

"Yeah, I'm with you Lobsang."

"And now, with Dolma, it's all coming back with a vengeance. Suddenly it seems like only yesterday that I unwrapped the bandages around my sister's head.

The second time I saw the Grandmaster was some twenty-two years later. I had been selected for guerilla training in *Dhumra*. Your father and I were already the best of buddies.

One day some honchos from the CIA's Far East Division visited us. I didn't really know much about the Agency and the way it was structured and I didn't really care. What was important to me was that we were trained and supported by the most powerful country in the world. Trained to take back Tibet, to once again be free."

From the onset mutual expectations had been out of sync.

"He was there. The Grandmaster. He called himself Brian Webb. I was shocked. How was this possible? The man responsible for my sister's death was now in charge of liberating my country. No way I was gonna shake that monster's hand. I felt sick, excused myself and retreated to our living quarters. No one thought much of it, except your father. Later that evening Jack came to check up on me. I told him everything. At first he didn't believe me. Said Brian had come up through the ranks of the agency, I must be mistaken. But I was adamant and convinced your father to use his connections and do a covert background check.

What he found changed his beliefs forever. You see, your father was like me; idealistic, that's why we got on so well. He believed in the moral superiority of his country, and the responsibility that came with it. America was a force for good in the world; combating evil and spreading democracy was a directive from God himself. One that he wholeheartedly subscribed to."

Scanner couldn't remember his father as being particularly religious. Somewhere along the way Jack Grant had deserted God or perhaps God had backed out of the relationship first?

"What had my father discovered?"

"Experimental Block Number Five"

"Experimental what?"

"Block Number Five. Dachau concentration camp."

MASTER RACE

Scanner poured himself a refill. A cold wind howled through the phone. He needed to fortify his defenses. What he was about to hear had made his father reconsider God. Unlikely to happen to him, since they had never been intimate. No, Scanner wanted to keep the devil at bay, prevent the last vestiges in his soul, where compassion and belief in humanity had found shelter, from being ransacked, plundered and violated, leaving only cynicism and nihilism in its wake. He made sure it was a double shot.

"Brian Webb was born Bruno Weber in early twentieth century Germany. When I first encountered him in Tibet, he was part of a scientific expedition tasked to collect specimens of animal and plant life, to map the country and study its people. But Bruno Weber apparently had a hidden, much more sinister agenda. You know that he never allowed anyone to photograph or film him, and his name doesn't appear in the records?"

Scanner recalled Lobsang's letter to Cathy Lee.

"Yeah, you wrote so. Why was that?"

"Bruno Weber was Himmler's man, you know, the head of Hitler's SS. Himmler was an ardent follower of everything occult and believed that Tibet was the birthplace of the Aryan race. The original master race had possessed incredible powers to move mind and matter, powers that had become lost

136

over the ages. Himmler wanted Bruno Weber to find out all he could about these psychic powers. The ability to control one's own mind, let alone the mind of others, would be a decisive advantage in any confrontation."

"How did Bruno Weber end up in the agency?"

"Because the US government was very much obsessed with acquiring these same powers. But not so fast Scanner, there is more.

"Your father's connections did not reveal whether the expedition had been successful, but Bruno Weber's quest continued throughout the Second World War. He was a driving force behind the methodically documented horrendous experiments carried out on concentration camp inmates at Dachau, in an area called Block Number Five.

I don't really want to go into details, it's too disturbing for an old man to recall, but no line of inquiry and method of experimentation was off limits. When we found out, we couldn't grasp how one could subject fellow humans to such horror."

Scanner knew the answer; the victims had been dehumanized. Untermensch, sub-human, the Nazis had called them.

"I thought we tried these bastards at Nuremberg."

"Some were tried and sentenced. It was required of the allied forces, as moral victors. Good over evil, you know what I mean? Others were brought to America."

"You're saying our government approved?"

"Yes. It was a top-secret program. Like I said, the Nazis had been very methodical, kept extensive records of the minutest details. At the end of the war, the US government sent special teams all over the former Third Reich, scouring for scientists and their records. You see, another war had started, an ideological war, and in the battle for hearts and minds, communism was a far greater threat than Nazism – at least to the industrialists and corporations who ran the government."

"You're no fan of communism."

"Would you rather die in an avalanche or from being gored by a charging yak? That is no choice. I'd rather live. All 'isms' are inherently about control, about influencing behavior. Control of the many, by a few, for the benefit of even fewer. War is control's last resort. Killing someone is a sure-fire way of influencing his behavior. But even the threat of war will most of the time accomplish this."

The Cold War, Scanner had grown up with it. At least with the proxy theaters in Asia. His dad always coming and going. Lobsang was right. War was one giant tranquilizer chair. It ought to be listed in the encyclopedia under world religions and ideologies. Warism. The idolization of perpetual war. It had been nearly ten years since the fall of the Berlin Wall. Soon another war would have to be invented.

"But back to the story now. In the end, it was the OPC who brought Bruno Weber to the US and established a new identity for him as Brian Webb."

"OPC?"

"The Office of Policy Coordination, the secret service of the State Department, later merged into the CIA."

"What happened after you and my father discovered all this?"

"Brian Webb committed suicide, after we had managed to get him off the team. Sent into early retirement. You know, part of the agency didn't know the true backgrounds of many of the war criminals that had been brought in under the Hundred Persons a Year Act. The CIA was divided. There were people for whom the end justified all means, while others possessed a certain moral fiber. Jack threatened to expose the rift; it would have caused a public outrage. Your father had enough support from his superiors to make it stick, fortunately, since whistleblowers are usually ranked below cockroaches by the government. Kill the messenger and delete the message. That would be the normal response.

Within two weeks of being forced out, Brian Web hanged

himself. We could only guess why. We didn't really care."

SHERRY OAK DREAM

Scanner's mind refused to settle down to a peaceful night. Death and destruction oozed from darkness' pores, like a saturated sponge, gluttonized on life's morbid banquet, slowly squeezed by an invisible hand. Scanner tried to drown the restless and tortured spirits in more shots of Maccallan, but the alcohol only emboldened them. Long after he had closed his eyes, the demons kept up their macabre dance.

***

Benjamin Rush chairs had replaced the entire front row pew. Leather straps constrained Lobsang and Scanner's father, both seated to his left. On his right side, Sue and Cathy Lee were immobilized in a similar fashion. Skeletons took up the remaining seats.

A giant roulette wheel occupied most of the altar table. In the alcove behind it, Max's motionless body, dressed in a school uniform, was tied to a life-sized cross. Paralyzed by drugs, only her terror-filled eyes bounced around like a black beetle imprisoned in a glass jar.

From the towering pulpit, Hideyoshi, The Priest, adorned in a long black cassock, seemed to deliver a fiery, yet speech-less sermon. A miniature skull pendant bounced playfully off his chest.

Now it was time for Holy Communion, but instead of wafers The Priest placed casino chips on everyone's tongue. The organ rumbled Night Fever and in danced Tony M followed by the two Indian tourists, dressed in matching white suits, each of them blowing the disco tune on a giant purple dildo.

The music accelerated towards an orgiastic NBA-like crescendo, the excited skeletons slid out of their loose restraints and, joined by Tony M and the Indians, congregated around the altar. The Priest telekinetically spun the wheel and all eyes and eye sockets were on the little white ball as it orbited hungrily towards final judgment.

Scanner detected movement along the edges of his peripheral vision. Two shapes, obscured by darkness, greedily witnessed the spectacle. The iron vice that steadied Scanner's head unfortunately prevented closer inspection. He could almost make out a face. Was it someone familiar?

Commotion erupted from the altar crowd. The two Indians jumped up and down and danced a victory lap around the table, purple dildos raised above their heads, swept into a frenzy by clapping and cheering skeletons. A couple of bony spectators lifted Max off the wooden cross and spread-eagled her across the altar.

"No." Scanner shouted. "Leave her alone. Don't you dare touch her, you disco dicks, you…"

Scanner looked at his wrists. Contrary to his assumption, they were not tied to the chair. All this time he had been free. His mind, resigned to a similar fate as his companions, had immobilized him, prevented Max's rescue. MAX! Empowered by his liberating realization, Scanner frog-jumped on top of the shocked Indians and knocked them unconscious with the purple dildos he had wrestled from their hands. The skeletons were next and utterly defenseless against the pummeling power of his silicone tool.

"Meditate on this, sucker"

Scanner grabbed a loose thighbone and aimed at the …

The Priest was gone. Now his attention turned to the two mysterious figures lurking in the dark. Who were they?

BANG. Just as Scanner reached the dim recess where earlier he had spotted the two voyeurs, a shot rang out. Tony M charged forward, blazing peacekeeper drawn and aimed in the direction of the ghosts. BANG BANG

"Don't shoot," Scanner shouted, "we need them alive, they hold the answers."

The two strangers started running, Scanner wanted to follow but his legs refused to obey. He became aware of a wet sensation emanating from his lower abdomen.

Shit, he thought, I've been hit. He touched his drenched shirt. Shit. It didn't feel like blood. It sure didn't smell like blood.

***

In the twilight zone of Scanner's dream one of the fleeing men stopped and turned around. Before Scanner could positively identify the vaguely familiar face however, it evaporated, leaving nothing but the lingering scent of sherry oak...

ASSETS

"SHIT!"

Now wide-awake, Scanner grabbed the bottle of Maccallan. All but one shot gone.

He had slumped against the headboard and fallen asleep, spilled the precious amber liquid all over his shirt. *Might as well finish it.* He took the final swirl straight from the bottle.

The dream. What was it all about? The more he tried to hang on to it, the more it retreated into the labyrinth of his unconsciousness, a place not for the fainthearted. On a good day Scanner might venture beyond the entrance. Usually though, the gate was firmly locked and, more often than not, this filled him with relief.

This time he wanted to go in, to chase after his dissolving recollection. If only he had dropped the whiskey a minute or so later. *That face.*

Trying to go back to sleep wouldn't work. It never did. Even if his consciousness let go and allowed him once more to travel into the boundary-free dream world, you couldn't just pick up where you left off. How often had he tried to do just that? Dreams frequently returned, but never on command.

Scanner got up, stuffed the single malt shirt into the laundry bag and adjusted the count. *Better go for a walk. Ass first, the mind might follow.* He smiled at the thought of the feisty stewardess. Cathy Lee, where would she be? Still at thirty thousand feet. She would be meeting Lobsang later. *It must be nice to have family waiting across the world.*

***

Scanner wasn't the only insomniac prowling the hotel grounds looking for a fix to chase away their demons. Plenty of drugs on offer too. One casino trip was all he could endure though. So he ventured down to the basement instead. There, a choir of angels promised instant redemption for hourly rates.

Most faces were familiar. Business was slow. Or perhaps the opposite held true. There usually was little incentive to hang around after the sex. Ebbed excitement laid bare the verbal desert underneath. It was extremely rare, if not impossible, to find the soothing post-coitus silence shared by lovers.

The standard argument that ordinary Johns weren't looking for intimacy, just a quick pop, had never convinced Scanner. As for the girls? For most of them it was strictly business. The more tricks they could turn in a night, the closer they came to realizing their material dreams. Nothing wrong with that, Scanner thought. He had zero tolerance for forced prostitution, but if a girl wanted to sell her body so she could trade up in the world, it wasn't any different from a teacher and certainly more honest than a lawyer.

Use the assets you've been given. Don't bury your talents. The Priest would approve.

And their maker had given these girls abundant talent. Which was not to say God was responsible. Asian women had embraced plastic surgery wholeheartedly. The reliable surgeons had their hands full. The unreliable ones changed address often.

"Hey mister, you want me."

Not only her assets were upfront. She could hardly be over

eighteen. Five feet was pushing it. *Especially with those heels.* The teenage girl's designer handbag swayed back and forth. Scanner imagined it to be filled with lead, providing the necessary counter balance. *And a useful weapon.*

"Not tonight honey. I am sorry."

"Mister. You. Want. Me."

Scanner realized she wasn't asking. He looked straight into the girl's black eyes. A cocktail of hope and fear stared back.

"My room. Now mister."

Scanner nodded his consent. Followed her to the elevator.

***

"What's your name?"

The ride up had been silent. Down the corridor Scanner had fallen a few meters back. Had they encountered anyone, he would have pretended to go for a different room. Now, with the girl seated on the bed, Scanner felt awkward. Usually he knew a woman's name before getting into the same room. Usually he knew a lot more.

"Joy."

Anything but. Scanner thought.

"I am Myanmar. Mister?"

"Me, America. Scanner, my name is Scanner."

"A-me-ri-ca," Joy pronounced with a longing exclusively reserved for those who'd never been to the United States. Scanner's name hadn't passed the professional filter.

The king-sized bed swallowed Joy. It was hard to believe she had seen eighteen summers. Scanner was afraid to ask. Joy did not volunteer. She sat on the edge of the bed, bare feet playfully dangling an inch above the carpet. Like a juvenile bird, ready to venture outside its nest for the first time, into the big bad world. Looks were deceiving. Scanner knew the world would never wait for girls like Joy to be ready. He decided not to press forward. The girl needed her own time. If and when she felt safe.

"Mister, my girlfriend you pretty. But very danger. Damage customer. Him not like. Only when no money him do."

"Scan-ner, call me Scan-ner please. Who? Who is he, your...boss?"

"Scan-ner."

"Yes, yes thank you. Look, you can tell me. I won't..."

"Scan-ner, my girlfriend you name?"

"Her name is Max. Is that why you brought me here? You know something about her father, did she show you a picture? Do you..."

Slowly, slowly. Scanner reminded himself that silence often was the most appreciated conversation partner. Not ignorant silence, or apathy expressed as silence. Inviting stillness, Lobsang called it, a rare quality very few possessed in this increasingly insecure society. The world was literally dying to be noticed, drowning in a tsunami of meaningless noise. Everybody wanted to be heard but there was hardly anyone who cared to listen.

"Max, I like. But very danger."

Like a bent bamboo stick suddenly released Joy exited the bed, feet moving upwards in an imitation of Max's debilitating kick.

"Aiyaaah!"

The Burmese girl landed safely on the plush carpet and threw a few consciously aimed air punches on the way over to the desk. She quietly slid open one of its drawers.

"Look."

Three full-length people filled the frame of the five by eight photograph. Depleted or perhaps excessively reused chemicals had aged the colors to a pale pastel, suggesting an era long gone. Joy's face said otherwise. The image could not have been taken more than a few years ago. Some cultures believed a photograph would steal a person's spirit, Joy's flat-chested family portrait reminded Scanner of the teenager's abruptly robbed innocence.

"*May may* and *phay phay*. Before two year."

It was a happy snapshot. A smiling Joy, flanked by her proud parents, defiantly dared the camera to take her soul. Yet there was also something distinctly ominous about the image. Scanner couldn't quite put his finger on it. Then he saw it. *The photographer.* A low angled, setting sun had cast another person's shadow over Joy's *longyi*. Soon all light would be blocked.

"Him took photo. Him say me work with family, clean house, make food. Him pay *may may*."

"Who is he? What's his name?"

"Him have many girls. Him name Uncle Ho."

DOING BUSINESS

Scanner spent the remainder of the allocated hour deciphering Joy's story. Uncle Ho had lured her out of the refugee camp on the Thai Burmese border with promises of work as a domestic helper. Right from the start, the Vietnamese pimp had closely guarded his new purchase. Made sure she got enough to eat, plenty of rest.

Several men along the trafficking trail had tried to force themselves on her. Uncle Ho had killed two with a bullet to the head. A third one lived, unable to tell the story, unable to procreate too. The Vietnamese people trafficker drew a swift blade and handled the weapon with surgical precision.

Though horrified by the bloodletting, Joy had been grateful to her protector. An illusion of safety that would soon be violently shattered.

Joy remembered the palatial house, the large iron gate that had opened by itself, the marble lions on either side of the door. She had pinched herself, not quite ready to believe she would be working there. That night, beaten into submission and repeatedly raped, she had held on to the lion's image. In a way it had protected her from her assailant. Though he had robbed her of her youth, he had failed to dominate her mind. All that Joy could recall was his hulk-like size and the putrid stink of his sweat.

When Uncle Ho came to collect her the following day he

had seemed concerned. Joy had been barely able to walk and the bleeding wouldn't stop. The Vietnamese pimp shot her up with, so Scanner imagined, a cocktail of antibiotics and sedatives before locking her in a room with a dozen other girls. Once the telltale signs of the physical abuse had abated sufficiently to be camouflaged under a layer of make-up, Uncle Ho had showered Joy with fancy clothes, shoes and other accessories. The next day he had her working the hotel shift.

Scanner shuddered at the efficiency of it all, the tormentor/benefactor dichotomy that had initially ensnared the young Burmese girl. Confused her into believing the scheming pimp was on her side. He had sold her virginity to the highest bidder and now would continue exploiting her on the way down. All the way down, as long as he could.

Still, Joy had kept a faint sparkle in her eyes. Scanner sensed a resilient spirit, not easily pimped into oblivion. But how much longer would she endure? Max's ball busting antics had perhaps been a wake-up call, a call to arms, to escape the tightening downward spiral that would squeeze the life out of her.

It wasn't Scanner's fight. However much he wanted to rescue Joy from the claws of the rapacious beast, he had other priorities. The world was a heavy place and it was impossible to shoulder everyone's burden. There was an endless supply of Joys to be purchased. If the money was right, nothing would be wrong. Everything, everybody had a price.

Stop being such a cynical bastard. To realize that you couldn't do everything was no excuse to do nothing. Even the mighty Yarlung Tsangpo river starts with a trickle, Lobsang used to say. Cold ice surrenders to the sun and forms a river feeding millions. *OK, OK old man, what can I do?*

Scanner looked at his watch. Nearly an hour had gone by. Sufficient to do one's business, not enough time to gain someone's trust. *Gotta speed things up.*

"Look, time's almost up. I'd better be going. Have work to

do tomorrow."

"Scan-ner no go. I know him where. *Phay phay* of Max."

Morning after

Scanner woke up with a thumping headache; bombs went off inside his head, perfectly synced to the loud bangs that emanated from the door. The LED display of the bedside console said ten, his mind screamed too early, his body refused to comment.

"You there? Scanner?"

Max's worried voice reached out from the other side.

"Scanner!"

"Yeah, yeah, ok, wait, I am coming."

Through the glass peephole Max appeared to move inside a fishbowl. It amused Scanner to observe her frantically pacing up and down. Even grotesquely distorted, she remained an absolute looker. Her dress was different, but the school theme had stayed. A charcoal suit-jacket/knee-length pencil skirt combo complimented by black opaque nylons and matching suede pumps portrayed an image of authority. Mess around with this head mistress and you'd be up for detention. Digress further and corporal punishment was almost guaranteed. *Could be fun.*

Just as Max's approaching fist had almost completely obscured his vision Scanner pulled open the door.

"Easy girl, easy. Can we tone down the drum solo a bit?"

"There you are. You got me worried. You know what time it is? Missed breakfast. Ah I see, bit of a hangover, have you?

Heavy night it seems, and somewhere along the way you lost your clothes."

Undaunted Max marched past the gradually awakening Scanner, only now becoming aware of his own nudity.

"Would be nice if you managed to lose a bit of weight as well, you know. Stay in shape, for when the Indians come knocking. Let's get rid of this."

Max grabbed the suit and laundry bag, exited the room and called out. Half a minute later she re-entered.

"Look, you're lucky I got here first, she was just on the way to cleaning your room. I told her to return in a few hours. Your clothes should be ready by tonight, and I got you a paper."

Max dropped the folded newspaper on the unmade bed and sat down cross-legged in one of the lounge chairs near the floor-to-ceiling window. Scanner, stunned by her whirlwind assault on his awakening senses, held on firmly to the half-opened door for another twenty seconds.

"You put on quite a show last night young lady. Knocking would be the last thing on the Indians' minds. I think they're gonna stay well clear of you."

Wrapped in an oversized towel he'd grabbed from the bathroom, Scanner positioned himself opposite Max.

"No, I'd be more worried about the local pimp. Uncle Ho is his name. Nasty character from what I've heard, not at all averse to using violent means if it gets him what he wants. A real manipulating low life, prowling the refugee camps on the Thai border and buying virgin girls with cheap money and even cheaper promises.

"Gotta give it to you though, I didn't think it would work but it seems your avenging schoolgirl act gave us a real breakthrough."

Short legs Leung

"So now we do what? We can't exactly barge in there. And there is no guarantee dad is still going to be there. In fact, most likely he isn't. What was he doing in the first place getting involved with scum like that?"

Scanner didn't have an answer. At least not one he would readily volunteer to Max. How did a Dutch cheese maker from Wisconsin on a business trip to Hong Kong end up being abducted by a Vietnamese pimp in Macau? He could think of a few possible scenarios, none likely to go over well with a daughter's unconditional and unquestioning love for her father.

"I am sure there is a straightforward explanation. However, the answer eludes me at the moment. My head... Did you bring any aspirin? Feels like a tap dancing convention inside."

"No, I didn't. But I'm sure there's a drugstore nearby. I'm gonna shoot down and get you some. Why don't you get dressed in the meantime?"

Scanner was grateful for the reprieve. A fully energized Max could easily crash a slightly vacuous brain, let alone one suffering from an alcohol induced meltdown of its synapses. How many shots had he downed last night? Perhaps it was time to sober up.

The dreadful thought of parting with his beloved Macallan was the spark needed to fire up his slumbering cells. Better keep them occupied now. Scanner opened the morning paper and let yesterday's reality dispose of the stubborn remnants of his inertia.

BLOODBATH AS RIVAL GANGS BATTLE FOR CONTROL.

In what appears to be the latest escalation in the territory's ongoing turf-war for control of the lucrative junket business prior to the handover to China, notorious local gangster and Soi Fong Triad member Ah Leung, better known as Short Legs Leung, was killed in a hail of bullets yesterday evening outside the Lisboa Casino. Two suspects were seen speeding away on a motorbike wearing full-faced helmets and black leather jackets. The Policia Judiciaria have yet to make an arrest.

Meanwhile a local government spokesman tried to reassure the public that its safety was not an issue as this hit, and the murders of the previous months, were carried out by "professional killers who never miss their target."

The rest of the article spread across three columns underneath a grainy and gritty picture of a body slumped face down on the pavement. The circular pool of coalesced blood that surrounding the gangster's body, combined with his disproportionately short shoeless legs, created the illusion of a man desperately trying to crawl out of some dark, bottomless pit. Maybe he had tried. The triads showed no mercy towards deserters. And with China breathing down their necks, everybody scrambled to save his own ass. Honor among thieves was a romanticized Hollywood notion in a cutthroat world where ruthlessly looking out for number one was the only ticket to the top. Or the only chance for survival.

Scanner smiled. You had to give it to the mobster. In life, he had probably killed men for mocking his physical appearance. Now, sprawled lifeless across the pavement, the gangster's stunted limbs transcended his cold murder into timeless art. Death had failed to obliterate Short Legs Leung.

Scanner read on. Besides receiving commission on bringing big fish to the casinos' private rooms, the triads' interests covered prostitution and loan sharking, protection rackets and contraband smuggling. All highly lucrative and the more so if it didn't have to be shared. The Soi Fong battled the 14K, rumored to have links to the Japanese Yakuza. Thrown into the mix were the Vietnamese, although they shifted alliances so often, no one knew which side they were on.

What an oddball comment, Scanner thought. To him, there was no mistaking the side the Vietnamese were on. That was why, throughout history, they kept on coming out victorious. Good chance it'd be no different here.

What is Uncle Ho's angle? Scanner recalled Joy's revelation that she had seen the Vietnamese pimp with a Caucasian man. At first he presumed it must have been Stuart, but the fragmented description he had managed to extract from a frightened Joy didn't fit. The photo Scanner had taken from Max's purse earlier erased all doubt.

A week earlier, Uncle Ho had commandeered her to his suite. Joy had gone up with trepidation, not knowing whether the extended hand would beat or feed. As it turned out, the pimp had showered her with gifts, nothing too expensive, obviously, and nothing that wouldn't support Joy fulfilling her job description.

Evil cunning and manipulating bastard. Self-interest wrapped in magnanimous generosity.

Joy had proudly shown Scanner the Pradda shoes and the Gukki handbag. They had seemed the real thing to her. She had proposed to take off the Chanale dress and couldn't understand why he wasn't interested.

On her way out from the pimp's den, Joy had glanced into an adjacent bedroom, before the goon guarding the door slammed it shut. But not before she had seen him. Thrust on the bed, hands and feet bound, mouth taped shut. Max's father.

But why?

For the second time that morning loud banging beckoned Scanner.

He opened the door and a visibly excited Max marched in.

"I'm back," she announced redundantly.

"Thought you might like some coffee too. Here, black right? Careful, it's hot. You haven't made much progress I see. It's all taped off outside and lots of cops. Apparently some mafia guy got shot last night. There's a big stain on the pavement. I don't think he survived."

"His name was Short Legs Leung", Scanner mumbled.

No Arranging

"The bastard doesn't seem to be after our money. By now we would have received some kind of ransom demand. I just came off the phone with Hilde. Nothing."

Scanner transferred half of the contents from the Styrofoam cup into a tall glass he'd picked up from the mini bar, swirled the coffee down to a palatable temperature, popped the foil on three aspirins and downed both drugs in one greedy gulp. May the best get there first.

"I also asked her to put in a visit to Mrs. Kowalski, see if there is anything she needs. I kinda feel guilty taking her good Samaritan away. I know you regularly did her heavy shopping."

Scanner wondered if Max was on some drug herself.

"Uh, OK, thanks. It's not exactly next door, you know."

"Just a short flight, business class on company expenses. Hilde jumped at the chance to go shopping in Paris on the Prairie and I think she's actually got some family there too."

Normally, Scanner avoided women who attempted to arrange his life like the plague. Nothing good could come of that. He had known a few. Attractive ones, too. Hot occasionally. And just like the next guy, he enjoyed giving in to temptation from time to time. But when the inevitable day arrived that he couldn't locate his favorite coffee mug in the remodeled cupboard or his peanut butter didn't spread because the jar had been relocated to a fridge set too cold it was time to let go.

Max was different. Scanner knew she wasn't trying to wriggle herself through some overlooked cracks in his outer shell only to start the demolition job from the inside. Max shot her arrows straight. Released them first, and what or whoever walked into their path became the target by default. It was an honest, here I am, live and let live approach. Unconditioned and unconditional. It was also dangerously naïve in an evil, crooked world.

"Like I mentioned earlier, your frontal attack yesterday did bear fruit of sorts, but it could have gone over differently. We're dealing with hardened criminals, in a climate of relative impunity. There's no saying what they could do to us. It's highly likely we're being watched by a plethora of nasties."

"I know", Max lowered her eyes. "It wasn't the smartest thing wasn't it?"

"No, not exactly. More akin to waving a red flag in the middle of the street during the running of the bulls. You're bound to get hit."

"Okay, okay, what do you suggest we do? It's so frustrating. Now we know who is holding daddy, it's even worse. We're so close."

Scanner was with Max all the way. The anger and impotence she felt had once been his, too. He had felt the fury raging, blinding all reason, ultimately set to self-destruct. If it hadn't been for Lobsang...

"We need to gain the upper hand, we need allies. When was the last time you went to confession?"

IN NOMINI PATRIS

"How did it go?"

"Good, I think. Surprisingly easy. It felt like, natural. I have always excelled at role playing you know?"

Scanner knew. Max's talent for metamorphosis was second to none. Changing character was as mundane as slipping into a different pair of shoes. And while her collection wasn't quite on par with Imelda Marcos', this girl carried more flavors than a Baskin Robbins outlet.

Because of Max's chameleon-like nature, Scanner had discarded his second rule, the one that said don't get the client involved in the case. Would he violate his first rule too? *Don't get involved with the client.*

So he had followed her, at a distance. It wasn't much of a plan, but Max was an accomplished saleswoman.

"More importantly, did Hideyoshi believe you?"

Scanner looked at Max. The question was merely rhetorical. Unrequited longing oozed from her every fiber. Wearing a short sleeve, black, button-down dress that descended slightly past knee length, long and loose enough to wipe and dust hard to reach corners yet short and tight enough to trigger lustful thoughts in distant regions of a celibate man's mind, Max had managed to perfectly project the image of a lonely and needy housewife. It was a distress call most men were hardwired to believe, an appeal to long suppressed fantasies of alpha dominance and sexual prowess, real or more likely, imagined.

The dress' row of nickel-size silvery buttons started just below Max's delicate neck and terminated halfway between hip and hemline, the remaining six inches of split fabric poised to part at merely a hint of movement from her slender legs. In a skilled woman's repertoire, controlled by the length of her stride, the bend in her knees and the width of her stance, this dark triangle of seduction was a formidable weapon; in Max's arsenal it became nuclear.

"Bless me father, for I have sinned."

Max crossed herself, before bending down, knees sinking into the plush carpet of Scanner's bedroom. Outside, darkness was winning the day's battle yet again. But tonight was no pushover. The dying day parted with wildly flailing arms. A drowning master, running out of time, forcefully squeezed tubes filled with paint, splattering a full palette of colors on the sky's canvas in one last defiant move. Screaming: I will be back. And if, by a cruel twist of fate, the night would not release its hold, at least the afterglow would shimmer on. A resonating echo of light, a reminder of what could have been.

What could have been. Nightfall like this usually got to Scanner. His life too had drowned in a violent explosion of light all those years back. A blackness nearly impossible to erase, like spilled crude stuck to feathers.

"Hey, you're not listening. What are you thinking? Magnificent isn't it? Look at those colors. Wish I had a camera."

Max was back on her feet and positioned herself next to Scanner.

"No, yes, sorry, I wasn't. Beautiful, yes. A photo won't do. Only your mind can keep… You're wearing Shalimar."

No wonder nostalgia had crept up on him so deviously.

"Yes, I thought it would help with The Priest, you know it's strong, evocative…"

Max fell silent. Her right arm grabbed Scanner around the

waist. She pulled herself closer.

"I'm so sorry. That was rather tactless of me. I should have thought about it. I am so careless."

"It's ok. It just hits me sometimes. Not your fault. It's good to have you here."

Scanner put his hand on Max's shoulder and silently they watched the sky, if not his memories, fade to black.

***

"Housekeeping!"

How long had they stood there? Two hurt souls seeking refuge in the shadow of each other's pain. Outside, all the day's warmth had disappeared, sucked into neon tubes regardless in what color they flashed. Even this high up, pale shades of red and green bounced off the room's ceiling, beckoning with a fake sincerity, claiming a false victory.

Scanner pulled the curtains on man's gaudy attempt to play God and for half a breath, life stopped.

"Let there be light. I'll get it."

Max turned on the bedside lamp and made for the door.

"It's probably your laundry."

PIECES OF THE PUZZLE

"They did a pretty good job. Look. Nicely pressed, too. And there is an envelope from the Mandarin, must be Lobsang's files."

"Ah, finally, I'd nearly forgotten. Let's have a look."

Scanner tore open the courier envelope.

"So I take it you made the connection?"

"He swallowed the bait. Devoured it rather, hook, line and sinker, the whole package."

Nestled inside, was another envelope.

"I mean it was freaky, you know. Even through the lattice. He has this kinda cuddly demeanor that makes people open up spontaneously, but I swear I could see his eyes bulge with lust, especially when I told him not getting any made me wanting, a terrible sin no doubt."

Increasingly impatient, Scanner opened the second package. Come on Lobsang. He understood the old man's precautions. *But six envelopes?*

"Deadly, and I am not kidding. If only half of what Tony M told me is true. Never let down your guard with this man. Never get cocky."

Scanner thought it strange how linguistic evolution had not produced a female equivalent of the word. The world was made of language and language was seldom grounded in truth. It was usually a projection of desire, a verbal image of how the speaker wanted the world to be. Come to think of it, the world was shaped and ruled by language. American society was about as patriarchal as it got - timid men would always be pussies and self-assured women cocky.

Six brown manila envelopes. Six names. Only Dolma was familiar. Penned in capital red on a weighty envelope, the name spelled a tragedy Scanner found disturbingly easy to visualize. He moved it to the bottom of the pile.

"I know, and I won't. What do we do now?"

"Wait. We're still moving the pieces, observing. I have a feeling that the end game will reveal itself soon enough."

Five faces. Five Tibetan teenagers. What did they have in common besides gender and ethnicity? Five lucky escapes from the claws of a beast they had no recollection of. Five lives proceeding in blissful ignorance.

Scanner and Max silently studied each girl's single sheet. At sixteen their history was a shallow grave.

Selective amnesia. What had they witnessed, partaken in, that someone wanted erased? Who?

"I don't see it. I mean, they're pretty and there's plenty of perverts out there, but every medical examination concluded they were untouched. They're all sixteen but go to different schools. Except for two girls who seem to be close friends, they don't even know each other. They are so, what shall I say, ordinary. In an innocent way, like you'd expect. Tibetan girls in Chicago, overprotective parents. Look. Piano lessons, tennis, cooking class. Don't know about you but I'm actually ravenous. Who'd ever think confession could make you so hungry? Let's order room service."

Scanner barely raised an eyebrow at Max's flawless transition. It'd be good to get a bite to eat, while he still had an appetite, before Dolma snuffed it all out.

The room service menu featured all the usual suspects. Scanner wouldn't have been surprised if the hospitality industry relied on some *uber* menu, locked in a Swiss vault, and cloned endlessly with a token hint of originality reserved for naming the dishes. He settled for a Signature Lisboa Club Sandwich, while Max chose the equally original Macau Special Fried Rice.

***

Dolma's file was every bit as nauseating as Scanner had feared. Lobsang had thoughtfully placed the most gruesome images in yet another envelope. Saving the worst for last. Despite the clinical language of the report, little was left to Scanner's jaded imagination. Vaginal penetration, presence of an as yet undetermined toxic substance, wrist and ankle contusions, cranial trepanation, pulmonary aspiration. Violated, drugged, strapped, drilled, drowned. The chronological sequence of Dolma's terrifying ordeal was inconclusive, the cumulative effect far from it: Death.

Water-filled lungs indicated the poor girl had been alive the moment the chair hit the lake. *Hopefully unconscious*. Immersion had erased all traceable evidence. No semen, no prints, no hair, no saliva. The only identifiable foreign object was the chair.

At first the investigation had entered a cognitive vacuum. Who would have thought that the wooden contraption had actually played a major role in the American healthcare system and was not just some device cobbled together by an S&M hobbyist in his grandmother's backyard? The lucky breakthrough, Sue had explained last night, had come when the psychiatrist, assigned to evaluate the missing girls' mental disposition, had introduced the police to Dr. Benjamin Rush and his hallmark treatment of the mentally insane.

Though an improvement from the brutal chains and damp dungeons of the past, the sensory deprivation advocated by the good doctor still showed, to Scanner's mind, a skewed but culturally accepted view of what constituted mental health.

Treatment was prescribed to those who made society uncomfortable. Who had Dolma made uncomfortable?

"Can I see that picture of the chair? What did you say it is called?"

"A tranquilizing chair."

Scanner passed Max the black and white four by six, taken after the removal of Dolma's corpse.

"Damn, I would be so *not* tranquil if I had to sit in that thing. They'd have to shoot me up first. I bet you that's what the sick fuck did. A sixteen-year old girl can put up quite a struggle you know. I would have."

No doubt, Scanner thought. But would Dolma have done the same?

With trepidation, he eyed the ninth and final envelope, the last known piece of the puzzle. Scanner picked it up; positive it wouldn't complete the picture.

EXPLOSIVE NEWS

Medusa. Scanner closed his eyes and tried, in vain, to eradicate the gruesome image from his mind. Greek mythology had been one of his favorite classes as a boy. The deeper meaning was, for the most part, lost on him, but the epic stories of bloody battles, invincible heroes and macabre monsters had provided refuge from the fierce storms raging in his head. The woman with the serpent hair.

Max had run off to the bathroom. *Silly girl.* She had insisted on seeing all the images. She could handle it. But the horror proved too much for her obstinate mind to stomach.

Scanner went through all the photographs once more. A wide shot of a crane lifting Dolma out of the water, divers surrounding the half-immersed chair. A full frame side shot of the chair ashore, the angle chosen to obscure Dolma's private parts. A close up of wrists and ankles bound by leather straps, a close up of Dolma's head, locked in the vise's deadly grip.

After the forensic team had meticulously documented every nook and cranny of the crime scene, they had unstrapped the body and laid it on a plastic sheet for further documentation. That was when the eels came crawling out of Dolma's hairless skull.

Medusa.

Behind the bathroom door Max continued to heave and

retch and flush in a dissonant and dark lament.

Scanner suppressed the urge to enter and comfort her. What could he say? It's alright? It was not alright. He dismissed the guilt he felt for not trying harder to withhold the images from Max's scrutiny. Her father had done that for too long. Time to face the world and confront the evil motherfucker, baby.

Scanner paced around the room, hoping for a moment of lucidity. Too early to call Sue or contact Lobsang. Had they managed to gain access to the Brian Webb files? Did the CIA recruited Nazi doctor hold the key or was that another dead end? The sooner they returned stateside, the better. He could work his connections.

Concentrate on the work at hand, Scanner. They were close, had to be. Joy had spotted Max's father, all they needed now was a current location. Then the plan set in motion this afternoon could run its course.

Scanner eyed the dry-cleaned suit suspended from the wardrobe door. It really was a good job. No trace of the stale odor of recycled cigarette smoke. Instead the air carried a faint hint of New Years Eve in Chinatown. *Gunpowder?* Intrigued he sniffed out the source and discovered a crumbled piece of paper in the right hand pocket.

A painted image of a rosy-cheeked Chinese girl dressed in a sleeveless cheongsam looked up at Scanner. Ruby red lips sealed in an enigmatic smile and thin, penciled eyebrows arching over almond eyes gave her the air of an oriental Mona Lisa. Perched atop a nearby rocky outcrop, a yellow and red pheasant looked eager to whisper or perhaps spit in the beauty's ear.

Silver Bird Brand, Scanner read. Neither one of the birds remotely fitted the bill though one was infinitely more precious. At the bottom of the label, underneath the *Yick Loong Fireworks Co. Macau* and next to *Made in China*, Joy had hastily scribbled her name.

MODEL SOLDIERS

A t eight in the evening, Taipa had already hunkered down for the night. A short distance but a far cry from the glitzy gambling dens and fleshy temptations of Macau, the old fishing village existed inside a time warp. Scanner couldn't imagine anyone living here. This place seemed the very antithesis of alive. Perhaps a black hole was a better metaphor. Even the street dogs had been sucked in.

"*Lento por favor.*" A few words from Scanner slowed the taxi down to a crawl. So this was it. *Rua Fernao Mendes Pinto.* The narrow street was named after a sixteenth century Portuguese explorer, Scanner had learned from one of the hotel's receptionists, a history buff named Joaquim. Pinto's astonishing adventures and accounts of life in the Far East, as chronicled in his book Pilgrimage, were often so outlandish that they earned him a reputation amongst contemporaries as a consummate liar. Had truth been stranger than fiction or had the adventurer embellished his reports to convince a gullible public the high price for his books was worth it?

Nothing new under the sun. Let's hope Max's and his truth would be more convincing.

To their right, a long wall loomed. About eight feet in height, it ran along a major part of the street, leaving only a narrow corridor of pavement for passing pedestrians. Moss had invaded the yellow plaster with dark irregular patches, most pronounced along the bottom few feet of the enclosure. Had water once come up this high? Streetlights placed at regular intervals cast their ghostly aura. Plenty of dim spots to choose from.

"*Aqui.*" The taxi driver turned to Scanner. "*Fabrica de Panchoes Iec Long.*"

Their destination. Two structures, flush with the rest of the wall, but much taller, stood on either side of an iron gate atop of which the name of the fireworks factory featured prominently in Latin and Chinese characters. Barred diminutive windows punctuated the thick wall. All but one, the guard or caretaker's quarter, Scanner presumed, consumed by darkness.

The taxi inched past the entrance. Through the bars, Scanner observed a huge vacant compound. An impenetrable fortress or, depending on your point of view, an inescapable prison.

"Don't stop."

Lacking sufficient vocabulary, Scanner gesticulated to the driver to continue up the road. He had seen enough. A real rescue would be impossible to execute, not without a small army and serious planning. Of course involving the police was out of the question. What would he tell them? What would they tell Uncle Ho?

And anyways, he abhorred guns, especially in the hands of mindless thugs, trigger happy marionettes controlled by devious paymasters. How much better to outsmart the puppeteer. No, no daring Hollywood-style raid or Rambo-esque rescue, a believable attempt would do just fine.

Scanner exited the taxi out of sight of the factory and detoured through the village until he was back at the start of the walled compound. He had spotted a couple of trees there that would facilitate scaling the wall.

***

With a soft thud Scanner landed inside the factory grounds. This close to the wall, the darkness matched his black tracksuit and sneakers and swallowed him whole. Inside the belly of the beast. He wondered about Max. Would she be able to pull off her part?

Their plan was not without risk, but Max had insisted rather forcefully in participating. At least Scanner had made her believe she had to. In all honesty, he had to admit to himself he needed her. Of course, to tell her so was out of the question. She was his client after all.

Scanner knew he was no action hero. To stand a chance, he'd better make the most of his manipulating mind and Max's assets.

Ducked behind a thick tree, Scanner switched on a flashlight and studied the rough sketch an excited Joaquim had drawn for him back at the hotel. To alleviate any possible suspicion Scanner had told the youngster he was a location scout on a recce for a blockbuster's final night time shootout scene. Hope you can keep a secret.

Iec Long Fireworks Factory had stopped production of its popular Duck and Silver Bird Brand crackers in the early eighties. Since then nature had invaded the two hectare plot and turned a thriving industrial village into a popular playground for weekend warriors. Joaquim was on one of the local Airsoft teams shooting it out in the compound on Saturdays and Sundays. Simulated war games for white-collar office workers. Battles without the blood, glory without the guts. *What's the point? Better here than running amok at the firm perhaps?*

With eyes adjusted to the darkness, Scanner gradually made for the far end of the compound. To minimize the danger of a massive explosion wiping out the entire factory, the various production stages were located in stand-alone buildings surrounded by giant trapezoid blast walls. It was easy to see the attraction this place exercised on the urban soldiers.

Ruined buildings, weeds reaching to above shoulder height, trees many times bigger. It was camouflage galore, a hooked arcade gamer's wet dream. You could park your car just outside and the mom and pop store down the road sold cold beer.

Where would be the best place to hide hostages? Joaquim had pointed to a cluster of buildings. Off limits he had said, dangerous. His lips mouthed the BOOM his separating hands described in the air. Scanner got the point. Someone wanted the kids to back off, and being model soldiers they naturally obeyed.

A sudden wind animated the lush vegetation. A choir of toads croaked a unified crescendo that ended as abruptly as it began. A squadron of ferocious mosquitoes circled Scanner's head. It really was a jungle out here! Scanner closed his eyes and for a carefree moment morphed into the explorer of his youthful dreams, re-enacting one of the old Jungle Jim movies he had so loved to watch with his dad. *Shake it Scanner.*

Scanner moved between derelict buildings, crawled behind gnarled trees and stealthily circumnavigated the few open spaces. There was almost too much cover.

Towards the far end of the factory grounds, Scanner noticed the signs. Large black skull and crossbones, DANGER EXPLOSIVES KEEP OUT printed underneath. Whoever had put up these warnings must have had no faith in their effectiveness. The eight feet tall chain link fence topped with a double roll of razor wire ten yards ahead said so. And the camouflaged motion sensor his trained eyes had detected a few yards further repeated it.

Undeterred, Scanner wiggled through the gap that had taken him a minute to cut. Rather clumsily, he tripped over the sensor, angling the beam outwards as he stumbled to the ground. If he had misjudged his opponent, death would come in an instant and freeze his face in eternal disappointment.

For a long minute, Scanner lay face down in the dirt, aware

of no other life but his own. His heart thumped in his ears, a reassuring signal he had been right. Now it was time to finish his mission so they all could go home. He missed Sue.

The heavy blow to the back of his head came just as he had pushed himself up on his hands and knees. It was of course fully expected and he had tried to steel himself for impact. Unfortunately that didn't make it hurt less.

TERMINATOR

"**D**o you believe in serendipity Mr. Grant? I don't. I think it is preposterous to think luck is on your side. That's all too convenient. Luck favors the prepared and I dare go a step beyond. The duly prepared control luck. And from where I am standing, Mr. Grant, you don't look particularly well prepared."

Scanner opened his eyes. How long had he been out? A string of Duck Brand crackers rapid fired in his head and he felt a trickle of blood run down his neck. *Some blow.* It was impossible to examine the damage, not with his hands tied to the back of the wooden chair.

A single light bulb attached to the opposite wall cast his captor's shadow right up to his feet. It was hard to make out the man's features. He looked well dressed, around five feet six and medium-built.

Scanner raised his head. "Uncle Ho, I presume."

"Take Joy, for example. She's such, what shall I say, such a delight to have around. When I met her for the first time, she wasn't prepared. I could say she didn't even know the meaning of the word. So I decided to change that. It took a little while; peasant girls have their own peculiar countryside stubbornness, but I am very pleased with the result. I prepared her well and she's grateful for it. Isn't that right?"

"Yes, Uncle."

Scanner strained his neck to look at the diminutive Joy standing off to his right just outside his peripheral vision. Unflinchingly, she returned his gaze.

"I apologize for the excessive force, Mr. Grant. My associate is, eh, old school and not exactly top of his class for that matter. For him, conflict resolution usually involves his hands and the occasional blunt object. It's eh, unfortunate you had to run into him."

Scanner would have preferred another way himself. He turned his head to his left where he presumed Uncle Ho's associate was standing. Judging by the size of the man and the smirk on the hulk's face, Scanner had, in a way, been lucky.

"I myself believe in the power of non-physical persuasion. It is infinitely more civilized to convince a man that what you want him to do is not only in his best interest but actually the right thing to do. Of course, not all minds are created equal and there are always some that can't be directed. In a way you disappoint me, Mr. Grant. I mean, you are obviously an educated man. You and I, we are not dissimilar. Violence is anathema to your convictions; you don't carry a gun and for a man in your line of work that is commendable. But how could you let yourself be fooled by a woman? One that you didn't even sleep with?"

The hulk to his left chuckled. "Yeah, really fucked you."

"Shut up Arnold, you're not here to participate in this conversation. I apologize Mr. Grant, for my associate's rudeness. His primitive cognitive faculties are occupied by two things only; muscle and pussy. I have the occasional need for the former and have limitless access to the latter. Thus Arnold's loyalty is assured, he'll do whatever I tell him. Isn't that right Arnold?"

'Yessir, uncle Ho, that right."

Good thug, bad thug. The lie Scanner had told Joaquim was not really that far from the truth. Up till now they'd stuck to the script pretty tightly.

"Now, where were we? Ah, yes, women. I'd really like you to volunteer the whereabouts of that pretty girl of yours, Max. I was kind of hoping you'd come here together. At the same time I am relieved you didn't. The mental qualities I assigned to you are at least partially correct, in other words you're not that stupid. And I hate being wrong. So where is she?"

Don't you worry, Scanner thought, she'll be here soon enough.

"I have absolutely no idea."

"Now both you and I know that that is a lie Mr. Grant. What you seem as yet to be unaware of, to your own detriment I'm afraid, is that I always get to the truth. Right Arnold? Maybe we should give Mr. Grant here a chance to refresh his memory. Go get him."

Scanner braced himself for the inevitable blow. Instead the Chinese terminator trudged towards a doorway to his right.

"I'll be back."

REMF

"You see Mr. Grant, I once claimed a strikingly similar ignorance. I must have been your age. My country went through a terrible ordeal. All we wanted was to be masters of our own destiny. But even that seemed too much to ask.

"During the war, I lived in Saigon. In between the occasional disruptive explosions, business was booming. And my customers, they too had a good time. My girls took care of them, you know. Scared to death and horny as hell, from the cotton fields back home to the killing fields of Nam, they came by the planeloads. Murder is the oddest aphrodisiac. Did you know that, Mr. Grant? The only way those boys could really forget the image of napalmed children etched into their minds was in the hazy embrace of Mary Jane or in between the bosom of a loving and caring May Lee. I provided both, an essential service during normal times, let alone for a mind coming off killing's high. Neither shrink nor chaplain could come even close. There was a helluvalot more singing done in my church.

"I didn't care much for the brass and the pencil pushers. Most of them never saw combat. They just fucked because they got bored. My girls could tell. I made sure they never refused service, a buck is a buck, no matter what dick is on top of you, but they didn't exert themselves. That's when I learned the acronym REMF. You know what that means?"

Scanner nodded. Rear Echelon Mother Fuckers. His dad used to hate them.

"Good things always end before you realize how good they really are. Ironic isn't it? I heard things. Sex loosens the tongue. And I prepared. Ah, there you are, put him down right here."

Scanner looked up. Uncle Ho's narrative was dangerously intoxicating. The man had a way with words.

Arnold heaved and growled as he placed the load he'd carried from the next room in the exact spot his boss had pointed out. An identical chair, occupied by a slumped over lifeless body of a man, held in place by a thick rope looped around the torso and the back of the seat. Despite the black hood placed over the man's head, Scanner knew who it was.

Oh god, he is not... Don't let him be. Panic tightened its strangling fingers around Scanner's throat and squeezed and throttled until reason was all but snuffed out. He swallowed hard.

THINK. BREATHE. SLOWLY.

Had it all been in vain? Would their search end with the realization that Max's father was gone forever? He had to stop Max. There was no reason to come here anymore. Only danger. This manipulating psychopath had as much humanity as a can of worms. How could he stop her?

Sweat gushed from his forehead into his eyes. A thousand salty needles stung his cornea, blurred his vision. He blinked forcefully, and in the temporary clarity that followed, saw uncle Ho handing something to Joy.

She straddled Scanner like a cabaret singer her chair. Hands folded behind his neck, her lower pelvis firmly placed on top of his. In one fluent movement Joy first arched back, hard nipples assaulting the fabric of her top, then recoiled, bringing her face within inches from Scanner's. She laughed mockingly and started to lick the sweat of his face. Finally she dabbed his forehead dry with Uncle Ho's scented handkerchief.

Scanner recognized the smell from the Happy Valley race-track. Uncle Ho had been there, directing or overseeing Stuart, another one of his pawns. And had he killed him when the Aussie punter had refused to execute Scanner? Had he killed Max's father?

Joy planted a wet kiss on Scanners sealed lips and dismounted.

"Relax Mr. Grant, your disgust is misguided. You force yourself to take the moral high ground. It is so obvious. But deep down you know there is no ground at all. Let's face it, we're all falling. And if you start higher you'll fall harder. So you see, in the end I'm guaranteed to come out on top. Now, let me temporarily assuage your anxiety. Arnold!"

Uncle Ho's stocky associate stepped up to the chair he'd set down moments earlier, put his right foot against the seat and pushed it over backwards. Wood slammed on bare concrete and a muffled primeval moan echoed in return.

Scanner swallowed a veritable canon of expletives. No reason to agitate this motherfucker. No reason to prove the damn bastard right either, at least not yet.

FOOLS

"Now, where were we Mr. Grant? Ah, yes, sex as a kind of truth serum. One day, I happened to listen in on a bit of gossip my girls were sharing amongst themselves. Usual stuff, John stuff. Some couldn't get it up, others kept talking about their wives, some were gentle, others liked to slap the girls around. I don't condone violence against my girls, after all, if there's anything that says used, it's a couple of bruises and a black eye. And no one wants to ride used. Bad for self-esteem."

Uncle Ho stepped up to Arnold's handiwork and returned the chair to its upright position. Scanner noticed a slight limp in the man's step.

"We had bouncers to take care of that. A couple of incon-spicuous alarm buttons, under the bed, behind the bathroom mirror, and the John exited, head first. I look after my stable and the girls appreciate that. Isn't that right, my dear?"

The pimp paced to where Joy was standing, motionless. He briefly hovered behind her before placing his hands on her shoulders.

"Yes, Uncle."

"So when I heard one of them, a feisty little stunner named Ivy, tell her colleagues how the satisfied colonel had spilled a lot more than his man chowder, I started to think. The war was a losing proposition, and unfortunately I was on

179

the wrong side. I mean it was the only place to be for intrepid entrepreneurs like me. The North's ideology was all about independence and sharing but even fifty percent of nothing amounts to very little.

My girls had done well for me; I couldn't stand losing what they had worked so hard for. The only viable asset preservation strategy was to slowly ingratiate myself with the enemy. So I started to drop bits of information while in the company of people I suspected of having ties to the North. Small things like travel plans of senior personnel. Towards the end, my girls were vigorously pumping their clients for information and I must say these guys spilled some real gems. More than sufficient to not only secure my survival in the new order, but actually put me in a very profitable position. Until this lot showed up and sent me to hell."

Uncle Ho hobbled back to the lifeless body, pushed down forcefully on the victim's covered head before grabbing a corner of the black bag.

"So Mr. Grant, I need to know where Max is. I'd like to reunite the girl with her father here. And then… what the fuck!"

A tiny red laser dot danced on the pimp's torso, roughly circling the area where his heart would have been. Alarm replaced the simmering anger in Uncle Ho's eyes, and without moving as much as an inch he called on his associate.

"Arnold, dammit. Go!"

Too preoccupied getting acquainted with his own little lively harbinger of imminent termination the brute enforcer failed to acknowledge his boss' command.

Too early, Scanner thought. *Why do you come too early? He is not here yet.*

"Take it easy." Uncle Ho shouted into the void.

"Easy." Arnold repeated incredulously.

"I am unarmed." The pimp raised both hands above his head, open palms facing outwards.

"Me too." Arnold took his cue from the boss.

It was all over in barely a minute. Uncle Ho lunged behind the nearby Joy, using the Burmese girl, too shocked to resist, as his shield. Arnold frantically weighed his options. Even if there had been another Joy, there'd be no hiding his bulk.

A salvo of shots cracked the coalesced fear like a hammer blow to a mirror. A second burst sent shards flying to the floor, Scanner could hear the pieces as they scattered on the concrete. Then it became silent, dead silent. For a full two seconds.

A stunned Uncle Ho released Joy, who scurried away into a corner, sobbing uncontrollably. Arnold patted his chest, searching for holes that hadn't materialized, hands coming up dry. Strewn across the floor in front of his feet Scanner counted dozens of tiny yellow pellets, wannabe bullets for wannabe heroes.

"That was frickin awesome man. We got them good."

Jaws went slack as all eyes zoomed in on the doorway where two figures, outfitted in mail order militia high fived their way in. Scanner recognized Joaquim, but not his exuberant friend.

"Yeah, like I told you Paulo, if we manage to impress these guys we might get a job."

The flustered weekend warriors approached Uncle Ho, sniper rifles casually slung across their shoulders.

You silly fools, Scanner thought.

Audition

"You must be the director."

Joaquim walked up to Uncle Ho with an extended hand.

"I told your location guy this was a great place. Don't you agree?"

"And we know it like the back of our hands," Paulo jumped in. "Been coming here most every weekend. Would you hire us? I mean it'd be so cool and we're pretty good shots too."

"Hiring you? For what?"

Uncle Ho had still not completely tuned in. Out of sight of the trigger happy teenagers Arnold readied himself to join the conversation. The gun in his hand told Scanner he wasn't likely to argue the finer points.

"The movie, of course. The final shoot-out. You do need extras don't you? There's ten of us in the club."

"Ten?"

Uncle Ho's raised hand and a barely perceptible headshake stopped a disappointed Arnold.

"There are more of you? Here?"

"No, it's just Paulo and me. The others are busy tonight."

"Ah, I see. Good, that's good."

The Vietnamese gangster turned to Scanner.

"Inventive, Mr. Grant, you really thought these punks could be of use? We're not so different you and I. We're both

182

result oriented wouldn't you say? It's all about make believe isn't it? And these idiots? Collateral damage right?"

"Make believe? What do you mean?" Joaquim's voice had lost its cockiness.

"Don't you fucking interrupt me."

Uncle Ho swirled around and buried his flat hand deep into the youngster's face with a force that sent the hotel clerk reeling backwards into the chokehold of the approaching Arnold.

"There is no fucking movie, you get it? This is real, as real as it gets. It's time to wake up. War is not a game for kids on their day off. It's a full-time occupation. You two punks don't have it in you and I'm afraid you never will."

"Please don't hurt us," Paulo whimpered. "Please let us go, we won't tell anyone and we'll never come here again."

"Oh I know you won't. But you see, Arnold, my associate over here, is not so easily persuaded. Can't really blame him either. He hasn't got much else going for him. Why don't you talk to him? Maybe you'll catch him in one of his reasonable moods and he'll send you home with a clean shot between the eyes instead of first breaking a couple of bones."

Paralyzed by fear and unable to push a sound past the blockade of Arnold's flexed forearm, Joaquim's frightened eyes jittered restlessly from Uncle Ho to Scanner and back, searching for a foothold against the rising tide of inevitable realization that truth was indeed stranger than fiction. Scanner held the youngster's eyes with a frozen gaze that offered neither solace nor encouragement, only a reaffirmation of the height to where the shit was piled up to.

"Hand me your gun Arnold and go get some more chairs for our trigger happy guests here. They want to see a movie, so let's give them a front row while we convince Mr. Grant that now is not a good time to change the script, and he'd better play the part we've written for him. On the floor you two, NOW!"

Like sand dumped from a pivoting backhoe. Joaquim, no longer muscled into Arnold's iron grip, spilled across the concrete next to the already deflated Paolo; audition definitely over.

Valkyrie

The water was almost refreshing. Without wind to do battle with the hot and damp air and force it to even consider retreat, mugginess ruled the territory with oppressive impunity. Even the mere thought of action made a man sweat profusely. Drenched clothes stuck to skin like a giant plastic wrap, one of those thin films Scanner regularly used to preserve the leftovers of a Mexican takeaway, though more often than not it became a useful barrier holding back the scent of food gone bad. He realized he was hungry. *Should have eaten before coming here. No knowing when the next meal might be.*

The water was almost refreshing, if only he could come up now, grab a bite before calling it a day. Darkness descended instead.

"You're killing him!"

Scanner violently breached the surface, water running off his face, cold wet siren fingers only reluctantly releasing him from their suffocating embrace.

"You're gonna kill him!"

Joaquim's desperate shrieking was strangely reassuring to Scanner. His oxygen starved brain cognized that death was still a future event. If he started to breathe again. He greedily gasped for air.

"You're stating the obvious, punk. I think your movie scout friend here has no problem visualizing the next scene,

185

right Mr. Grant?"

Scanner opened his eyes to reveal an upside down world. Water was floating above him. Dancing on the surface waves, rhythmically in tune with the drops of water that shot up from his head to pierce the liquid plane with decreasing frequency, was Uncle Ho, who appeared again, less jittery this time, suspended from the ceiling a couple of feet further. After a few disorientating seconds, Scanner realized that gravity had not reversed itself but that instead its forces had him precariously balanced on life's edge. He strained to lift his head. A flustered Arnold, enjoying himself no doubt, held Scanner's chair by the two front legs, shifting it back and forth over its pivot point, the edge of an old zinc tub, water up to the brim. The musclebound brute's face shone with a childlike glee, full of wonder at discovering the principle of equilibrium for the first time. Scanner's equilibrium.

"What you idiots don't realize is that you're next if you don't shut up. And I don't care if you know less than Arnold over here, which in and by itself would be no mean feat, you will be begging to tell me everything you don't know before I'm done."

Now would be a good time, Scanner thought, not really fancying another dip. He glanced around the room. Off to his right, seated and bound front row, in front of a hooded and barely alive Mr. Zwoelstra, Joaquim and Paulo whimpered quietly. Directly at his feet, Arnold, absorbed in Newtonian wonder, was fine-tuning Scanner's precarious position.

"Look boss, no hands," he beamed gleefully before halting the chair's descend inches above the water.

Standing a few feet away from Uncle Ho, Joy shifted uneasily from one leg to the other. Her face, though upside down, carried undeniable traces of disgust and fear, born out of the realization that this was no longer a game. For a moment, Scanner pitied her. Was there still enough left to bring her back? Then his line of vision trailed upwards to the girl's breasts, which, given Joy's position, seemed to have settled in the wrong direction. The mind, under extreme duress, seeks comfort in the familiar, Scanner recalled. He missed Sue and her particular ways of comforting him. When this was all over, he'd go and see her, straight from the airport.

"So Mr. Grant, have you made up your mind? It's Max I am after. What is she to you? Give her up and I'll let you go. A woman can't be worth this."

"You'd never know, you pathetic piece of pimping shit!"

Scanner steeled himself against what undoubtedly would follow. Unless…

A muffled and synthesized rendition of Valkyrie interrupted the interrogation. It most definitely lacked the martial impact of a full-blown orchestra, according to Scanner, but he welcomed the reprieve.

"What!" Uncle Ho screamed.

"It's the phone boss." Arnold fumbled in his pocket, one hand holding the chair, unsure what course of action to take.

Clearly not a multi-tasker, Scanner thought. To his relief Arnold put the chair back on all fours before cutting off Wagner mid-assault.

"It's for you boss. The Priest."

MAX DARROW

"So Mr. Grant, it appears I thought wrongly of you. You are more conniving than your actions seem to suggest. I can almost admire your audacity though it seems to be firmly rooted in an archaic notion of idealism. I hate to bring it to you, but gallantry as a moral code is overrated and hopelessly outdated. Of course with the Japs you never really know what motivates them, Samurai honor and all that nonsense."

Uncle Ho had been on the phone for a couple of minutes gesticulating heavily with his free arm and occasionally turning to Scanner. He had been out of earshot but Scanner had no doubts about the nature of the conversation.

"From what I have been told your Max has ample motivation to bring to bear on any argument, all the more so with a pervert like Hideyoshi-san, whom I believe you've had the pleasure of meeting. Lesser men would have utterly lost the plot, I have to give you that, but not Yoshi. He's got such a great racket don't you think so? A priest? Nice try to get Max to convince him to come to the rescue, though doomed from the start, really. If only you had thought it through a bit more."

Who said he hadn't?

"They are on the way, shouldn't take long. Yoshi is my customer, has been for a long time. And quite satisfied too, I believe. He's never returned any of my merchandise."

So Max had succeeded. Scanner had counted on it. Had put his life on the line. He loved it when a plan came together, especially considering the alternative.

"Arnold over here seems a bit disappointed, now that there is no longer a need to extract Max' whereabouts. Aren't you, Arnold?"

Since handing over the phone to Uncle Ho, the bulging enforcer had stood off to the side, sulking, like a kid whose game console had been confiscated, wondering whether it would only be a temporary measure.

"Normally I would have consented in letting him have another go, just to keep him happy. Alas, I am under instructions to stop short of termination. Sorry old boy."

The Vietnamese pimp turned to Arnold and addressed him in Chinese. He spoke slowly, carefully articulating the words. For a brief moment Scanner wondered what transpired between the two crooks. The twinkling that brightened Arnold's eyes combined with the look of terror frozen on Joaquim's and Paolo's faces radically reduced most of the guesswork from that equation.

***

"Ah, Grant-San, *komban wa*, how nice to meet you again."

Hideyoshi strode towards Scanner with martial resolve. He offered his outstretched hand only to retract it immediately upon noticing Scanner's predicament. Instead he stood to attention and slightly bowed his head.

"Somewhat unfortunate situation it is I'm afraid, but I pray you do remember that the Lord works in mysterious ways. *Fear thou not for I am with thee.*"

Uncle Ho jumped in before Scanner could counter.

"Yoshi, Yoshi, please cut the crap. No one here needs proselytizing, though perhaps these kids here might want you to administer the Last Sacrament. Where is she? You said you'd bring her along."

"I did and I did. But you'd have to appreciate that she is rather a handful, more likely two actually. *Thy breasts shall be as clusters of the vine.* King Solomon had a way with words hadn't he? It'd be rather rude to drag the girl in here without formally having greeted Grant-San over here, even though he is the one who conspired to lead me into extreme temptation."

"Your politeness annoys the hell out of me, Yoshi. Please bring her here, now. God knows I've been waiting long enough."

"Don't…"

The Priest started to protest Uncle Ho's deliberate mocking, then thought the better of it and pressed the speed dial on his phone.

"Ima, now," was all he said.

***

"Put me down, you mindless idiot! Keep your filthy hands of me. Let me go!"

Max' loud protestations heralded her imminent arrival. By the sound of it she was putting up a good fight. Scanner knew it was all show of course, though her captor would no doubt fail to appreciate the fact that Max didn't target his eyes, or throat or any other vulnerable points he didn't know he had.

The Japanese thug carried her like King Kong holding Ann Darrow. Built like the side-by-side Whirlpool Scanner had once, as a kid, used as a hideout, much to the distress of his mother, he moved with about the same amount of grace. Even Arnold looked impressed.

"Put me down now, you brainless Sumo primate mutant Godzilla offspring."

Now Scanner was impressed.

Muscle manifested itself in remarkably identical ways all over the world, he mused. Hopefully this beefcake's wiring would also prove the cliché right. It was getting crowded now and too many variables tended to screw up carefully crafted plans.

"Oh my, have you grown since the last time I saw you. Finally we meet again. I don't suppose you remember me. That's close enough, keep her secure right there."

Word of Max' acrobatics at the Lisboa no doubt had reached Uncle Ho, and he made sure she was kept at bay by the Priest's associate who put her down well over a leg's length away from him.

"Where's my father? What have you done to him? What do you want from us?"

"All in good time, my dear Max. Don't worry, there'll be plenty of opportunity, you're not going anywhere very soon. Arnold, be a gentleman and offer the lady a chair."

Exam

Scanner studied the room. All was in place now; the cast complete, he prayed, though not everyone on set. Sure, there were a few unexpected extras but they had actually bought him some welcome reprieve and had probably prevented additional abuse Arnold would have meted out in his physics 1.1 class, since the Priest's call came later than expected. *Cut the crap Scanner, who are you fooling?*

If he was being honest with himself he had only narrowly stopped short of inviting Joaquim to the party. Cunning and manipulative indeed, it was a fine line that separated him from the bad guys, a line he had knowingly crossed a couple of times in his career. After all, you can't dispose of shit and expect to keep your hands clean. What stood him apart, or so he kept telling himself, was the absence of pleasure as both motivator and reward for his transgressions. He'd better make sure no harm would come to the two boys.

So this was it. His self-professed expertise in reading the human psyche put to the litmus test. Pass and you get to live, fail and a quick death would be a welcome punishment. With ten people gathered in the small, dimly lit space it could easily get messy. At least only the bad guys were left standing, for now.

Uncle Ho limped over to where Max was seated, on Scanner's left. Though she was firmly bound to the chair he took no chances and approached from behind. The back of his left hand trailed across Max' face down her neckline before turning and resting on her left shoulder.

"I can't begin to express how elated I am having you here. It's been what? Twenty-odd years. I often despaired during all those years in isolation, and thought about killing myself, but the pain of dying without having cleansed myself in the sweet waters of revenge kept me alive. YOU kept me alive."

"Don't touch me, you psycho. Who are you? You should have done yourself a favor, all those years back. Where is my father? What did you do to him? If you as much as…"

Uncle Ho placed his hand over Max's mouth and cut her short. Not a smart thing to do, Scanner thought.

"Shhhh, you've got quite a spirit, I must say. I should have offered to buy you when I had a chance, though somehow, I think your mother would never have acquiesced."

Scanner cringed.

The Vietnamese pimp realized too late just how far Max's spirit could take her. She abruptly lifted her head and with the ferocity of a starving Pit Bull chewed down on her captor's hand.

Uncle Ho's face turned a yellow shade of pale, Scanner could see the bulging veins at his temples pumping frantically, before jumping to a scarlet electric red, thus covering the full spectrum of national colors. What he didn't do was scream. He suffered the fierce assault silently. Scanner wondered whether such was the ingrained, almost instinctive reaction of a man who had endured physical torture while denying his tormenters the pleasure of witnessing the inflicted anguish.

"What the fuck do you know about my mother? WHAT DO YOU KNOW!" Max exploded with volcanic intensity, spitting blood and words and bits of skin, a violent, scorching eruption blasted at anyone foolishly enough to get in the way.

Scanner was relieved she was firmly bound to her chair.

Uncle Ho circled around to face Max. His right hand

flicked open a 5 inch hardened steel switchblade.

"Your mother was a whore, nothing but a cheap cunt, and you, you are history," he spoke quietly, murderous intend in his eyes.

"Whoa, chotto, chotto that's enough. Why don't you calm down?"

The Priest stepped forward and grabbed Uncle Ho's arm. Arnold reacted as conditioned and drew a Colt Anaconda. The priest's associate, not wanting to look sluggish, threw himself into the fray holding a more modest though equally deadly Glock 32.

"What is she to you?" Uncle Ho snapped at the Priest, "you do this all the time."

"Not with her, she's… she's perfect. The others, they were expendable."

"Yoshi, Yoshi," Uncle Ho sighed. "You brought her here, remember? What did you think I was going to do, have a romantic candlelight dinner? Ask you to bestow the Lord's blessing on us? I see she actually got to you. I am disappointed. I thought we had a deal."

Scanner shifted uneasily in his chair. The situation was spiraling out of control. He weighed what few options he had. The four goons were standing in close proximity to each other, weapons exposed. Joaquim and Paulo were off to his right, obscured in darkness, probably scared stiff. They blocked Max' father, which was a good thing, Scanner thought, since it also thus far prevented Max from knowing he was right here, in the same room, highly combustible information that would have made her go nuclear instantaneously.

That left Joy missing. Where was she? Scanner prayed the Burmese girl had had the wherewithal to retreat somewhere relatively safe, the adjacent room perhaps?

It was no small miracle that the hot and humid air, excessively saturated with accumulated fear, hatred and testosterone, still managed to carry the tiny particles of a familiar scent into Scanner's nostrils. It was an aroma he'd never expected to be so relieved to be smelling. In the movie reel of his mind, the clapperboard slammed shut. Final take, it read.

CUBAN SHUFFLE

Scanner noticed the dot before anyone else. He was expecting it. He quietly leaned as far to his right as the rope would allow, loading the spring, knowing that he'd only have one take, no rehearsal.

In front of him, the gangster's argument had reached a silent and dangerous impasse. Whirlpool-San had his Glock trained on a visibly strained Arnold, who was digging down deep for an answer as to why he shouldn't pull the Anaconda's trigger and send The Priest, still blocking Uncle Ho's arm from executing a cut and slice on Max, packing off to Kingdom Come. It was a perfect Mexican standoff, Asian style.

"Boss, loo-look," Arnold stammered. He had seen the light.

"Nani?," the fridge quizzed as the red dot now circled his double doors.

"Not again, you idiots," Uncle Ho shouted into the dark.

"I'm the only one unarmed," The Priest fired off.

NOW, Scanner thought.

With all the speed he could muster Scanner shifted his upper torso to the left, creating a momentum that toppled his chair, which, in turn, slammed a surprised Max onto the concrete with a loud bang. *Out of the way.*

Scanner's own, well executed version of the domino theory immediately reverberated as four shots, fired in quick succession sent two guns flying and two goons crashing to the floor, both holding their knee caps and writhing in agony.

Of the two men left standing, Uncle Ho reacted first. He raised his blocked arm followed by a swift downwards twist and turn that set him free from the Priest's feeble grip. Next he slashed the switchblade upwards, cutting Yoshi on the forearm, before circling around the shocked Priest, locking him in a chokehold, knife at the jugular.

That pretty much severed their relations, Scanner thought.

"I know what you want," the Vietnamese pimp shouted.

The laser target searched but found no foothold.

"He'll be dead before me. As dead as your equiphile partner, and you'll have nothing to show for your friend's sacrifice."

Uncle Ho was quick witted, Scanner realized, and well informed. How had he made out the identity of his hidden opponent this quickly? There was definitely more to the pimp than met the eye. Earlier, he had alluded to someone wanting Scanner to stay alive. Hiding in the shadows. It had only been a dream, yesterday, though Scanner knew better than to naively dismiss such alternative realities.

"What's going on?" Max whispered

"Stay down," Scanner commanded nervously, his mind temporarily oblivious to the absence of a credible alternative.

"I was just about to levitate," Max joked. "Have you seen dad?"

"No."

Technically it was the correct reply. It would have to do for now. *Better not start a fire in your own backyard if you can't extinguish the flames.* He hated being so utterly hamstrung. *Just get that pretty little thing of yours out of the way* Tony M had told him, *keep her calm while I return fire. I'll be a quick shot, I promise. Don't worry 'bout a thing, done this at least a hundred times.*

That did worry Scanner. Who was Tony M, really? Who did he work for?

"You arranged my partner's death, perhaps even killed him yourself, why would I let you go?" The sharpshooter shouted out from the dark.

"Because you see the bigger picture, you guys always do. You can't let something as trivial as your partner's death ruin the assignment; you'd be out of a job tomorrow."

"I can get another job. I am highly employable."

Tony M stepped forward, night vision and Socom pistol firmly trained on Uncle Ho and The Priest, who had both retreated against the far wall. He stepped over Scanner and Max, circumvented the two moaning enforcers, picked up the Glock from the floor with his free, gloved hand and shot Arnold in the head, never once taking his eyes off the real target. "That's for Stuart. And you, you'd better shut up. Or I'll put you in touch with my little friend."

No doubt what M Tony had morphed into now.

The fridge instantly jumped into energy saving mode while Tony M eyed the Anaconda, hesitating momentarily before nonchalantly kicking the weapon into the furthest corner.

"Now, what was it you wanted to discuss?"

A PLAYER NOT A KILLER

"Easy, easy now, big fellow, no reason to get angry."
"I'm not, I'm getting even."

"What do you want? Name your price. Why don't you come work for me, there's a job opening, someone just got laid off. They can't be paying you that much. And don't forget the benefits, as often as you want."

"Enough, they pay me enough. Lemme tell you what, you let The Priest go and you'll live, I'll hand you over to the authorities."

"Stop right there or I start cutting, and if not?"

"I'll put a nice pristine slug in both of you. Hell, if I'm lucky it'll be the same round. Shit happens. I'll square it with my bosses later."

"You're bluffing, you…"

BANG.

Discussion terminated, Scanner thought, though from his vantage point, Tony M filled most of the frame and he couldn't see anyone dropping to the floor.

"I am bleeding," The Priest clutched his throat then stared in horror at his blood soaked hands before easing away from Uncle Ho. "Help me, I'm gonna die."

"Yoshi, Yoshi. Stop lamenting like a pig in a slaughterhouse. You disgust me. That ain't your blood."

Hideyoshi turned around to Uncle Ho, frozen against the

wall. The knife in his right hand was gone. Most of the pimp's right hand was gone too. And still not a sound.

"I don't understand," The Priest said.

"Nice shooting kiddo," Tony M approved.

'I told you I was an ace," Joaquim announced proudly as he stepped into the arena, carrying Arnold's Anaconda at his side. Joy followed closely, the pocket-knife in her hand explained all that needed to be.

"Why didn't you go for the head, a much bigger target from where you were standing?"

"I'm a player, not a killer. There is a difference you know."

"Good on ya kid, if you ever wanna play with the pros, gimme a shout. Uncle Ho is not the only one hiring. Now let's sort out this mess. Hand me some of that rope of yours."

Joy proceeded towards Scanner and Max. On the way she paused and gazed intently at what was left of Arnold before finally bending down to poke the corpse repeatedly with her knife, too scared to trust her own judgment, exorcizing demons until she was satisfied they'd never come back.

"Scan-ner. Thank you." The Burmese girl planted a kiss on Scanner's cheek. It was a child's simple gesture of gratitude, a world away from the provocative lap dance earlier.

Not too far gone, Scanner thought and for the first time that evening he found a reason to feel good about himself.

"Max, me like. Aiyaaa!"

It was a joyous, celebratory kick, spirit awakened after a long, cold, dark and comatose night. Max, cut loose now, hugged Joy. The girls' embrace dispelled all remnants of make believe, all barriers created by the mind to guard the tiny spore of hope against the world's rapacious intent. Tears ran freely, watering a new life, with a bit of luck and an awful lot of caring.

In the distance, a crowing rooster picked up the vibe and cautiously heralded the morning light.

HAI KARATE

Some things are better kept hidden in the dark, Scanner thought.

The night's battlefield displayed its victims with graphic clarity. Tony M had covered Arnold's body in a large plastic sheet that Joaquim and Paolo had retrieved from a nearby building. On an empty stomach, the blood and gore were nauseating but the plastic actually made it worse as it stuck to the most pulped and bloodied parts and reminded Scanner of the shrink-wrapped offerings in a supermarket's meat section. Maybe he should become vegetarian. Lobsang would approve.

Fortunately, Max and Joy had moved to the adjacent room, taking care of Max's father. He had survived the brutal kidnap ordeal but was badly dehydrated and floated in and out of consciousness. He had yet to speak and Scanner wondered how the man's mind had held up. During the late night stand-off, Joy had used the obfuscating chaos to cut loose both the boys and together they had lifted the Dutch cheesemaker out of harm's way.

A quick-witted Joaquim, deducting that whoever was out there had to have night vision, then returned to hide in the shadows and had managed to signal Tony M for Arnold's gun, which he consequently used, thanks to his own night goggles, with such debilitating precision.

It was an improbable sequence of events, Scanner reflected, and it was a miracle it had concluded the way it did. He had relearned, through Lobsang's intervention, to once again believe in miracles. Yet to act upon them prematurely, as if their occurrence was all but guaranteed, was perhaps pushing the boundaries of faith into entirely unknown territory. Maybe he'd just gotten lucky.

"It's all in a day's work." Tony M wiped the sweat from his forehead.

Together they had propped up the three surviving gangsters against the back wall. A few lengths of rope had all but stemmed Uncle Ho's bleeding. The anaconda had chewed off most of the pimp's right hand. By comparison, Max's bite to his left had been a Chihuahua's nibble.

"You're a stone cold motherfucker, you know? Even for a Charlie. And I knew me a couple, back in Nam."

"At least what you see is what you get," Uncle Ho said, his first words that morning, "not like this religious pussy pushover." He turned to his right to face The Priest. "You shouldn't have stopped me, you moron, we would have had a chance, he was all by himself."

"Speak for yourself, if I'm not mistaken my fortune is about to take a turn for the better, isn't that so, Lone Ranger?"

"What's he alluding to Tony? You're not going to let him off the hook are you? You know what he is capable of, you told me yourself." Scanner didn't like where this was going.

"Yeah that's right, The Priest over here is an evil son of a bitch but, from now on, if he makes the right decision, he is our evil son of a bitch. Do we have a deal Yoshi?"

"Ah, the intricacies of US foreign policy, why are you so surprised, Grant san?" The Priest mocked. "Still harbor those illusions? The American Dream is only for those who are asleep. Time to wake up."

"What is he to you Tony? Who are you working for, really? And don't give me more of that Peace bullshit."

"I work for a special branch of the State Department, that's all I am allowed to say. We specialize in the acquisition of sensitive foreign assets, before some hostile forces scoop them up. The Priest, Hideyoshi-san, has been on our most wanted list for quite some time now, I'd say for well over fifty years."

"That's impossible, he was just an innocent toddler fifty years ago."

"You're square on the dot man, but his father, Priest Senior, was anything but. Ever heard of Unit 731?"

The steadily rising sun could not dispel the ice-cold wind now howling through the abandoned fireworks factory. Scanner shuddered as Tony M filled in the gaps he'd rather he had left blank. It was an eerily familiar story of unfathomable dread and spine-chilling horror, the twin tale to Lobsang's gruesome account of Experimental Block Number Five.

"Daddy Yoshi directed some of the most promising chemical experiments. The Japs meticulously kept extensive records, just like them Nazi dudes. Call them what you want, but they were no slackers. You don't need to be an Einstein to know the damage those records could do in the wrong hands, enemy hands. That's where I come in, secure and procure, at any price."

"But this is not a new policy. The procurement should have been completed in the immediate post WWII period."

"You'd think so, but you'd be mistaken. The Japs really never 'fessed up to this whole sordid business. Most of the scientists involved went on to lead comfortable lives in postwar Japan. Mind you, we went soft on them of course, at the war crimes trials. Execution or imprisonment wouldn't exactly help the cause and uncover the hidden records. It all kinda backfired though, as we couldn't really offer the right incentives. Them Krauts could easily be integrated into our civil society, Zipperheads would stick out a lot more."

Civil indeed.

"So we've always had the hunch they were holding out on us, notwithstanding the immunity we gave them. The files we got? Just the tip of the iceberg, man."

Despite the night's victorious conclusion, Scanner felt utterly defeated. He had led Tony M to The Priest, thinking justice would be served, believing the Dream. Lobsang's and his father's revulsion towards Brian Webb at Camp Hale suddenly acquired an intensely depressing familiarity.

But of course, family. Why hadn't he, he must call, they must find out.

Fragments of ideas swirled in his head, like shards of a broken mirror carried by a violent whirlwind, sometimes, during a rare and brief moment of lucidity, hinting at the bigger picture before turning and slicing it all to pieces, obfuscating any attempt at clarity.

He had a son, or a daughter. No doubt.

"Look, I've said probably more than I should have. Perhaps y'all should get going. I'll clean up the mess. You don't wanna stick around for the authorities. I like you, man and I have to thank you. In the end we both got what we came here for. It's time to part. The old man needs medical attention, Uncle Ho's girl needs a new home, the boys are pretty shook up and need to be debriefed to keep their mouth shut and you and that pretty Max of yours should share some quality time, her being no doubt extremely grateful and ready to show it, if you get my gist."

Scanner did and wondered how anyone could even contemplate sex after all the carnage. What was it Uncle Ho had said earlier? Scanner turned to the deflated pimp.

"What were you going to do to them?"

"Nothing that they didn't cause to happen to me."

Judging by the man's accumulated bitterness and inner emotional wasteland, it wouldn't have been pretty.

"There will be a blacked out van waiting by the time you get to the gate." Tony M clearly had come prepared. "There is no security, you can get in without anyone noticing. The driver will take you wherever you want, no questions asked. Just in case though, I wouldn't hang around Macau much longer."

"We'll pick up our stuff and make straight for the heliport," Max said, "I've already arranged the chopper. There is one more thing you can do for us though."

"Call it lady."

"Make sure Joy can go with us."

"Consider it done."

As the motley group of survivors made for the exit, Scanner remembered one final question he needed answered.

"What's that after shave you're sporting Tony? I recognized it from the casino, it really perfected my timing."

'That's eh…"

Was the blunt agent blushing?

"It's *Hai Karate*. Very popular in the seventies. They had some great TV commercials, especially the Brits. *Be careful how you use it*, was the tagline. You should check it out if you have a chance. The lead actress was this incredibly hot, total knock-out bombshell, Valerie Leon. Come to think of it, Max is kinda like her, if you get my meaning."

OFFSPRING

"I am soo very much relieved to hear your voice. I was really getting worried when you didn't call yesterday."

Sue edged ever closer to tears. Even though it was in the middle of the Chicago night, Scanner had called her as soon as he got to his room and vividly recounted his harrowing ordeal of the past, turbulent, twenty-four hours.

"Me too baby, me too."

"When will you guys fly back?"

"I am scheduled tomorrow, Max and her dad are gonna spend one or two more days here in Hong Kong. He really is too weak to travel. The medical didn't show any physical issues other than exhaustion and dehydration, but the real damage might reveal itself later, mentally."

"He's in good hands though, right?"

"Absolutely. Max hasn't left his side since we checked in to the Mandarin this afternoon and Joy is right there to assist if needed. I certainly feel redundant right now."

"You won't get laid," Sue paused deliberately, "off over here, you know that right? There's just too much, uh, work to be done. Have I got a job for you if you think you're up to the task."

"I will be, I will be, don't you worry baby."

"I am thrilled to hear, I'll be even more thrilled to experience it uh, first hand. I miss you… A lot."

"I miss you too."

"So in the end it was all about revenge and a chance encounter at the delicatessen fair?"

"That's right. Uncle Ho has his fingers in many pies; gambling, loan-sharking, prostitution, you name it. Illegal wildlife trading and the obscene but legal shark fin business brought him to the delicatessen fair. Funny thing is that Max would have never let her father participate had she known there would be fins on display."

"As they say, revenge is a dish best served cold, but well over twenty years is a long time to be carrying that kind of grudge. What exactly happened to him?"

"Not sure, but it must have been very unpleasant I imagine. What I've been able to piece together so far is based on the limited information Max's father has been able to share. After baby girl Max got rescued from the sinking boat it transpired that the political commissar on board, Uncle Ho, had, in fact, been masterminding the entire escape. For a fee of course. That didn't go down well with his Party superiors and a prolonged exposure to re-education followed. I think the curriculum was mainly physical and psychological torture. The guy walks with a limp and seems completely pain free."

"And what about Tony M? Is he really going to take The Priest stateside?"

"No doubt, no doubt. What a guy. I'd love to hate him, but I can't. He's a misogynist asshole, but he really came through when it was absolutely vital. The man's an anachronistic seventies relic, I mean his fashion sense, his choice of after shave, god, you wouldn't believe how awful that stuff smells, though I'd love to see the commercials, especially the ones over in England. See if you can find some Hai Karate. And then his ideology. An unfaltering belief in the goodness of America, us versus them, you know the rap. But he quite possibly saved my life, saved all our lives."

"I am so glad he did, baby. Though this Priest seems to be

a real psychopath, it's giving me goose bumps thinking what might be in those files."

"Yeah, but you know what, none of this is a coincidence, I am certain. Call me a whacky new-age head-in-the-clouds day dreamer if you must, but the revelation that the son proceeds along his father's path is a real eye opener."

"Oh baby, I would never call you that. You're straight, middle aged and fully awake and there's nothing wrong with having your head in my cloud."

"Go ahead and make fun of me all you want. You had better get your hands on the Brian Webb files. I am absolutely positive that's where the answer to your case can be found and I'd be willing to bet it involves his offspring. Any other news? How's Lobsang and did you meet Cathy Lee?"

IMPECCABLE TASTE

"Lobsang's been calling in favors, old agency connections, friends of your father. So far he's coming up empty-handed. If Brian Webb's records still exist, they're buried pretty damn deep. It doesn't help of course that the OPC – CIA rivalry continued even after they merged. Who knows, it might still be a problem, in some form or the other, to this day.

The trip we did down to the lake, you know, where Dolma was found, didn't produce anything new. You have seen all the pictures right? Anything we overlooked?"

"I don't think so, but to be honest I should probably take another look. Yesterday kinda got in the way."

"You could do that on the way home, take it easy for now. You've got a long flight ahead of you tomorrow. I'm gonna try to catch a few more hours of sleep. The boss just increased my workload. Some graduate student from the Wisconsin National Primate Research Center turned up dead at Lincoln Park Zoo early yesterday morning. One of the zoo keepers discovered the body inside the Great Ape House."

"Natural causes ruled out?"

"Pretty much, unless you consider being naked and drugged inside a full body gorilla suit natural. Poor guy suffocated to death. Whoever put him in there didn't realize or didn't care that slumped over, the breathing holes get obstructed. Don and I are off to Madison later today, to see what we can find out at the university."

"Alright baby, go back to sleep, looks like you need it. I'm gonna head over to the bar, see if I can engage a gentleman in a conversation."

"This gentleman happens to be Scottish?"

"No, no, these highland guys don't talk back until much later. It's the bartender, a really nice man I met last time. His name is Trueman Wong."

***

Going down, the canned elevator lady announced.

"Tell me something I don't know," Scanner addressed his reflection, neatly split right down the middle.

He dreaded being alone this evening. Max was reunited with her father, Joy got a new lease on life, he had just kissed Sue goodnight and it really was too early to disturb Lobsang and Cathy Lee. He felt aimless, alone, orphaned, depressed.

His hand wandered inside his jacket pocket and brought up a slightly faded three by five color photograph. *I got something for you Scanner*, Tony M had said on the way out. Scanner had been the last to leave and the government agent had called him back. *You're okay, you know that. I wasn't sure at first, but you're okay. This is something I found in Stuart's drawer. Thought you might like to have it. It's your dad I believe. Him and Stuart were good buddies, it seems, back in Nam.*

***

"A double Macallan, right away sir, and this one's on the house. It's good to see you again sir. I heard you got lucky sir, in Macau."

Was he just guessing?

"Trueman Wong, you have an extraordinary ability to uncover what I can only describe as sensitive information. Are you sure you're only a bartender?"

"Sir? Been serving all my life, sir. With the best I may add. Here's to your return, and the lady's too, of course."

The four Scotsmen touched. Their clinking armor reverberated around the Captain's Bar and continued to echo inside Scanner's head long after they had abandoned the scene.

"A refill please, Trueman, and help yourself too, my bill of course."

"Thank you sir, much appreciated, but I think I'll decline. I have to keep an eye out for my customers. A Scotch Mist should remain a drink, not a condition. Something bothering you, sir?"

Scanner sighed and put Tony M's picture on the bar. If Trueman recognized any of the four people in the photograph he managed to keep it to himself.

"You see the officer on the left?" Scanner slid the picture towards Trueman, "that's my father."

"A fine looking gentleman sir, I can see a likeness there." Trueman turned over the image. "Jack Grant and I on a double date, Saigon, March 22, 1973," he read slowly. "Is that Jack?" Trueman pointed at Stuart.

"No, Jack is my father, I got this picture this morning from a friend of Stuart, the other guy."

"Ah, I see, how's your father doing sir?"

"He's not, I mean he's dead. He died in an accident when I was fourteen."

"I'm terribly sorry to hear that sir, please forgive my intrusion, that was rather tactless of me."

"It's alright Trueman, it's not your fault. You know, you never really get over it. My dad and I, we were close. Seeing this picture brings back so many memories."

"Memories are good sir, you are keeping his spirit alive, your father deserves nothing less. And if you don't mind me saying so sir, your father would be proud of you."

Scanner stopped reading his Macallan and looked up at the bartender. Did he know? Or was he just being kind? Telling his customer what he needed to hear.

"I would hope so, but to tell you the truth, Trueman, I am not so sure. Life puts all these choices in front of you that you'd much rather not have to make and once you have, it's hard to shake the consequences. People die, Trueman, Stuart is dead because I am my father's son, because I came here, and a lot more people could have joined him."

"I am just a bartender at the Mandarin in Hong Kong sir, I've never been to your country and I probably never will. But I've seen my share of human folly parading by. You don't strike me as belonging in that category, sir. Stop beating yourself up over what has passed and you'll actually have time to appreciate what is. Take this picture for example. Two fine gentlemen and two gorgeous ladies. I'll bet you a Scotsman you hadn't noticed the striking resemblance between your girl and this stunning beauty over here posing so elegantly at your father's side. You both have impeccable taste."

***

Scanner stared in silence at the picture on the bar. Faded though it may have been, there was no denying the accuracy of Trueman's observation. Now that the bartender had gone off to serve newly arrived customers, Scanner tried to grapple with the revelation by himself. He violently swirled his Macallan to just below the rim, reaching for thoughts on the verge of escaping and gratefully watching them drown. The more he drank, the harder it became to reign in his wildest speculations. Of course it was possible, considering Lobsang's penchant for orchestrating coincidences. Scanner had not seen the likeness earlier because he hadn't been looking. But now that it stared him in the face everything started to make sense. There was really only one way to find out.

HOME

"No, that's not possible."

"Oh, come on Max, that's such a knee-jerk reaction. Of course it is. Possible."

"You and I? Family? I...it's... You're my brother?"

"Half. Half-brother."

Of course Trueman had been correct. The likeness was uncanny. Once you actually noticed, once you were ready to accept the possibility, however far removed it might seem.

It had taken Scanner a final drink to grab courage by the neck and push it in front of him. That had made it four doubles. It would be a lively talk show later tonight.

Joy had answered the door and immediately planted a kiss on his cheek. *Scan-ner, Scan-ner*, she had turned around unable to hide her excitement. Max exited one of the bedrooms and with a gorgeous girl on each arm, Scanner had entered the lavish Mandarin suite.

"You have been drinking."

"Yes, yes, but if anything, it paved the way for the revelation. Look for yourself, there is no denying the resemblance. It all starts to make sense, in some disturbing and at the same time delightful way. You meeting Lobsang for the first time at the airport. That surely was no coincidence. Why? Why has he held out on me for that long? If it is indeed true. We need to question your dad. How is he?"

"He's sleeping. He seems fine. He talked a little to me, earlier. Thank you, thank you so much. I've not had much of a chance to tell you how grateful I am. And now this. No more client relation bullshit. Thank you... Brother."

Max threw her arms around Scanner and hugged him long and hard. Joy, seated on the other side of him, followed suit. It was difficult to breathe but Scanner couldn't care less. *So this is how it feels,* he thought, *coming home.*

LIGHT MY FIRE

For the best part of the next hour the three of them sat in silence, absorbed in thoughts that, had they been voiced, would have been remarkably similar. Yet the need to express themselves had evaporated together with the boundaries it had taken each of them a lifetime to construct. Scanner knew it was an all too rare moment of one-ness, three people plugged into the Gaian Overmind as Lobsang would have called it. Scanner had often, though never openly, dismissed his teacher's philosophy as new age fairy-tale – cut the crap and get real – bullshit and no doubt he would be justified to do so again on many future occasions. People were, for the most part, dark and predictable. But not at this moment. Right now he felt it too.

Max finally broke the spell.

"Let's go and speak to dad, I can't wait any longer."

She entered the bedroom first, while Scanner waited in the doorway.

"There you are, my little princess. I thought I was never going to see you again. I should have done my homework. You know they were selling shark fin. I was ready to pack up when I found out. I wanted to make a statement so you could be proud of me. But then…"

"Oh daddy, it's ok, it's all over now, we got you back, Scanner and I."

Max turned to the doorway and nodded for Scanner to enter. He drew up a chair next to her, beside the king-size bed on which Mr. Zwoelstra looked almost lost.

"Daddy, this is Scanner, Scanner GRANT."

She emphasized the last name. And waited.

The silence that followed spoke volumes and when Max's father at long last addressed them both, it was only to confirm what had become, to both Scanner and Max, abundantly clear.

"I have been waiting for this day to arrive for a long time. I am so sorry princess, I should have… I… I was afraid to lose you. I knew it was wrong, but I just couldn't bear to see you go. I need my… Where is my suitcase? Did you retrieve it, from that hellhole back there? It has a hidden compartment, behind the lining on the inside. Luckily that bastard never found it.

When I rescued you, that fateful day, and brought you down to the ship's infirmary, there was something your mother had hidden inside the tablecloth. Scanner, can you get it please, it belonged to your father."

***

"What is it?"

Max inspected the matchbox size metallic object Scanner had retrieved from her father's suitcase.

"It's a Zippo lighter. It was standard issue during the Vietnam War and for a lot of soldiers it became a talisman. They had it engraved with all sorts of texts and images; a proverb perhaps, or a favorite cartoon character, the name of a loved one, or something to remind them of home. Others chose something to symbolize the madness that engulfed them. Look!"

WHEN THE POWER OF
LOVE IS AS STRONG

AS THE LOVE OF
POWER THEN THERE
WILL BE PEACE

Max pronounced the salient text on the lighter's lid aloud. Another line, lower on the Zippo's body, read:

TOI YEU CO LAM

"That's Vietnamese for I love you Miss Lam."
Max flipped over the lighter and read:

NAM 72-73
J GRANT

After nearly three decades the Zippo still had the power to ignite a firestorm. It was as if the doors to an inner purgatory had suddenly burst open. Flames leapt and twirled and engulfed Scanner, not to consume him but to try and cleanse his cynical heart, burdened by guilt, hardened in that other, deadly fire that had ripped him away from what he had loved so unconditionally.

It was, by no means, an easy proposition, but if there would be anything up to the task it would have to be these few square inches of polished metal. His dad's lucky charm carried a message, like a tiny beacon of light beckoning from a distant horizon. It was time to set sail.

PART THREE
CHICAGO

INTOXICATION

"You knew?"

"I knew."

"When were you gonna tell me?"

"I wasn't. I couldn't. I promised your father."

"For Buddha's sake, Lobsang, she's my sister. I could have ended up in bed with her."

"Not enough time. Before the barley is fermented, *chang* tastes like *dzo's* pee Scanner. You know it and I know that you do. Besides, you have strong work ethics."

"Ethics have been known to shift occasionally, especially when a woman is involved."

"Would you? How about Sue?"

"Damn you Lobsang, leave her out of it. It's not about Sue or my relationship with her. Your loyalty to my father and the promises you made back then are commendable. On the other hand, you should not have withheld this information from me. It sucks."

"It would only have caused you more anguish, knowing you had a half-sister, but being totally in the dark when it came to her whereabouts. You see, I didn't know where Max was until the day I met her at the airport."

"You're serious?"

"Of course. That day I followed a hunch, a premonition as you might say. I'd like to call it inter-dimensional seeding.

221

An energy flow not bound by time or space was reaching out. We all have receptors you know, though in most of us they are culturally neutered, cut off courtesy of the sanctioned version of reality.

"Anyway I knew better than to dismiss the call, but it wasn't until I saw Max that I knew why I had to come to the airport that morning."

"Amazing story, Lobsang, and I do believe you. Which is not to say that you shouldn't have informed me. I do like to make my own decisions."

It was great to be back in the city. Surrounded by the familiar aroma of Lobsang's taxi, listening to his old friend's arguments, trying to find fault in his actions and always failing. Was it any more manipulative to withhold facts than it was to share them? *All in good time* his father used to say, *just keep your eyes open.* Scanner smiled. And your ears, your nose too, and don't forget your mind, he thought.

"Gotta quickly pass the apartment and drop my bags off. It's pretty late already. You'll drive me to my rendezvous after that? I guess you're right; I would have let Sue stop me, even though she would never object, actually more likely because she would never try to. She's working on a new case, did you know that? Sounded like monkey business to me. By the way, where's Cathy Lee?'

"She got a call this morning. Could she fill in for a colleague who called in sick? So she's off flying. A short trip, she'll be back tomorrow. We all can get together then."

"That'd be wonderful. She's an amazing woman, they seem to gravitate towards you, old man."

"That's why you're sticking with me aren't you? To see if some of my charm would rub you off."

Scanner laughed

"You should say rub off on you, but yeah it wouldn't hurt, I guess, as a back-up plan."

Lobsang decelerated the taxi to a stop in a quiet side street.

He pulled open the glove compartment and reached for a 12-oz plastic container.

"Before we proceed any further let's express our gratitude. Come, step out for a minute."

Nothing needed said. There was indeed a great deal to be grateful for. Scanner flicked a few drops in the air before emptying the shot glass in one, large swig.

"Aarrgh," he spit a mouthful on the pavement. 'That is absolutely disgusting, horrible. It's not done yet. This is rubbish, sorry, but you have to let it ferment longer man."

"Exactly," Lobsang laughed. "I knew you would say that. There was never any danger of you getting intoxicated by Max, at least not yet. And now, here's to family."

Lobsang retrieved a second bottle from the car. Scanner sipped cautiously of the milky white liquid. This was the real stuff, nothing he had ever brewed came close. He looked Lobsang in the eyes.

"You devious devil. Let's move. It's getting late."

Scanner slammed down the remaining contents of his glass and entered the taxi. Someone was dying to see him.

ITCHY

"So give me the lowdown on all that you've found out so far. Especially about Brian Webb. I don't know if Sue mentioned my hunch, but he must have had children. That's the link. That's why it's all returning."

"His records have all but vanished. I got a lot of *misplaced* excuses, which is, of course, agency talk for none of your fucking business. It's hard to believe that, after so many years, they continue to be this evasive. Unless they're still at it."

"And we know they are. Tony M is living proof of that. His relentless pursuit of The Priest Senior's diaries tells us."

"Yes, so until yesterday I was going nowhere. The girls blissfully oblivious, the restraining chair untraceable, collective intelligence amnesia amongst my connections. Then, this morning, as I was easing along Michigan Avenue during rush hour, someone tapped my window. Soon as I had it rolled down enough, an envelope came flying through. Looking up, I just managed to catch a glimpse of the bicycle courier zigzagging up the road."

"What was in the envelope?"

"Not much. An early Dachau camp record of Bruno Weber. There is a photograph of him and it lists his vital statistics, his unit and rank, but most significantly it says he was married to a female prison guard named Hildegard Koch."

"Children?"

"It doesn't say. But it's certainly a likely proposition."

"Anything about her?"

"Nothing. Just a photograph."

A meager result indeed, Scanner thought. Still, the appearance of the file meant that Lobsang had an unknown ally on the inside. Perhaps more information would be forthcoming.

The vibrating sensation emanating from his pocket caught Scanner off guard. He had switched on the phone after landing just in case Max needed to get hold of him. He hadn't expected her to call so soon, and as it turned out she didn't. It was Sue and she was in avalanche mode.

"Hey baby, you've landed on schedule, that's great. I spent last night in Madison, we needed to talk to a few more people today. It's so exciting, it's all connected, it's unbelievable, but we found stuff. You know the guy in the monkey suit right? It appears he is, uh, was working for one of the country's leading experts on behavior modification. We had a look at his lab. Horrible. You know they had all these monkeys there with electrical wires sticking out of holes in their skulls..."

"Whoa, whoa, calm down. Where are you? I thought we were going to meet."

"We are, we are. Oh baby, I am so excited. I am on the way to our place now, just dropped off a bunch of lab documents at the station. I will tell you everything, it's all connected in some macabre way. We found papers, shipping documents from Hong Kong, numbers that seemed to have been tampered with. We also found drugs, though the lab obviously had the required permits. The guy had received threats from the Animal Liberation Front, and it's likely they made good on them. And you know what, I am not supposed to say this, but I can totally understand why. To call these people animals is actually an insult to animals."

Sue was fired up. Could be a fun night, Scanner thought.

"Look, we'll meet soon and you can go over everything."

It was Scanners turn to wordplay.

"We will baby, don't you worry and don't make me wait too long."

"What was that all about?" Lobsang quizzed.

"The scientist, the one found dead at the zoo the other day, was experimenting on monkeys. Drilling holes in their heads and wiring them up, feeding them drugs. It's uncanny, isn't it. This can't be a coincidence."

Scanner and Lobsang continued their journey immersed in oppressive silence. Dreadful images, like endless waves swept up by a violent storm, rolled in relentlessly; unfolding a Technicolor kaleidoscope of horror neither one of them knew how to switch off. Relief arrived, at last, as the cab drew up in front of Scanner's apartment.

"I'll wait in the car while you carry your luggage inside. Say hi to Mrs. Kowalski, tell her I'll be at the club next weekend."

"Oh Mr. Grant, you're back. It is good to see you. You look well. Did you have a successful trip?"

Scanner knew the fragile concierge's observation to be false. But her intention was genuine and that, Scanner thought, was what counted.

"Yes, yes, all went well. Amazing city really, Hong Kong. But you know Mrs. Kowalski? There really is no place like home. It's good to see you keeping the fort."

Scanner bent down and gently kissed the aging Polish immigrant on her cheek.

"I thought so, seems I returned just in time. You went through that bottle pretty quick, didn't you? Still trying to charm those gentlemen at the club? I brought you something new. Should be an absolute hit that only a sucker would ignore. Here, this is for you."

"Oh, Mr. Grant, you're too kind to an old lady like me, you shouldn't have. Thank you so much. What is it?"

"It's called Rive Gauche, it's French. It's very flowery, which I think goes extremely well with the dresses you like to wear."

"Don't you make fun of my choice of fashion, young man. I like those floral patterns. I couldn't possibly wear the kind of outfits you want your women to sport, Mr. Grant."

Scanner couldn't agree more.

"Look Mrs. Kowalski, I've gotta go. My girl's waiting. Just keep my luggage here, will you? Lobsang's going to drive me there. He's parked in front. He says hello and he's looking forward to dancing with you at the club this coming weekend."

"You're such a bad liar, Mr. Grant. Really, did he say that? Oh, I nearly forgot, I need to tell you something that's been bothering me. You know, while you were away someone..."

"Can we continue the conversation when I come back? I am late already. Sorry, Mrs. Kowalski, I really need to go."

"I know, you've got an itch. Where I couldn't possibly scratch. Forty years ago, yes, I'd have no scruples with such a fine gentleman as you. Go on then and don't show your face here again if you fail to make her happy, lucky girl."

FACING THE MUSIC

"How is she?"

"You've gotta ask her yourself old man, you know that? She's fine. Said she really wanted to dance with a genuine gentleman such as you at the club this weekend so you'd better practice your moves. No good disappointing her."

"Nice try Scanner. Really, is that what she said? She's a sweet-talking woman. I used to be a fairly good dancer, did I ever tell you?"

More than once, Scanner thought.

"What, in Tibet?"

"No, no, at The Garden. We pretty much had to entertain ourselves. Secrecy was strictly enforced. There was no staff, we cooked for ourselves. I usually made momos, that's all I knew how to prepare. Your father taught me how to dance. We had an RCA record player and we listened to all the greats: The Count and Duke, Glen, Woody, Benny and Dizzy. Of course, in the absence of women, we had to rotate. That, believe it or not, actually was the key to rising above the pack. Put yourself in someone else's shoes, literally in our case, and you'll learn to appreciate their point of view. The team effort was much better for it."

Lobsang stared ahead into the night, as the ghosts from Camp Hale took their nostalgic Blues to the dimly lit streets in full big band line-up. It was blazingly obvious, the hold Dumra still exercised, all those decades since.

"We better get moving, Lobsang, Sue should be there shortly, if not already."

Lobsang nodded silently and put the taxi in gear. The car edged away from the curb and its driver turned over his shoulder towards Scanner.

"You're right, it's time to dance. I can see you're in the mood to do right."

He sure was. How long since the last time they were together? So much had transpired in the days past that he found it hard to recall that last passionate encounter, but judging by the intense longing now so fiercely consuming Scanner's heart, the separation had been much too long.

**

Despite his efforts to stealthily ascend, the wooden staircase squeaked with more gusto than a JAV starlet on nitrous oxide. Perhaps it was genuinely excited that Scanner was back; its steps urging him upwards, spurring him on to the third floor rodeo and his own fiery cowgirl.

Pausing briefly on the second floor landing, Scanner suddenly found himself engulfed in music. The entire hotel had been transformed into a giant stage on which a full orchestra was getting ready to perform. A violin yielded to sensual stroking behind the door nearest to him while in the next room a horn loudly heralded someone's imminent arrival. Further down the corridor an ardent percussionist banged the timpani to a rumbling crescendo before stopping abruptly, only to restart the buildup a few seconds later. It was, for the most part, a pleasing and stimulating harmonic symphony Scanner thought, though the occasional false note escaping in a muffled staccato defined it as a practice session; the undress rehearsal for the Wiener Philharmonic. Sue would appreciate the pun.

Barely able to contain his own artistic desire, Scanner raced up the next flight two steps at a time. The door to room 304 stood slightly ajar. Sue, no doubt, would be on full alert, crouched down behind the door and hopefully, by now, equally ravenous and ready to devour him whole.

"Smell this you creep!"

The words were the usual, the voice rang a bell too but it wasn't Sue's. Besides, she couldn't possibly have gained this much weight.

Scanner tried to shake off his attacker. He was such an idiot. Blinded by his desire for the woman he loved, he had run straight into a trap. How pathetic. All the twisting and turning failed to thwart his powerful, unknown assailant. Just before succumbing to the potent anesthetic, Scanner confronted his sorry reflection mirrored in the opposite wall. Defeated, for real this time. By… No, this was not possible. He caught a glimpse of a familiar Bavarian blond.

"Hilde?"

Milky way and monkey business

Dozens of Friesians levitated about six feet above the spring green meadow, like four-legged black and white spotted zeppelins. Scanner wondered whether this was due to a malfunctioning metabolism or had someone actually suspended gravity? Whatever the cause, the result greatly facilitated milking them the traditional way. He sauntered towards the nearest floating bovine. Right now, nothing would please him more than to squeeze the pinkish two-inch teats protruding from the full, Rubenesque udders hovering in front of his eyes. He didn't have a whole lot of experience with farm work, which was not to say that he didn't know a thing or two about teats.

"Go on then, there's no reason to feel embarrassed," Max encouraged him. "You should get to know the family business first hand."

Scanner needed to get accustomed to this new reality and now was as good a time as any to start the familiarization. So he stretched out his hands and cupped two of the massive udders. She sure was warm blooded, he thought.

"Not like that, Casanova," Max laughed. "It's all in the teats, squeeze them gently in a downward motion and the milk will flow freely."

It just wasn't his day. As soon as he touched the cow's nipple she took off to the sky, like a child's balloon let loose and propelled by a big fat noisy fart. Luckily for Scanner, the animal's exhaust fumes turned out to be odorless. Soon the sky was swarming with flatulating Holstein Friesians, buzzing in a mad directionless dance. Teats started lactating and in a rare moment of existential clarity, Scanner grasped all there was to know about the origins of the Milky Way.

"Stop monkeying around," Sue exclaimed, which, to Scanner seemed kinda odd as his girlfriend was the one sporting a headless monkey suit.

He was inside a laboratory room now. Devoid of furniture except for the walls stacked ceiling high with little glass cubicles. Biology had never been Scanner's strongest subject but he did recognize some of the species on display: a bewildered rhesus monkey held Scanner's stare unblinkingly, an impressive feat he thought, until he spotted the permanently clipped open eyelids. The majority of animals were macaques, all strapped into miniature restraining chairs facing the front of their glass box. It reminded Scanner of a picture he had seen once, in one of the glossies, of a temple carving somewhere in Asia: hundreds of little Buddhas serenely contemplating existence. Humans sure had come a long way meditating.

A white-coated scientist hunched over an enormous control panel in the middle of the room. His moves resembled a crazed DJ mixing psychedelic trance tunes at an all-night rave; feverishly turning knobs and shifting levers, manipulating his wired-up primate audience according a master plan only he was privy to.

Though the man's face remained obscured, Scanner recognized the spinmeister from a previous trip. It was the same man who had been watching him from the shadows earlier, with Max and the Indian Disco Dicks. The same man who had been watching him all this time. All his life. The same.

Scanner strained to lift his head and raise the heavy curtain that blanketed his drugged out brain cells. Reality was, if anything, a state of mind.

"He's coming to dad," Hilde announced somewhere in the distance.

SEEING THE LIGHT

Scanner had no idea exactly how long he had been under. For the second time in a week, he found himself utterly incapacitated. Unlike in Macau, his current predicament, the direct result of a severe bout of amorous myopia, frightened him. He had no plan B, hell, he hadn't even contemplated a plan A. Perhaps he ought to retire and take care of the farm, if he were given the opportunity. Objectively assessed, that seemed a very big if.

No one could possibly have the slightest clue where he was. No one would even start wondering for at least another eight hours. Max was either in Hong Kong preparing for her departure or somewhere over the Pacific, Lobsang had just dropped him off, Cathy Lee was not due back till tomorrow. The only other person aware of Scanner's rendezvous was Mrs. Kowalski but she had long since stopped raising the alarm whenever he failed to show up for a few days.

For all the world knew, Scanner had temporarily transcended the mundane in the arms of the only woman capable of accomplishing this. Who would dare to disrupt their ecstatic journey?

But where was Sue? Dread instantly vanquished the stubborn remnants of mental inertia that lingered in his head in the wake of the retreating drug. He came down hard.

"Sue! Where are you?" Scanner's panic-stricken voice filled

the void. "What have you done to her? By god, I swear if anything happens to her I'll kill you. I'll kill you all!"

He had yet to get formally acquainted with his abductors, so it seemed best to stick to the plural.

"And how exactly would you accomplish that, pathetic loverboy?"

Hilde appeared from the shadows and leaned forward over the gurney-strapped Scanner, her face mere inches from his. Had it been more than just a dream earlier, he wondered? Max's assistant had shed her secretary image together with almost everything else and replaced it with a black leather... what exactly was it? To call the miniscule strips of charcoal colored tanned cow skin accentuating Hilde's abundant curves a dress, one would have to rewrite the dictionary. His female assailant had put the heat back in hot pants while simultaneously scaling new heights with her push up brassiere.

"If you thought you and your officer had it bad you should try me. You and I, we'd go places you never even knew existed."

By now Hilde had climbed the gurney and straddled Scanner at knee level. She straightened her elbows and pushed her palms into his inner thighs. A calculated move no doubt, as it required her to angle forward from the hips and advance her mammary assets even further towards a full ocular eclipse.

Where do they learn this stuff? Scanner wondered. It was both kinky as hell and calculatingly cold.

"Hiking stark naked across the arctic in mid-winter during an ice blizzard would be infinitely more appealing. You're not my type. WHERE IS SUE?"

"Looks like a part of you disagrees lover boy. A *substantial* part."

The black spotted cowgirl was right of course. Mind over matter. It continued to be a struggle. The spirit was willing but the flesh was..., well, speaking in a metaphysical way at least, weak.

"Tell you what darling, if you unstrap me I'll do my very best to convince you. I promise I'll make it quick."

For a moment, eyes sparkling with obvious glee, Hilde contemplated the challenge.

"What makes you think you're a match?"

"Bravo, bravo. Mr. Grant, you do not disappoint me. Hilde, my dear, that's enough. Dismount! Now! Let's put Mr. Grant in a more comfortable, upright position, so we can see eye to eye."

It was him. Without an ounce of doubt. Hiding in the shadow, like always. Scanner didn't have to see to know. He felt the same eerily familiar presence.

"Do excuse the rather theatrical display of my eh, relative, Mr. Grant. Or may I call you Scanner? Such an appropriate name for a man with your qualities, wouldn't you say? I feel like I've known you forever though eh, circumstances never allowed us to be properly introduced. It's such a pleasure to finally meet you."

Someone adjusted the gurney to a seating position and switched on two rows of fluorescent ceiling lights. The instant brilliance, bouncing off every tiled and polished surface in the room, practically blinded Scanner. When, seconds later, he opened his eyes again, the voice had materialized and stood, bathing in overwhelming brightness, a mere foot away from Scanner.

Impressive, Scanner thought, a revelation executed to perfection. The Priest would have approved of the theatrics, but Scanner wasn't ready to be star struck by the man's messianic illusions and neither did he care to contemplate redemption, at least not his own.

"And you are?"

COOK'S KITCHEN

"Yes, yes, of course, forgive me my rudeness. Ralph, Ralph Cook."

The lanky scientist looked older than the photographic likeness Scanner remembered and was about a foot taller than he had assumed, but there was no mistaking his identity. Second generation German immigrant. The background checks Scanner had been hired to run. Cook. Where else had he come across that name?

Scanner's brain fired on all synapses as he attempted to process what he had learned so far; files he'd read, conversations he'd had or overheard. What was it Sue had said? *It's all connected.*

"What I can't quite fathom yet, Mr. Cook, or may I call you Webb, Ralph Webb or perhaps you prefer Weber, Rudolf most likely? What I am wondering is whether your audacity is merely stupidity parading as cockiness or do you honestly believe you can get away with abducting those girls and murdering Dolma? And now Sue?"

Might as well be the bull in the china shop, Scanner thought. There would be no other way out than through verbal brinkmanship. Maybe, just maybe, if he could keep the man occupied long enough someone might be able to figure out what had happened.

"But I am, Scanner…"

Ralph Cook stepped forward and leaned on the gurney. Scanner much preferred the other cook's aroma.

"…Getting away with it. You obviously have connected the known dots leading back to my father. But are you aware that I am also the psychiatrist assigned by the various school boards to evaluate the girls' health? There is hardly a better way to ascertain the validity of my experiments wouldn't you say so?"

Scanner only nodded. He was aware now. That was where he'd read the name.

"I must applaud your powers of deduction. Of course I always knew you would eventually discover the truth, perhaps not this soon, but that doesn't really matter now, does it? You're hardly in a position to cause me any trouble with your recently acquired gnosis. This then begs the following question: what do you really know if you're the only one who knows it? And wouldn't you be so much better off to not know? Imagine being able to choose what stays and what gets erased. Who wouldn't want that opportunity? For a start, there'd be no more reason to chastise yourself over anything, no more oppressive guilt complex keeping you awake at night. Sleep lost over the what-ifs and should-haves. You'd finally be free to reach your full potential. And when you screw up, as we all do occasionally – though some are more naturally inclined fuckups than others – the right treatment will unburden you and set you free once again."

"You had to permanently erase Dolma, you fucked up, just like your father. Did you rape her before or after? And what did you do to Sue?"

"On the contrary, one out of six? Are you kidding? That's an incredibly low casualty rate, considering the variables. We wasted a lot more monkeys when we first started out years ago. They don't come cheap, do you know that, Scanner? And their trade is considerably more scrutinized; non-human primates don't just cross international borders by themselves, with a ticket and a fake work permit or a marriage certificate. Besides, just about every monkey out there has an NGO campaigning on its behalf. Save the gorilla, save the orangutan, the chimpanzee.

Have you ever noticed that we humans are never quite so motivated when it comes to saving our own species? Why is that, do you think? Freeing yes, all the time. Government policy. Free the Tibetans, free the Koreans, the Cubans, the Vietnamese. We gladly accept casualties as long as they die while we try to liberate them. Collateral damage, a rather poignant phrase isn't it? I ask you, what is the collateral for? What's a few dead bodies in the grand scheme of things?"

The scientist's rhetoric was intoxicating. Scanner generally agreed with the diagnosis of human mental bondage, though not with the prescription Ralph Cook proposed. Top-down liberation would always lead to oppression by a different master. It was just too tempting not to take advantage of the innate insecurity and vulnerability of those subjects looking towards leaders as a source of inspiration and redemption. The desire had to come from within. To expect or even wish a doctor, a teacher, a guru or a government to deliver would doom the entire enterprise from the start.

"What did you do to Sue?"

"Nothing harmful. I'm sorry, I understand your anxiety, but your lady friend is fine. She had to undergo a few minor attitude adjustments, what one of my dear mentors used to call depatterning. All for her own good of course. It's amazing what a bit of probing can accomplish – and the drugs of course. The alternative would be rather more dreadful, as she got a bit too close for her own comfort, and for ours, I should add. The Wisconsin National Primate Research Center should have erased those records when I told them to.

"Try to look at it from a positive angle Scanner, isn't that your forte? You and her can get reacquainted all over again. All very exciting, don't you think?"

"Just like the first time, loverboy, I bet just thinking about it makes you hard. Let's hope for your sake she takes a liking to you, again," Hilde chimed in.

"Nooo, you bastards, you didn't, you manipulating psychopathic Nazi head fucks," Scanner screamed at the top of his lungs, "I'll kill you both. You're dead. I'll spoon out your sick brains and feed them to the primates at Lincoln Park Zoo."

Staring into the face of the animal inside scared the shit out of Scanner. He hadn't seen that one coming. A destructive shockwave of raw anger ripped through his mind, an emotional tsunami, tearing and shredding and obliterating in an instant the precious few safe havens it had taken Lobsang and him years to construct. Once again he curled up in his dad's Maverick, shaking uncontrollably, the door blasted shut this time, no way out. Why hadn't he accompanied his father inside that day? Life would have turned out so much better.

Get a hold of yourself Scanner. Now.

Losing Sue was not an option he had ever entertained. Could not. He had to get through this, if only to make good on his promises.

"Why don't you let me help you forget her? Can you see now how that would be a desirable procedure?"

"I'd like to help too," Hilde offered.

"What makes you think you can change my mind, even if I wanted?"

"Because, my dear Scanner, I already have."

GAME

"My father was an extraordinary man, a true visionary who realized early on in his life that power didn't advance through the barrel of a gun, but rather flourished with the ability to harness one's psyche against unwanted intrusion while simultaneously gaining full access to other people's minds. Military might, in his vision, was a blunt manifestation of what was essentially mental incompetence. Only necessary insofar as it would allow for the natural progression towards a grand psychic order, a society benevolently ruled by guardians, exceptionally gifted minds with the power to directly influence and instruct those lesser humans not sufficiently developed to be trusted with making their own decisions.

"Not exactly a revolutionary thought. After all one can argue that the third chapter of Genesis documents the first attempt at selective mind control, one that my father ardently pursued to its logical conclusion. It was my father's manifest destiny to become an explorer of man's inner terra incognita and in that capacity he covertly partook in Himmler's Tibet Expedition.

"The turbulent years that followed proved exceptionally fertile for scientists in Germany and incredible advances were made in my father's field. Yet all of that would have ultimately amounted to very little if not for the foresight exhibited by certain high ranking US government officials after the war.

"As a boy, I was completely unaware of my father's activities. All I knew, and proudly expressed whenever I was asked, was that he was doing important work for the government. Not unlike your situation, am I correct?"

Scanner wondered where this was going.

"What do you know about my life?"

"Everything there is to know, Scanner. When my father died I was only fourteen. I don't need to describe the rage, the feelings of abandonment and despair that consumed me, do I? You see, though we've never met, I often think of you as my little brother. Ours is a bond stronger than blood, which, after all, is merely an involuntary connection."

"You don't say. Nice way to treat your family."

"Yes, yes, I do apologize. Yours is only a temporary restraint, for your own good. I figured it would take some work to get my point across."

"Damn right, you're mad. You and I have nothing in common."

"Winters. The Bucks. We're rooting for the same team. Always have. Hilde my dear, can you get Scanner some water? He looks a bit dehydrated, and then please go and see if Don has made any progress with the girl."

Which Don, Scanner wondered.

"Which Don?"

There was, of course, only one possible answer. Scanner closed his eyes and watched in horror as the last imaginary lifeline slipped from his trembling hands. Only his willpower could keep him afloat now, as dark waves of amnesia assembled on the horizon and threatened to pull him under once and for all. Don Cockburn, Sue's partner. He had been part of it all along. Now there really would be no one coming to the rescue.

"Now, where were we? Ah, yes, the game. You're not the only one who remembers April 30, 1978. I too, wouldn't have missed game six of the playoffs for anything in the world."

PARADISE LOST

"What do you know about April 30?"

"We'll get to that, don't worry. All in good order and in due time. Not until I was eighteen did I fully understand what had driven my father to commit suicide. When I finally got to read his diary, the desperation, like a highly contagious super virus, infected my every thought. I resolved to make it right, to correct the dreadful mistake my father had made in Tibet, whatever it would take.

He should have killed that girl immediately, erased the error he committed in a rare unguarded moment of weakness. Instead of drawing *shakti* from the *Karma Mudra* during the Tantric rituals, my father was robbed of all he had accomplished the instant the girl absorbed his semen. He did wipe clean her memory, using a rather primitive though surefire method I must say, a compromise with the monastery, but the baby girl she birthed annulled that desperate attempt.

It was too late to make amends. The war had started and Tibet became inaccessible. All my father's efforts never returned him to the height of his powers. So he signed up for Operation St. Circus as his last chance for redemption, if only he could find his child. Your father, Scanner, and that Tibetan friend of his, Lobsang, denied him that chance."

A chance for what? Scanner thought. To snuff out another mind and destroy another life? Scanner had met a plethora of despicable nasties in the course of his career, but this cold and evil motherfucker occupied a realm all by himself. If Ralph Cook ever discovered the identity of Cathy Lee… Where was she? Lobsang had said she was filling in for a colleague. Scanner prayed that was the truth. Prayed she stayed away, never to meet the devil's henchman.

"I have been watching you from the day you were born, Scanner. Your father and Lobsang made me an orphan. I swore revenge on my dad's grave. I studied hard and worked my way into the agency. My father never revealed to anyone the game-changing scientific advances he had made during the war. Not even to bargain his way into the US. Now I am encouraged to carry on with his legacy."

"Your father was a cold blooded murderer, a manipulating psychopath who got what was coming. And you are the same and…"

"Scanner, Scanner, you need to see the larger picture here. To control the minds of their subjects is every self-respecting government's Holy Grail. A benevolent dictator's wet dream. What are a few wasted minds in exchange for the real opportunity to build a peaceful world? A world where everyone is content with his or her allocated place. You can join me as we establish the vanguard of a new world order, now that we realize Shambala is not a physical place, but a state of mind. A mind that we are on the verge of controlling. In the meantime, as we are not yet able to make people consistently do what we want them to do, we focus on making them forget. That way WE can do what we want. Selective amnesia is a much easier proposition, especially since it is what most people long for in the first place. Either way, full control will be ours eventually.

And once we have achieved that, wars will become archaic aberrations. Imagine all the money freed to erase poverty; finally everybody on this planet can lead a productive life. Paradise is only an alteration away."

Scanner didn't care much for the deranged psychiatrist's version of paradise. It was far too damned cold for him.

"There is no you and I, and there never will be. Nothing forcefully gained is worth having, and that includes love and loyalty, and other such human qualities you would not possibly be familiar with."

Ralph Cook drew up a chair next to Scanner's gurney.

"What will it take to convince you my position is the correct one? You believe that circumstances shaped you into who you are now. No one would disagree. But have you ever asked yourself who created the circumstances?

"I realized early on I would never be able to manipulate Lobsang's mind into telling me what he knew about my father's bastard girl, but I was desperate to find out what I could. After all, that girl had stolen my birthright. As a mixed breeding abomination, it would be highly unlikely she would develop those powers, but why take that chance? I needed to find her and stop her once and for all.

"Unfortunately, your mother couldn't tell me all that much either. I did manage to extract from her the existence, if not the whereabouts of your half-sister. Why on earth your father had volunteered that simple transgression beats me to this day. From what I gathered, the woman was nothing but a stupid Vietnamese whore, certainly not worth the domestic aggravation.

"It is very possible I would have found out more, but well, you know what happened. I had no time to clean up properly so I had to improvise. It seemed best to leave no trace before leaving to watch the Bucks' victory."

Ralph Cook sighed. "You see now how much we have in common?"

"You… You killed them, you killed them both. You… I…"

Scanner thrashed around like a wrongfully convicted death row inmate seconds from receiving his lethal injection. If granted a stay, he would use the chance to make sure he didn't go down an innocent man. Startled, Ralph Cook jumped up from his seat and plunged a needle deep into Scanner's shoulder.

"Relax my dear Scanner, surrender is inevitable, it's up to you how hard you want to make it."

For the second time that night, Scanner crossed the threshold into chemically induced oblivion, his mind a pressure cooker bursting with evaporating expletives. This time though, he greedily embraced the dark embryonic void that welcomed him to the other side.

MUSICAL CHAIRS

Ten outward facing Benjamin Rush chairs formed a neat circle in the middle of the circus ring. Ten people had taken up positions along the outer periphery. Scanner recognized them all, but only five he knew by name: his father and mother, Lobsang, Sue, and Dolma. The five remaining girls matched their file pictures, though they behaved a lot less animated than the black and white headshots would suggest. It looked like photography had indeed robbed them of their spirit.

The loud commanding crack of Hilde's whip edged the reluctant performers forward, barely noticeably. A dark and palpable dread saturated the air, inversely matched by the gleeful enthusiasm of the leather-clad mistress in the center of the spectacle. It was obvious that Hilde enjoyed being in control.

A second crack echoed around the arena and everybody sat down simultaneously. Dozens of monkeys entered the ring through the back door and carried off all but one of the chairs.

"Bravo, bravo!"

Somewhere in the grandstand a single pair of hands clapped approval. Scanner looked up. It was him again. Ralph Cook descended and stepped out of the shadows. He no longer had the need to hide his identity as the puppet master.

"You see Scanner, almost everyone has capitulated. Dead

or alive. Their choice, really. Join me. Join Hilde, she'll be everything you'll ever desire and more. Forget your past, it's only keeping you shackled. Erase your sadness. Come with me, come."

The magnetism of the psychiatrist's voice soothed Scanner's worn down mind. What would it matter? How often had he envied those whose ignorance kept them in a permanent state of bliss? Why couldn't he be like them? How tempting it was, to wake up with a clean slate, expecting nothing from life but the frequent opportunity to copulate and to accumulate as many gadgets as possible, thereby substantially increasing those sought after instances of getting laid. After all, nobody liked a poor fuck.

"Stay strong Scanner, you're not the only one resisting. What about Max? She's counting on you."

Lobsang's familiar voice rang out and penetrated the twilight zone of Scanner's retreating hallucination. Was Scanner's trusted friend really there? It was both a reassuring and a frightening scenario. If Lobsang had been captured, he would be in grave danger. Ralph Cook had a rapacious appetite for revenge.

"Shut up old man. One more word and I'll perform a full frontal on you right now. Heck, I should do it anyway since you're not likely to change your mind voluntarily. I've been waiting for a chance to probe that righteous brain of yours. Hilde! Donald! Come over here will you, and bring the tools, I think it is time for a Lobsangotomy."

"Don't you fucking dare touch him. Don't you…"

In a desperate attempt to obliterate the nightmarish visions tormenting him, Scanner willed his eyes open. The image of his Tibetan friend, rather than dissolving, appeared in front of him with heart stopping clarity. *Lobsang, oh god, what have you done?*

Lobsang smiled and seemed to slightly nod his approval at Scanner's return to the real world. Or maybe Scanner only imagined the miniscule movement to reassure himself. It really was hard to tell, now that Benjamin Rush had the ageing Tibetan master firmly in his grip.

"Leave him alone, he is harmless. I'll do what you want, I'll surrender, if you let him go"

"How touching. Each of you volunteering to save the other. Didn't the old man use the exact same words when you found him, Hilde?"

"Verbatim father, uncanny isn't it? The night shift guy at that seedy love hotel called me right away that someone was sniffing around. It's been such a great night and there is more; you've got to hear what Don just pulled out of that cop bitch."

There was no way Lobsang would let himself get caught, Scanner thought. Unless he wanted to. Unless he had a plan.

LIGHT

"That's fantastic news. It's… I can't believe it. All these years. Not a trace. And now… Finally all that surveillance has paid off. Nothing can stop us now. It's obvious, isn't it? Hiding in plain sight. My gut feeling was right, to hospitalize that old hag of a secretary and get you into that cheesy office. Hilde, my dear, do you realize what this means? I'm about to claim what is mine."

"And what is mine too, right, father?"

"Well, technically, hmmm, not quite, but we'll get to that some other time. It is of utmost importance to capture the girl and bring her here. Have you managed to locate her yet?"

"Yes father, ever since she showed up with the old man a few days ago, we've been keeping an eye on her – call it a premonition if you will. We even arranged for a flight attendant to get sick yesterday so we could separate her and her uncle; put her on a flight out of the area. Right now, she's on her way back. About to land, actually. Two of our agent contacts will quietly escort her over here. They sounded pretty psyched, about you reaching full potential. It will definitely make the next budget allocation to the foundation a no-brainer."

"Well done Hilde dear, you truly have your grandmother's genes. The agency, on the other hand, really is made up of a bunch of penny pinchers, all of them. Not everything in life is quantifiable you know. Isn't that right, Scanner?"

Scanner thought it wise not to agitate the crazed scientist again. Right now, more than anything, he needed his wits about him. Provoking another drug-induced blackout would be counter-productive. Ralph Cook's quest to reclaim Bruno Weber's lost psychic powers was about to culminate in the imminent capture and likely termination of Cathy Lee, one of the five women alive he really cared about. Lobsang's and his own fate wasn't likely to be any rosier.

"Like family, for god's sake man, that girl's mother is your sister. What are you going to do to her?"

"Half. Half-sister. And a far inferior half at that. Whatever it takes. Believe me, I'll be doing mankind a favor."

For the first time since his capture, Scanner wondered where exactly they were being held. Maybe there would be a way out. There had to be a way out. Darkness had thus far obscured those parts of the location beyond the reach of the ceiling lights, a very limited reach, as it turned out to be.

The place was huge. High above Scanner, perhaps fifty feet overhead, a faint orange glow peeked through dust covered windowpanes, two off-center rows of which ran across the full length of the curved roof. Like a novice swimmer getting wet feet on the edge of the deep end, the dawning day hesitated before taking the plunge.

Once committed though, there was no turning back. Streaks of morning light jumped through the fuzzy windows, projecting slowly descending search light ovals on the brick wall to his right. It reminded Scanner of the Jacob's ladders he'd loved to look for with his father after a rainstorm had passed. Would they be able to get him out of this hellhole?

They were in some kind of warehouse or abandoned factory. Plenty of those around Chicago. The stripped interior provided no clue as to its original purpose. What Scanner had earlier taken for the ceiling were in fact rows of fluorescent armatures suspended from long steel rods. The roughly five hundred square foot area they had illuminated throughout the night was but a small raised island in the centre of a vast tiled floor, spread across which were at least a dozen similar, non-elevated work stations. Scanner noticed gurneys and dissecting tables, even the occasional Benjamin Rush chair. Was that Sue in the far corner, strapped, motionless?

"Do you like my kitchen Scanner? Courtesy of the US government and the people's insatiable appetite for cheap goods, there is no shortage of suitable accommodation to conduct our experiments. The Far East is flooding us with substandard products, have you noticed? Wal-Mart is full of it and we love it. But over here the factories close and the jobs disappear, and even at bargain basement prices the Chinese made crap will become too expensive. Still people dream of coming to the US, can you believe it? Such is the illusion we have projected around the world.

That's what I love about this country; there is an almost infinite supply of inferior people for my experiments. No need to monkey around with primates and all the animal activists. I mean, the current air of general stupefaction benefits us, but change is coming, it is inevitable, and we will be on the forefront, the vanguard of the new order, filled with purity of purpose."

Let the guy ramble on with his fascist crap, Scanner thought, time was running out. He looked at Lobsang. His Tibetan friend didn't seem the least bit perturbed by the situation. If it wasn't for Lobsang's interference earlier, Scanner's mind might have capitulated by now, surrendering to the alluring promise of amnesia Ralph Cook had dangled in front of him.

Lobsang exuded calmness only a fool would mistake for resignation. What did his teacher know? Would anyone come to the rescue?

"Look Scanner", he whispered barely audible, "It's getting light."

It was by far the most trivial statement Scanner had heard

Lobsang make in a long time, but because his old friend was anything but, it offered Scanner the reassurance he had so desperately searched for.

TERMINAL

On the face of it, Ralph Cook's version of Block Number Five was no different from any other medical college lab Scanner had seen. If anything, this place felt distinctly underfunded. The absence of sophisticated equipment beyond the occasional microscope communicated "rudimentary", the ubiquitous white ceramic tiles and stainless steel surfaces said "anatomy", a spider web of gutters that connected all work stations and converged at an oversized drain near the centre of the room, screamed "murder".

The only access to the psychiatrist's morbid playground was through a small steel door in what Scanner deducted to be the Southeast corner. If indeed the light coming through the atrium windows belonged to the morning.

The vastness of the space and the glass-clad vaulted ceiling reminded Scanner of the Great Hall at Union Station. Unlike Chicago's famous landmark, no one came here to travel. A terminal in the truest sense of the word, Scanner thought, even the light balked at entering, afraid of getting snuffed.

Make no small plans, they have no magic to stir men's blood, wasn't that what the architect of Union Station had said? Ralph Cook definitely had megalomaniacal plans but he was merely serving his paymasters. The blood he stirred ran down the gutter all the way to Washington. Hadn't it always been that way? No matter how well it was packaged, wrapped in flag and religion; it was still the same old dirty blood-soaked shit it had always been. The hubris of the powerful knew no limits. The public was, for the most part, kept paralyzed by fear and placated by toys.

Scanner seldom gave in to fear. Fear was reserved for those who had something to lose. After his parents' deaths, he had constructed a wall around his emotions, refused to let anyone enter. Without attachments, the fear would never return.

Lobsang had been the first to slip through the cracks and make Scanner realize his fear of separation was in essence a fear of living. If you want to take control of your life, Lobsang had taught him, accept the necessity of transition. Without relying on wings, the golden eagle can soar to even greater heights. Or something like that.

But this was different. The two people Scanner had let closest to his scarred heart were in mortal danger. By all accounts, Sue was no longer the woman he knew and Lobsang, in spite of all his wisdom and talk about flight, sat opposite him, severely shackled and restrained. Cathy Lee would be next. *The necessity of transition.* No fucking way, Scanner thought, not as long as I'm alive. But how? What could he do? What cruel fate had brought him here? Front seat, death row.

Once more, Scanner sought Lobsang's help in stemming the encroaching tide of terror for which his mental defenses, however shored up they might have been, would be no match.

"Never doubt the power of flight, Scanner," his Tibetan friend muttered cryptically.

***

"They're here, father, they're here!"

Hilde's excited voice snapped Scanner out of his oppressive revelry. In the far corner of the lab, Don Cockburn pulled open the solid steel door and let in the captured stewardess, flanked by two standard issue agents, suits, sunglasses, earpieces, the whole shebang.

"At long last, the blemish on my father's record shall be erased." Ralph Cook announced. "The power, of which he was so callously robbed, will return to me, and unlike this racially mixed fuckup, I actually know what to do with it. Let's get on with it, we've wasted too much time already."

FLIGHT AND FIGHT

Cathy Lee's composure exuded calmness on par with Lobsang's stoic serenity. Still dressed in her in-flight uniform, she made no attempt at resisting her two captors. Scanner knew what she was capable of, having seen the black belt and the trophies in her apartment. Judging by the nonchalant way her chaperones held on to the stewardess's arms, her martial arts prowess hadn't made it into the Agency's database.

Ralph Cook, on the other hand, made no effort to hide his growing excitement. Last time Scanner had witnessed a grown man practically come in his pants from anticipation was at the races, with Stuart.

"Yes, yes, hold her there, so I can get a good look. Hmmm, at least you don't look like him, that's a relief. How old are you now? Thirty-one, right? That's almost twice what I am used to. I'm afraid I can't do this the pleasurable way, which is likely a good thing though, since you'd probably manage to fuck me over just like your grandmother did my father. The question then, really, is how much do I need to make you forget and is it worth the effort? What do you think Hilde? Or shall we just dispose of her right away?"

"No, no, that would be such a waste, father. She's so pretty, let me have my way with her first."

Ralph Cook's daughter stepped forward to within inches of Cathy Lee's face.

"I promise, it'll be an experience you'll want to remember for the rest of your life, however short it might be."

Hilde's black lacquered fingernails sensuously caressed the flight attendant's motionless face and, after lingering a few seconds over Cathy Lee's curvy and voluptuous mouth, parted her red glossed lips by playfully rolling down the lower half. Hesitating an instant for dramatic effect, the Bavarian mistress seemed to contemplate a delicate nibble or perhaps a full-on French adventure, before deciding against either and retreating one step, curved tongue trailing the full length of her own parted lips instead.

"Yeah, baby."

The agent on the right shifted legs, maybe more. The colleague on the left flexed his head backwards, struggling to breathe against the choking tightness of a collar starched to kill. The job had its perks.

Don Cockburn looked appropriately bored. He'd seen it all and was just here to augment his rapidly approaching pension, and to keep the wife happy.

"What you gaping at, dickheads?!" Hilde lashed out. "Don't get any ideas. I'm way above your pay grade. You think you're sexy? You're not. You've got to have brains for that. You don't, you follow orders."

Hilde turned to face Ralph Cook.

"It's not my day, father. I'm surrounded by horny robots and limp old farts. The only man up to the task is foolishly committed to a woman who's forgotten all about him. I need some fun, let me have her, please."

For once Scanner found the Teutonic dominatrix slightly agreeable, her tirade uncannily Max-like, albeit in a different context. He missed his younger sister. Their current predicament could do with an infusion of Max's no holds barred youthfulness, her gung-ho approach to conflict resolution. He had run out of viable options a while back; since the ambush at the hotel yesterday.

Lobsang still seemed to believe escape from the beast's claws was possible, if not imminent. But that was Lobsang, a man who no doubt would label his own death auspicious.

There, that awful smell again.

"Alright then Hilde dear, you truly take after my mother, if dad's diary is even halfway accurate. I'm so glad I followed his instructions."

"What instructions, father?" Hilde seemed puzzled.

LIMP OLD FARTS. That's what it was, Scanner thought, someone was having a seriously bad stomach day. The stench was getting stronger, almost unbearable really. Surely, he was not the only one noticing.

"Oh, eh, I'll explain some other day, dear. I eh… What? I can't believe it, you fucking barbarians. You know I hate this, why do you have to come in here and stink up the place? It's fucking disgusting. If there's one thing I detest above all else it's some punk polluting my lab. It's one of the reasons I was glad the monkeys were gone, and now this. Who? Who of you? Get out! Before I terminate your miserable, flatulating existence!"

The agency twins turned to each other and shook their heads in synchronized denial. All eyes settled on Don now as the most likely chemical warfare agent.

"Who? Muh-muh me?" he stammered barely audible, not accustomed to being on the receiving end of flying accusations.

Scanner watched the unfolding drama with increasing glee. It played out just as Lobsang had said it would, back when the boy Scanner loved to listen to his tall spy stories. It was, in other words, all part of the plan.

***

Ralph Cook continued fuming, consumed by olfactory rage.

"I want you gone, OUT. You are contaminating my lab and turning it into a shit hole. It's un-fucking-believable. My whole life I've been working towards this day and you, you come and ridicule my efforts. Can't you fucking control any of your bodily functions anymore, you gaseous Yankee moron?"

"Whoa, mind your words, baby kraut. I don't know where that awful stench is coming from but it isn't me. You're paying me well, but you don't fucking own me. In fact I've about had enough doing your dirty work."

"Getting a conscience now, are you? In here, of all places? It's a bit late for that. And don't you dare call me that you... you..."

"Father, father, calm down, we need to keep going."

Hilde tried to dampen the heated dispute and maneuvered herself in between the raging Ralph Cook and the indignant Don Cockburn.

It was the confusion Cathy Lee had sought to create when she unleashed the chemical equivalent of a few pounds of steaming fecal matter, by spraying the unsuspecting Don Cockburn with a stink weapon originally developed by the OSS during World War II.

The spy crap surrogate bought the flight attendant a few extra seconds. In a move that would make her father proud, Cathy Lee somersaulted backwards and slipped out of her stunned captors' grasp. Before she landed next to Scanner's gurney, she had unsheathed a small blade from her concealed bra holster and proceeded to slice through Scanner's restraints.

"What the..." agent one exclaimed in awe. Wondering what would have happened had they had frisked the stewardess more rigorously.

"Take care of Lobsang, Sir, and both of you, cover your eyes."

Combined with all the sulfur extracts already in the air, it sounded biblically prophetic.

"Fuck," a shocked agent two chimed in.

A massive black shape appeared in the portion of the sky visible through the atrium, projecting an even larger ominous shadow on the laboratory's brick wall, slowly gliding across the eroded landscape like a rapacious Pteranodon stalking prey.

At first Scanner thought some imposing cloud formation had obscured the sun's generous attempt to shine a little light in this hellhole. Perhaps it was how the gods admonished the sun for sharing her energy so wantonly. But of course, no such justice existed in this world, and Scanner knew that the gods would, at best, treat the wicked and the just with equal generosity.

The first pararescue jumper ripped through the glass atrium dead center, the other two gutted what was left of the dilapidated roof. All three rapidly descended in an apocalyptic hail of shattered glass and rusted iron.

"Holy shit," Don bellowed.

"You bitch," Hilde shrieked.

"Kill her, kill her now!" Ralph Cook commanded.

Scanner grabbed Lobsang and Benjamin and pulled both on top of him, letting the wood bear the brunt of god's unleashed wrath. It had been a while since he'd been this close to his Tibetan teacher. There was barely enough room to safely witness the pandemonium in all its terrifying glory.

"Get down father." Hilde shoved the rabid and delirious Ralph Cook out of harm's way.

"Terminate her, terminate her, term…" The murderous psychiatrist smashed into the floor like a power-tackled Running Back.

"My eyes, shit, my eyes. I can't see." Agent one drew his gun and blindly started eliminating his fear.

"Shoot the fuckers!" His partner joined the melee.

"Don't shoot. I surrender, I'm done, I…"

There was nothing friendly about the bullets that lacerated

Don Cockburn's body. By the time he hit the floor, his retirement was permanent.

Cathy Lee, taking cover behind Scanner's overturned gurney motioned Scanner to stay put. She knew what was coming. Like the loud explosion guaranteed to follow the minor bursts of a string of Chinese firecrackers, two more shots rang out, echoed by two thuds, as both agents crumpled to the floor.

Three down, two to go. Where were Ralph and Hilde Cook?

At last a muffled, vaguely familiar voice, broke the dead cold silence. "All clear, we got them, you can come out now, bro'."

Scanner's jaw dropped. Bro'? MAX?

JUMPING CLOWNS

"Max, is that you? What on earth are you doing here? How did you know?"

With Cathy Lee's help, Scanner returned Lobsang to the upright position. While the stewardess busied herself unstrapping her great uncle, Scanner stood and admired the surreal landscape.

Tiny specs of glass covered Ralph Cook's workstation like an early spring snow. The foul air had dissipated; replaced by a scent Scanner had no problem identifying. Sunlight joyously hopped around the sparkling crystals and had, at places, forced the thin opaque blanket to retreat, revealing a riot of colors brought forth by nature awakened; crimson red patches expressing life's enduring defiance. If only one overlooked the three bodies.

Don Cockburn had succumbed first, Pollocking the scene with his blood, tissue and brain matter. The two loose cannons responsible lay on top of him, equally dead. The only thing professional about them, Scanner thought, was the way they'd been silenced.

"I'm so glad you're unharmed, it didn't take long for you to get into trouble without me, didn't it?"

The shiny, black leather body armor molded to Max's contours like a second skin. She stepped towards Scanner with the excessive sway and aggressive cockiness of an inebriated and coked-up fashion model, paused just over two feet away, and gingerly extracted her head from the purple Bonehead helmet before holding it up high for a few infinite seconds, testing the lateral stress limits on her suit's frontal zipper.

Agent Provocateur.

"Give me a hug."

"What are you doing here?" Scanner repeated, still clumsily new to the intricacies of fraternal love. Especially with a woman as hot as Max.

"Who are they?"

Now that he had firmly embraced his baby sister, it became a lot easier to scrutinize the rest of the cast. Max's fellow tribe members dressed in identical black skins, though with torsos resembling Batman rather than Catwoman. Each man trained his M45 SOC pistol on a member of the Cook family, both grounded, Ralph reduced to a whimpering heap of misery, and Hilde a cornered and seething wild creature, hissing and cursing.

"Scanner, meet Baba and Jamba, or, as their trainers at Camp Hale called them, Bart and Jame, together forming the incredible Lama Clowns. Baba and Jamba, meet Scanner Grant P.I., my recently found and soooo endearing Big Brother."

Max planted a big red kiss on Scanner's cheek.

Lama Clowns? Well done Lobsang, well done.

"Great to meet you guys, it's been eh, a testing time. Didn't see that one coming. How did you…WATCH OUT! SHIT!"

For a split second following Max's introduction, the clowns' concentration veered towards Scanner. It was the chance Hilde had been waiting for. With the ferocious agility of a ravenous panther she leaped forward, eyes zoomed in on Cathy Lee, mind set to murder, hands clawing for revenge.

"DIE YOU BASTARD BITCH. I WANT MY POWER. I'M GONNA BREAK YOUR FUCKING NECK."

"Not on my watch you won't."

Max swiveled around and raised her right hand, still holding the Bonehead by its chinstrap; she hadn't let her guard down. With a powerful underhand swing, Max connected the high impact helmet to her secretary's jawbone. The loud, dry crack gave Scanner goose bumps, Hilde's agonizing drawn out scream lingered in his ears long after she'd gone down, blacked out on top of the recently deceased agents.

"No more mind games for you bitch. You're fired."

Max turned to Scanner.

"Let's go home, bro'. I think I've seen enough action for a while, it's been quite the week."

"Sue, I need to see Sue right now, where is she?"

"Let Cathy Lee and the clowns take care of her." Lobsang approached. "She is physically unharmed but eh, I don't know how to say this any other way Scanner, but her mind is... not what it used to be. She won't remember you, and this sick place is hardly the right location to get reacquainted."

Scanner sank to the floor, arms clutching the shins of his drawn up legs, head on his knees. Sue, his Sue... Gone. The best thing that had happened to him, obliterated, reduced to a memory no one shared. How long would it be before he himself started doubting it had ever happened? She might as well be dead.

"You've killed them all you murderous monster."

Engulfed in raw rage Scanner jumped to his feet and mercilessly started pounding Ralph Cook's face.

"You fuck, you fuck, you..."

"Stop it Scanner, he's not worth it. You're better than him. Let it go, let it go."

Max came up behind Scanner and flung her arms around him in an effort to stop the demon from taking hold of her brother.

A bloodied Ralph Cook looked up and grinned.

"You and I have much in common, you see it now?"

"Oh, shut up!"

Once more Max unleashed her purple wrecking ball, with the same devastating result.

***

For most of the ride to the airport, Scanner, Max and Lobsang remained silent, absorbed in thoughts and inner battles better left private.

You're coming home with me, Max had said with a forcefulness that tolerated no defiance.

Upon receiving the all clear from Lobsang, his trusted agency contact had dispatched two vans to the secret lab and Cathy Lee and Lobsang's St. Circus team members had taken Sue to the hospital for an extensive evaluation.

"She will be looked after well, Scanner, we'll do everything in our power to bring her back."

"I know, my old friend, Sue couldn't be in any better hands. Thank you, thank you so much, I shudder to think what would have happened had your guys not descended from heaven. What I still don't understand though is how did you know I was in danger?"

"I didn't. You'd have to thank Mrs. Kowalski for that."

"Mrs. Kowalski?"

"Yeah."

"But how?"

"Last night, after I dropped you off I returned to the apartment, to visit Mrs. Kowalski. I knew you had been liberal with the truth, telling me how she looked forward to the dance and all that, but it got me thinking. I really like her, you know, but I kinda needed your encouragement. When I arrived, she nearly ran me over, that's how anxious she was to tell her story."

"What story?"

"When you were in Hong Kong, Hilde visited her. You remember? Max had told her to. Mrs. Kowalski recognized

Hilde, even though fifty-five years had passed."

"That's impossible, fifty-five years? Hilde is barely twenty years old."

"I know, but Mrs. Kowalski was adamant, absolutely certain that she had been visited by Hildegard Koch; her erstwhile tormentor, the sadistic Auschwitz guard, Bruno Weber's wife.

As you will recall, I carried Brian Webb's agency file. Mrs. Kowalski's reaction upon seeing the photograph of Hildegard Koch left no room for doubt; Max's secretary and the notorious Nazi camp guard were one and the same."

"You mean their likeness was striking, right?"

"No, no, the same, Scanner."

"That's… How?"

"You heard what Ralph Cook said. He never once referred to Hilde as his daughter. She had all her grandmother's genes, literally. She was an exact genetic copy. That was the secret Bruno Weber never revealed to his captors and later employers. Hilde was a clone. Brian Webb and Ralph Cook had mastered human cloning.

Ralph Cook never really knew his mother. After the war she was tried and executed. Bruno Weber abandoned her, she was too much of a public enemy, he was afraid insisting on her immigration would jeopardize his."

"But he extracted cells?"

"Yes, and when Ralph found his father's diary, after the suicide, he set out to create the mother he never had."

"He needed a partner in his quest to recapture his father's lost powers."

"Exactly."

It was all thoroughly fucked up, Scanner thought. He too had lost his parents. He too would once have given anything to get them back. *Anything?* We have much in common, Ralph Cook had said. Had the psychopathic psychiatrist been right?

"Creepy, I mean I don't know anything about my mother,

but I have found my family. Trying to reverse what happened gets you stuck in the past forever. That would be such a waste of your life."

Max was right of course; Scanner had all the family he needed.

"So you knew Hilde was involved, how did you figure Sue was in danger?"

"Once I realized Hilde had the same surname as the psychiatrist who popped up in the girls' files, the pieces started to fall into place. A friend at the Tribune did a search and uncovered photographs of a gala fundraiser Ralph Cook attended some years ago, in the company of his beautiful daughter Hilde, it said in the caption. It was a fundraiser for his foundation, advanced research into the causes of memory loss. The article also mentioned the controversy surrounding the foundation, with animal rights activists protesting the use of primates as test subjects."

"And I had already told you about Sue's trip to Madison."

"Yes, it would only be a matter of time before she made the connection to Ralph Cook."

"With Don on the inside, the Cooks would have realized this."

"Your relation with Sue wasn't exactly a secret, it was the perfect trap."

Scanner thought about Mrs. Kowalski, the fragile Polish immigrant who couldn't detect the cat switch he had perpetrated with her beloved Misty.

"She's nearly blind, Mrs. Kowalski, she would not be able to see any likeness."

'We all have our own way Scanner, in how we cope with the unimaginable horrors in our lives. Her failing eyesight was Mrs. Kowalski's protection mechanism to never again have to witness the unspeakable evil she had encountered in the camp."

"How did you know the location of the lab?"

"Have you ever noticed how many taxis there are in Chicago? It's a perfect shadow network."

"Shadowing, Lobsang. That reminds me, you know Ralph Cook mentioned surveillance, how he had been watching me for years. You think my phone is tapped? Or perhaps someone has been trailing you? I know you check your cab for bugs all the time but you could have easily been followed that day you met Max. Ralph and Hilde are no loners; they couldn't have operated all this time without covert government support.

"I know, the old rivalry persists. It's a precarious balance Scanner, we'd better watch our backs."

"What about you Max, you were not supposed to return till later. Why did you come back so soon?"

"The monkey connection. Tony M called me in Hong Kong. Said he had seen my Friesian Gold commercial, I reminded him of that buxom actress he has a crush on. And he appreciated how I cared about animal welfare. He had dug up evidence that linked Uncle Ho to the illegal wildlife trade. He mentioned a Chicago based foundation and maybe I could put a stop to it.

"If there's one thing I learned from being around Lobsang it's to not dismiss coincidences out of hand. I had to go to Chicago immediately. I tried to call but couldn't reach anyone, so I hopped on the next flight out. I went straight to your apartment and Mrs. Kowalski filled me in. It was the final piece of the puzzle.

"Uncle Ho had supplied the Cooks for years with test animals. When dad got kidnapped, Ralph Cook feared the possible fallout of an investigation. He had no idea who I was other than a daughter looking for her missing father. It's possible Stuart's moonlighting for Uncle Ho was in fact a secret agency assignment, trying to keep all bases covered. With the agency's tendency to compartmentalize, Tony M wouldn't have known.

"So Ralph Cook had me followed to Chicago. Imagine the surprise when they spotted Lobsang picking me up at O'Hare. Once Hilde was maneuvered into my office, they were always a step ahead. I had put everyone in harm's way. So you understand how no one could dissuade me from jumping with the clowns."

"What about your dad?"

"He'll arrive this evening, with Joy. So we can all be together tomorrow, I'm going to throw a dinner party at our house. Lobsang, you're coming right? And you've got to bring Mrs. Kowalski and the rest of the crew. I'll send you the plane tickets today."

TEAM PLAY

"*La Gyalo.*"

Lobsang stood up and solemnly raised his glass.

"We have completed our arduous journey victoriously. Along the way we have battled demons and overcome our fears. Friendships were forged and family found. There is much to be grateful for. *La Gyalo*, Victory to the Gods."

"*La Gyalo.*"

In unison all guests, gathered around the table, followed Lobsang's example and flicked drops of *chang* in the air, before downing the homemade Tibetan brew in one gulp.

"Let's not forget the Goddesses."

Max circled the table refilling the empty glasses.

"Last I checked, guys didn't hold the divine monopoly and let's face it, without some crucial female input, we wouldn't be celebrating. We are here tonight because we are family, some of us bound by blood, but all of us connected by choice. Here's to each and every single one of you and especially to the absent Sue, though most of us have never met her, this is where she belongs and…"

Max fell silent, she swallowed hard, on the verge of crying.

"To Sue!"

Scanner hooked his left arm around his sister's shoulders, raising the next glass of chang with his right. He felt a little soft himself and could do with the support.

"To Sue!" the family chorus replied.

"And now, let's eat. Joy and I have been in the kitchen almost the whole day. You all have to try the Friesian Gold momos, they are absolutely heavenly."

***

It was a truly enchanted evening. The food an adventurous fusion of Dutch, Tibetan and Asian dishes, the company a motley and colorful lot.

Scanner ambled around the table towards Cathy Lee, carrying two glasses of the finest Macallan sherry oak. He had yet to thank the stewardess for her courageous interference.

"Ah, there you are. Am I correctly assuming that duty won't be calling tonight?"

"Who knows, sir, it's not called duty for no reason. I guess I'll have to inebriate myself to the extent that flying, in an airplane at least, would be a breach of safety regulations."

"I might just have what you need, chief purser Cathy Lee."

"I never once doubted that, sir."

"You know, you really are an angel, snatching me from hell's clutches a second time. You could have overpowered those two goons any time, yet you waited until you were in the belly of the beast."

"That was the plan all along, sir, someone had to get you and Lobsang out of harm's way and I was the most qualified."

"You certainly are, chief purser Cathy Lee. Thank you."

Scanner gingerly kissed the stewardess on her cheek and ambled on.

"You know where I live, sir, if ever you feel in need of air, liquid or otherwise."

***

Mrs. Kowalski was trying to talk to Joy when Scanner drew

up his chair.

"She's such a lovely girl, Mr. Grant, Max has told me a little of what she had to endure. I feel for her. You're going to keep her safe, aren't you?"

"Of course Mrs. Kowalski. I um… You… always knew about Misty?"

"Oh Mr. Grant, you are such a gentleman. I knew, but how could I disappoint you? You have always treated me with nothing but kindness, you're like the son I never had. I'm so glad it's all over now, and those horrible monsters will be locked away forever."

"They will," Scanner replied forcefully, though the knowledge that others were waiting in the corridors, supported by dark and powerful forces, somewhat dented his conviction. If Mrs. Kowalski noticed, she didn't let on.

"You're wearing Yves tonight – irresistible, like I told you. Would you do me the honor of dancing with me?"

***

Mr. Zwoelstra, Lobsang, Baba and Jamba had congregated at the far end of the dining room, admiring photographs of award winning Holstein Friesians and trading tall spy stories.

"It's your turn, old man."

Scanner had deliberately shuffled Mrs. Kowalski into close proximity of his Tibetan friend. With his battle-hardened pals around, Lobsang realized he was cornered. On cue, Max changed the music.

Why don't you do right, Peggy Lee questioned Lobsang and when Benny hit the high notes, Lobsang turned to Scanner and mouthed a barely noticeable thank you, before gently swaying his girl off into the night.

"You guys were unbelievable, how did you know the roof would cave in?"

"A calculated guess, right, Baba? Not that we had much

choice; it was the only viable way in."

"Me and Jamba, we do this all the time," Baba joined in. "We like crashing parties. We're the Lama Clowns."

Both Tibetan warriors took a wide stance and simultaneously raised their arms in wide V's. The deep bow that followed would perfectly compliment any Barnum & Bailey act.

"Trying to liberate humanity since nineteen-fifty-nine, at your service."

"Bravo, bravo. You guys are the best."

Max floated across the room in her designer silk dress. *Like a watercolor in the rain.* Scanner smiled. He hadn't had much chance to talk to Max this evening. But he'd had plenty of opportunity to observe her.

Tonight the Ronettes, all three of them together, would have been no match for his drop dead gorgeous sister. Max's flaming auburn shaded beehive would make a bear's legs go wobbly in an instant. Emerald eyes suggested depths far surpassing the Mariana Trench and the dark grape color of her velvety lips promised the lushness and intensity of a full-bodied Grand Cru.

A large gumball sized natural black pearl resided comfortably in the hollow of her jugular notch. Had it been allowed to roll freely it would have come to rest in the lucky slot of her natural cleavage. *Faites vos jeux.*

With Max, all bets would always be off, Scanner thought.

"I've talked to dad. That hotel where you and Sue met is up for sale. Someone will likely tear it down. So we bought it and we'll keep it for as long as it takes. You know the doctor thinks there's a fair chance Sue will regain her memories if lovingly coaxed to relive some of them. Whenever that time comes, your old love shack will still be there.

And there is something else I want to show you. It's in today's paper, look."

Scanner's eyes followed Max's finger as she pointed to a tiny column, buried deep in the international section, amidst the ubiquitous and voyeuristically comforting foreign suffering and misery.

POLICE OUTGUNNED:
VIETNAMESE KINGPIN ESCAPES
IN DARING DAYTIME RAID

In what Hong Kong police sources describe as a surgically executed strike, a notorious Vietnamese gangster escaped yesterday when the ferry he was being transferred on was raided by heavily armed men in two high-powered speedboats.

No one was harmed, and no shots were fired when the masked and machine gun wielding pirates took control of the ferry traveling between Macau and Hong Kong, before whisking away the gangster, nicknamed Uncle Ho, to an unknown location believed to be the gang's hideout somewhere along China's Southern coast.

"Somehow I don't think we've seen the last of Uncle Ho."

"Exactly what I fear, you know bro', I've been thinking, we make a good team you and I. In Hong Kong, in the Captain's Bar, you told me you worked alone, you remember? But that was before we knew we were next of kin, and anyway, I think I deserve some credit, don't you?"

Scanner didn't like where the conversation was heading, but in all honesty he had to admit Max's contribution to both cases had been quite a bit more than peripheral.

"Yes, you uh… really went for it, pulled out all the stops."

"So what do you say we team up? I have access to resources, I'm good in role-playing and you, well… you are the voice of reason, you can reign me in. We compliment each other well."

Working together with Max, he hadn't seen that one coming. The idea frightened Scanner, but, somewhere deep inside he also found it strangely reassuring.

Author photo by Kraig Lieb

Jonathan H Kemp is the author alter ego of award winning photographer Hans Kemp. Hans' photography books, documenting culture and life in both known and remote parts of Asia have sold well over 100,000 copies worldwide. His first crime novel, A Nose for Trouble, is the answer to a question long occupying his mind: How difficult can writing a book be?

Certainly not a walk in the park, Jonathan compares the writing process to the hard work of being on the road. When you set off you may have a sense of direction but the logistics will seem daunting. Along the way you will meet an array of extraordinary characters whose very existence was unacknowledged only moments earlier. Even the final destination remains obscured until you actually turn that last corner.

A Nose for Trouble is the first book in the Scanner & Max Mystery Series. New adventures loom, the empty screen begs, just as all the roads not yet traveled.

Wondering about the various fragrances mentioned in the book, or the songs referred to? Follow Jonathan and learn more about A Nose for Trouble on his facebook page: https://www.facebook.com/JonathanKempAuthor

Acknowledgements

I never thought I would write a book. I have always considered myself to be more of a "visual guy." But of course, the years spent on the road with my camera and all the encounters along the way proved a solid foundation upon which I could build this story.

The search for the catalyst that set me off on this mad adventure will surely expose my good friend and author extaordinaire Tom Vater as the main culprit. Was it a bout of envy that energized me into trying to emulate his exceptional mastery of the language? From the onset, an impossible task, I quickly realized, though that only encouraged me more.

Equally eloquent and a treasure trove of minutest facts, my editors, Cameron Cooper and Reed Resnikoff, skillfully improved upon the manuscript.

Writing A NOSE FOR TROUBLE, I felt like a crazy alchemist, standing over a magical cauldron, mixing exotic locations with flamboyant characters, historical events with fictitious dark matter, stirring it up, throwing in some red hot sex spices, dead bodies too, of course, then heating it up over a crackling fire, all in order to create something precious. I don't know if I succeeded but it sure was fun and I hope you enjoy the result.

Word-of-mouth is essential for any author to succeed.
If you enjoyed A Nose for Trouble, please consider
leaving a review on Amazon.
Even a couple of lines would make a difference
and would be extremely appreciated.

If you enjoyed **A Nose for Trouble** you may want to check out other exciting books on our website:
http://www.crimewavepress.com
Subscribe to our newsletter and you will be amongst the first to learn about new **Crime Wave Press** titles and free advance readers copies.

Crime Wave Press is a Hong Kong based fiction imprint that endeavors to publish some of the best new crime novels from around the world.

Founded in 2012 by acclaimed publisher Hans Kemp of Visionary World and seasoned writer Tom Vater, **Crime Wave Press** publishes a range of crime fiction – from whodunits to Noir and Hardboiled, from historical mysteries to espionage thrillers, from literary crime to pulp fiction, from highly commercial page turners to marginal texts exploring life's dark underbelly.

Follow us on Facebook:
http://www.facebook.com/CrimeWavePress